Up Fool's Hill and Almost Down

All Rights Reserved, Copyright © 2013

Published by Old Goat Publishing Company

Up Fool's Hill and Almost Down

This book is dedicated to Miss Winston, my 5th grade teacher who told me to write a story and then approved of what I had written, leaving me with the belief that I could write.

To Mrs. Clemons, my high school English teacher who gave so much of herself to me, and to whom I gave so little in return. Many times she chased me from her classroom, but she always brought me back.

To all teachers who inspire others to read and write and to all grandchildren who inspire grandparents to tell stories.

Joe M. Berry

Table of Contents

Forward

Most of my life I have had the urge to write and publish—an itch that finally needs be scratched. Over the adult portion of my past eighty years, I have regularly written simple stories and poems, shared these with family and friends and then discarded, misplaced, or lost most of what I have written. But I have kept a few of them. Most of these stories are based on my life experiences. Some are fictional.

On rare occasions, others have tickled my vanity by suggesting that I publish some of the things I have written. A nagging doubt that my writings would be of interest to anyone, other than those I personally know, has held me back. Talking to myself in 2009, I said, *Old Fool, these are the twilight years of life. If you are ever going to try to publish some of your stories, you need to do it now.* (I don't know if this came from my head or my heart.)

Finding much truth in this notion, I sought the opinion of a wonderful poet, author, and teacher, sending her one of my recent stories. This kind and gracious lady not only encouraged me to publish some of my stories, but also provided wonderful suggestions and editing benefits. To her I am greatly indebted.

I am equally indebted to my grandson, Ethan Berry Clanton, for his many hours of proofreading my manuscripts and his many splendid suggestions for improvement; and to my granddaughter, Anna Kate Coffey, for her cover illustration. Thanks kids!

My head tells me these are my twilight years of life; yet, my spirit reminds me daily that *I love dogs, and cats, and birds, and children, and old people, and babies, and wrinkled hands, and happy eyes, and crying eyes, and that I have a writing itch that needs to be scratched.* Thank you for allowing me to share my stories with you.

Instant Wealth And Everlasting Debt

I guess Daddy had already left our family when I went on my crime spree, but I can't be sure about that. I have spent little of my life thinking about the man I never knew. Maybe that sums up my attitude about him—he was simply a man I never knew. I have no way of missing someone I have never known. It would be like missing a train you never caught, or hitting a ball that was never thrown. So it does not matter whether Daddy was around or not when I got into crime and saw the inside of hell.

With no warning or explanation, Daddy just pulled up stake one day and left. It was the years of The Great Depression and many daddies just walked away. Mother and her five children were left to grub out a living for themselves. Frank, my brother, was the oldest; Betty, my older sister, was the gentle one; Don, my younger brother, was the mysterious and distant one; and my sister, Mary, was the baby. Early on we nicknamed Mary "The Queen." I was the middle child.

Frank was the best of us. I'll never forget his sacrifice. Aged only into his early teens, Frank stepped forward, taking hard labor jobs to help feed the family when Daddy left. He didn't get much education, but he gave himself for us. What greater gift? He put food on our table, shoes on my feet, and left me with a debt of gratitude that can never be repaid.

But, my brothers and sisters had nothing to do with my stealing the money. I was the one who put that hurt in Mother's eye and made that mountain-size lump appear in her throat. She was close by when I ventured into crime. In those days, I knew Mother would always be close. She was a happy person, a smile seemingly painted on her face. The burden of five hungry kids never seemed to take her happiness away, and she never acted tired. I know she must have been many times, but she never let me see it. She was my rock, a special rock. She laughed, sang, and whistled; a whistle that stayed with her throughout her life, except for the time I was caught in crime. I shall never forget the day when my theft stopped Mother from whistling *Amazing Grace*, and other church songs about the *Sweet By and By*.

The other kids called her "Mama." I usually called her "Mother." Don't know why I did, but I did. Guess I was strange that way, different from the others. I was different in another way too. I turned out to be the thief in the family. As far as I know, I was the only one of us that did any stealing, except the one time my brother Don helped me steal some of Old Man Moore's sugarcane.

Mr. Moore was a grouchy old cuss. I have never regretted stealing his sugarcane. Even now, these seventy years later, I'm glad that my friends Murry, Rufus, Raford, my brother, and I got that old man's cane. Oh, he caught us right enough, but seeing that we had already snapped that cane off where it met the ground, he gave us a good cussing and let us keep the cane.

Old Man Moore had a pistol in his left front pocket when he found us in his cane patch. We never actually saw the pistol, but why else except to finger his pistol to be sure it was ready to fire, would he have put his left hand in that pocket several times while he was cussing us? After we left his field, carrying the cane he had given us, there was unanimous agreement that a pistol was in that pocket. That got bigger every time we told our friends about getting caught and almost getting shot.

Another reason I don't regret taking the old man's sugarcane was that Mother did not see me do it. I guess a large part of how you feel about stealing depends on whether a mother is watching or not. For sure, having your mother know that you have been stealing makes one hurt a lot worse. It is a feeling that one carries for the rest of life.

So my brother Don did a little stealing too. But as far as I know, I was the only big time thief in our family. I do not think God got too upset about boys stealing Old Man Moore's sugarcane, seeing as how he was a grouchy old cuss.

At the time of my stealing the money, I was not fully aware of how difficult our family situation must have been. I well knew that even a penny was a prized possession. Since that time, I have learned that Roosevelt was seeking re-election, promising that he would raise cotton prices to selling for at least twelve cents a pound. He got the price up there for a while, until he won the race, and then it went back down to a nickel again. Wool was a nickel, too; corn seven cents a bushel; oats a dime. More than twenty-five percent of the people in this country lived on a farm at the time of my big caper in crime.

Even though I had no interest in presidential elections at the time, I was interested in gypsies and hobos. I had seen both. The hobos had secret code signs; signs they would put on the gatepost, or the mailbox, or any post they could find to let the other hobos know how good the picking was at someone's house. A vertical line with an intersecting slash said that the place was slim picking. Two vertical lines with an intersecting slash said things looked pretty good. Three vertical lines meant *man you have hit pay dirt. This is the mother lode.* An "X" indicated *buddy you may as well move on down the road, these folks are as poor as you and it wouldn't hurt if you prayed for them.* There were no hobo signs at our house. We could not afford any kind of post for it to be marked on.

Besides, it was not our house. It belonged to Judge Robinson, a good man who would not throw you out if the rent did not get paid. Lots of folks got evicted because they would not pay the rent and others lost their houses at mortgage foreclosures and had to move out. Folks getting thrown out of their houses kind of changed as the Depression lasted longer. It got to where a lot of the empty houses were being burned down by the folks that had been tossed out. So landlords figured it was best to let the folks just keep on living there even though no rent was paid. Folks living in a house became a kind of an insurance policy to protect a house from being burned.

Mother would never think of burning a house, and even though I did some stealing, I would not have burned a house either. Maybe it is best to just say that Judge Robinson was a good man. He never thought of throwing us out when the rent could not be paid.

I guess I kind of wish we had lost our home at foreclosure, or Judge Robinson had kicked us out, so then I could use that as an excuse for what I did. I kind of wish we had been ill-treated that way, so I could have felt like Jesse James did when he was robbing the rich to give to the poor, and I could state that as my reason for crime. That way I could say I was trying to get even, that society had made me a mean, bitter, and vindictive person. I wish Judge Robinson had been an ugly, old man, just like Old Man Moore, and that I was a modern-day Jesse James, wanting to even the score.

Heck, I can't even say that. There were no mean, stingy, ugly, low-down, no-good creditors in our lives. Just the opposite. The creditors were good, very good, to us. I do not know how much rent went unpaid to Judge Robinson. He died before I grew up and got enough money to offer to pay any that was owed. I guess I could look up some of his grandchildren, or great-grandchildren and offer to pay the back rent. But, they would not know what was owed, so I have not even tried to pay that debt. Besides, I would not know what to offer and I would have a hard time figuring out the interest owed and the percentage of the debt that went to each great-grandchild. You can see how complicated all that would be.

I do not know any of those people, nor where they live. His children, the ones I knew, are all dead, and I never knew any grandchildren. You can tell by the way I talk that I feel bad about the possibility that Judge Robinson did not get all the rent that was due to him. But that excuse does not satisfy my need to pay what is owed. I guess my feeling that way indicates that in spite of the stealing I did, I am not a completely bad person. I hope that is the case.

Not even knowing if any rent money for our house went unpaid, and not being able to settle the family account with Mr. Daniels, I sometimes now look for ways to pay old debts. Now and then, I give some money to folks who seem to need it. I had rather give it directly to those in need, those who may be on the brink of crime the way I was, than to some charitable organization. I'd rather do it directly and miss the tax deduction. Somehow, a tax deduction on a piece of paper does not satisfy the need to pay an old debt. I want to see the little boy who gets it, to see the light in his eye. A canceled check to the United Way does not have any light in its eye, or any smile on its face. Sometimes when I give it directly and catch a smile, I think, "Maybe this child does not get to smile too often." Yet, even when I give something directly to some kid or his family that does not satisfy my need to repay some debts. Some debts just ride on your shoulders to the end of the road. Maybe even beyond the end of the road, I do not know about that part, yet.

I did offer to repay Mr. Frank Daniels. He was also one of those creditors that I wish I could count as mean and greedy, but that does not work either. He owned a small grocery store in Carrollton and extended credit to those who were unemployed and hungry. I know he gave credit to Daddy. Mother let that slip out one day after Daddy had left. No one knew where Daddy had gone. He was just there one day and gone the next, and Mother let it slip that money was owed to Mr. Daniels.

Even extraordinary mothers slip up sometime. Good mamas do not want their little boys to know there is no food in the house and no daddy to get any. I guess good mamas are kind of funny that way. I guess that is just part of being a good mama. Of course, I am just guessing, seeing as how I have never been a mama. Any way, Mother let the cat out of the bag about the money Daddy owed to Mr. Daniels for groceries. I do not remember what it was that was needed, but I know it was in the grocery line, something to eat. I knew we didn't have it and we needed it. Knowing the feeling of needing something in the grocery line sticks with you forever, it seems. That feeling is a double first cousin to knowing an old debt has not been paid. I was not all that good of a kid, but on that day, when Mother let the cat out of the bag, I was trying to be good. "Mother," I said, "I will run down to Mr. Daniels's store and get it for you."

Mother stopped her work and looked at me kind of funny. Her smile was still there, but not arranged like it usually was. Little boys know when things aren't just right. With that smile kind of pushed to one side, she explained that we owed Mr. Daniels a lot of money for groceries that had been bought on credit before Daddy left town. I could tell it hurt Mother to tell me about it. It hurt me too. It still does. She explained that Mr. Daniels was a good man and that he would still let us have groceries on credit, but she did not want it that way. Even as a little boy, I did not want it that way either.

I start telling these stories and it makes me see lots of old faces, like the face of Mrs. Daniels, the grocery man's wife. Eventually she would be my sixth grade schoolteacher, but that was later on in my life, after I had done my big-time stealing. I don't reckon Mrs. Daniels ever knew about my stealing. She never let on like she knew. As I said, I don't know why I mention Mrs. Daniels. I guess it was because she was the grocer's wife, and I feel like when there is a husband there is supposed to be a wife. But Mrs. Daniels's face, just as if it were yesterday, came to mind when I thought about the grocery bill that went unpaid.

I do not know if Mother ever got any more groceries from Mr. Daniels after Daddy left us. She probably did. She probably had no choice. I am sure that if she asked, the good man did not refuse. I do know I went back to see Mr. Daniels more than twenty years after I did my stealing. I had worked during that twenty year interval and saved a little money for college and law school. But I still had that feeling of things not being right.

I knew we had eaten Mr. Daniels's groceries and that he had not been paid for all that was eaten. I knew Mother never had the money to pay him. Mother and Daddy were back together by then— but Daddy was not the paying-back kind. Maybe Mother had gotten more groceries from Mr. Daniels after she gave me that funny look and let it slip out about the money that was owed. Maybe she had to go back to that store and I did not even know it.

There were several years, after my stealing, that I lived away from my family, living with others, so I do not know what took place during those years. But years later, after I had worked awhile and saved a little money, I went back to my hometown and talked to Mr. Daniels about the money that was owed.

At least I tried to talk to him about the debt. I told him I knew we owed him for the food. He would not even talk about it. He told me that it was a long time ago, that it was not even my debt. We all look at things with different eyes. He would not discuss what was owed. He told me that it was a long time ago, that he had thrown all the old records away, and that he would like to forget those Great Depression Years. He told me that I was just a little boy then and said, "Joe, that is not your debt." He was moved by my willingness to pay, I could tell that. He was grateful for my offer, but he said it was not my debt. How could that be? I ate part of the groceries and my family ate the rest. I owed Mr. Daniels for the food. I still do. Some debts are never paid.

It would be nice if someone had treated us badly so I could have had a chip on my shoulder, and I could claim that I wanted to get even, and that is what led me to committing my crime. I guess I would feel better about my stealing if I had someone to pass the fault onto. But, such was not the case. My big-time stealing was for one reason and one reason only—greed . Pure greed. Knowing that I stole the money, that the groceries were never paid for, and that some rent may still be due hurts. Maybe there were other creditors that went unpaid that I do not know about. I am glad I don't. I have got a full load to carry as it is. Some things hurt forever.

I don't know why I still think and talk about the hard times and the unpaid debts, and about Daddy leaving and all those things. Maybe it is to get you feeling sorry for me. Accomplished crooks like me, folks who will steal, are manipulative. We try to turn a person's thinking away from the subject. If we can get them to feeling sorry for us, we've got them right where we want them.

Of all my stories, I guess the one I am about to tell you hurts the most. Maybe that is why I keep beating around the bush and not getting to the main point.

Not finding any mean creditors, not being able to pretend I was acting like Jesse James by robbing the rich and giving to the poor, I will tell you about my greed and great theft. It was not the Devil that made me do it. He or she or it, whatever the Devil is, if there is a Devil, did not have any hand in my caper. I feel bad enough about what I did the way it is, so making some false charge against the Devil would not help. Now some of the fancy-talking folks would call it cupidity, avarice, avariciousness, avidity, or even rapacity. But the speller of such vague sounding names would be just like the good thief that I am. They would be trying to throw you off the trail, off the scent. So to help you understand why I did the stealing, let's just call it pure, virgin, unadulterated, simple greed. My greed, Satan had nothing to do with it.

As soon as I saw it, I knew I was going to steal it. No sooner than I had gotten into Mrs. Hogue's house than the greed just took control of me. I had never seen so much money before, at least not that I can recall. Believe me, I have tried to recall any time before in my life that I had seen such a fortune right in front of my eyes, and I cannot. That money looked as if it were stacked six feet high. There it was, right before me, as big as a mountain. Bright, new, and shiny. I guess I was about six, maybe a year older, and it was right at my eye level. I had gone with Mother to the neighbor's house. Mrs. Hogue was her name, but all the grown folks called her "Pinkie." To me, she was "Miss Pinkie."

The details of the trip and my crime remain etched in memory. Miss Pinkie was in the bedroom, off to the right of the living room, when we arrived. She had seen us coming up her sidewalk, and before we could even get onto her front porch, she had called out to us through the open window, "Just come on in, I'm in the bedroom sewing."

We walked into her living room and turned right into the bedroom. Miss Pinkie had her Singer sewing machine all rigged up. It was one of those foot-pedal jobs where the right rhythm of the foot on the machine's treadle would make the machine sing and hum along better than a church choir. Miss Pinkie had her back turned to us when we walked into the room. Scraps of sewing material were scattered on the floor around the machine. She continued her work as she talked.

Miss Pinkie dipped snuff, Garrett snuff. She said Brewton snuff was too sweet. Her small, tin can of Garrett snuff was sitting on the left side of her sewing machine, just beneath that little silver colored wheel that had to be given a spin to get the machine going in rhythm with the foot rocking the treadle below. Unlike some folks who used a sweet gum snuff brush, made from a sprig broken from the limb of a sweet gum tree, Miss Pinkie took her snuff straight, inside the lower lip. Miss Pinkie already had that sewing machine going in high gear, and over to her right side, out on the end of that top leaf of the sewing machine, I saw what I knew I had to have. It was that moment when my greed juices started flowing. It was love at first sight, and I knew I was going to steal it.

There it was, right at eye level. It looked as big as a mountain. It was bright, with a new look, and it was mine for the taking. No one would ever know I'd gotten it. I could be quick and sneaky about it. If I planned and executed properly, no one would see. I was sure about my plan. I had never done it before, but I already understood good planning and sneaking. A virtual fortune was right before my eyes, and all I had to do was catch Mother and Miss Pinkie looking the other way. See how a good thief thinks? I have been there. I speak from experience. A good thief just knows it can be done and never expects to get caught.

Now, if one wants to test their greed factor, just get in that situation. Like I said, I cannot charge it to a mean landlord or a calloused grocery man, or even to the Devil. I cannot even charge it to an empty gut growling for food, Mother always managed to put food on the table. All those things aside, I knew I had to have that shiny, new dime. I had never seen so much money before and soon it would be mine.

I planned, I executed, and I got it. I put it in the right front pocket of the short pants I was wearing. I got it quick, and I got it out of sight. I made a clean snatch and take. Perfect plan, perfect execution. Suddenly, I was rich. I never before had so much money. I was fixed for life, ready for an early retirement. I was all primed for a clean get-a-away.

About then, things started coming unraveled. Things started happening that I had not planned on. Miss Pinkie started looking for her dime and that was not part of my plan. Miss Pinkie claimed that she knew it had been right there on the end of that top leaf, that she had put it there intending to send one of her kids to the store for some sewing thread.

At this time I had to start improvising, making quick moves, and doing things not included in the master plan. But I seemed up to the occasion. I was right proud of my quick thinking and dexterity. I "joined" in the search for that dime. I said I thought it might have rolled under the bed, so I got on hands and knees and looked. I next "thought" it might be under some of the scraps of cloth on the floor, so I shoved them aside and looked. See how a good thief works? They turn your head by helping in the "search." That is the way it works, turn the heads, get them looking the other way, get them confused, and get yourself looking good. Of course, Miss Pinkie could not find her dime. Equally of course, I knew where the dime was, but I was doing only the looking and none of the talking. I had made a clean grab. That dime was right where it ought to be. Everything was looking good. I had stolen and I had improvised. I was on my way to living on easy street.

I do not recall the purpose of Mother's visit to Miss Pinkie's that day, but it was soon time to leave. I had not planned on committing a crime as we had walked the one-fourth mile to Miss Pinkie's house. My stealing had been a crime of opportunity, my greed just suddenly grabbed me and I grabbed the dime. I do not recall having done any stealing before, unless one considers hiding his younger bother's toys stealing.

Not too long after I helped "search" for the dime, Mother and I went out the front door, across the porch and down the steps. Miss Pinkie had a concrete sidewalk that ran the length of the front yard, between the hedges that sat on either side. At the end of the sidewalk, where the hedges parted, Mother and I stepped onto a gravel turn-around driveway. The small gravel circle had been there since horse and buggy days. The dime was secure and out of sight in my right front pocket. I had committed the perfect crime. I had made a perfect snatch and a clean getaway.

Now comes the painful part, the part that will never go away. Now comes the part that more than seventy years later brings a shortness of breath and hurt to my spirit and soul. It is painful to speak of this enduring hurt and grief that lives deep inside me. The thief's guile in me urges me to turn your head by saying my long lasting pain stems from a repentant heart. My deceit prods me to say that I feel guilty about my stealing and that I see the error of my way and that I will never steal again. In fact, I never did steal any more money after that day, but I got some apples, peaches, pears, and watermelons. So you see, I did do some more stealing, and some of it I feel good about. I never did think God got too excited about a boy stealing apples and peaches and Old Man Moore's sugarcane. God could see how grouchy that old man was too. So, the redeemed sinner syndrome has nothing to do with the hurt that never goes away. It was something else.

It was right in the middle of that circle driveway that it all came unglued. That circle drive made of river gravel was such a small place. Mules and wagons had first made that circle. The Model T Ford later modified it. The circle was about half the size today's cars would need. So, you see it was not a big place, yet it was large enough to hold the entire world. Any place where the world comes apart is a big place, how else could the entire world be there?

Right there was when and where the world started coming apart and flying in all different directions. Not only was the entire world there, so was that place we call "Hell". That is, if Hell is not a part of the world. No matter where it is, it was there too. I saw the inside of it. I was right in the middle of it. Right in the middle of that circle is the middle of Hell. It was in that circle when my Mother completely lost her smile. It just left, completely gone. It was not even lopsided, or crooked, or twisted, or misplaced. It was gone, completely gone. There was not a trace, not a smidgen of that ever-present smile left. I had never before seen Mother without some kind of a smile or grin on her face.

Right there, right in the middle of Hell, Mother stopped and looked down at me. "Joe," she asked, looking down at the son she trusted, "do you know where Mrs. Hogue's dime is?"

Now in telling about this, I could twist things around to get you feeling sorry for me. I could turn your head and try to make you find understanding about my life of crime. I could tell you about the hard times, about Daddy leaving the family, and about my older brother having to drop out of school and become the daddy in the family, and about him nearly breaking his back working on the section gang of the railroad. There are lots of things I could tell you to twist your head and move your heart in my direction.

But there was one thing I could not do. I do not know where the streak of decency in a criminal like me came from, but it was there. I could snatch that dime and crawl around on the floor, deceitful scamp that I was, acting like I was helping look for it. But somehow, someway, a redeeming quality came to the top. Maybe it saved me from a life of repeated crime. But that is not yet to be said. Life is not over, and there is still time for more stealing.

I could, and did, do all the bad things I have told you about. But there was one thing I could not do when Mother looked at me with sadness in her eyes and the smile gone from her face. It was a look of crying inside, a hurting, a wishing, a wanting look. There was no look of anger, just the look of a loving mother that had trusted her son. Mother already knew, but she asked me the question anyway, "Joe, do you know where Mrs. Hogue's dime is?"

"Yes ma'am," I answered.

"Where is it, Joe?"

My heart wanted to burst. My lungs lost all taste for air. My guts were on fire. But I had that small streak of decency left. Thief though I was, I could not lie to my mother.

"It is in my pocket," I said.

It was right there in the middle of that driveway circle that the dying began, and I have been dying ever since. It was right there in the middle of that circle that the folks who wrote the Bible got the idea of what Hell is all about. That is where the nether world comes from, that is where it is. If anyone wants to know where Hell is, I can tell him or her. It is Miss Pinkie's gravel driveway. I have been there, I have seen it, smelled it, and tasted it. At least that is the front side of Hell.

The other part of Hell was in Mother's face, in her eyes, and on her lips. The smile of Heaven was gone and the remainder of Hell had taken its place. If you want to see the backside of Hell, just see my mother's face that day. See the smile gone from her lips, but mostly see her eyes. Those gray-blue eyes, like mine. But you will never see that kind of hurting in mine. I have not walked the hard miles that she did, I have not struggled to feed five little kids the way she did. My eyes do not have the capacity for sadness that hers had that day when I was six years old. She had eyes that had seen too much misery in life, but she always wore a ready grin. And now, it was gone.

It was there when those eyes showed a look that won't go away. Happy eyes, now sad. Eyes that danced, now still. Eyes that always showed confidence and challenge, now puzzled, confused, bewildered, confounded, perplexed, and hurting. Many times I have tried to find the words to describe what I saw that day. I have struggled to find words that adequately describe the backside of Hell. Many times I have thought if I could just write down what I saw, it would help relieve my heavy load. But the words do not come. The words I find do not rid my spirit of its burden. I guess, most of all, those always happy eyes, now sad, said, "I trusted you. I believed in you. What has caused life to go so wrong?" I guess that is mostly what they said. Those eyes seemed to say, "You let me down, you broke my trust."

There was no anger in those eyes that looked down at me for what seemed like nine hundred years in the gravel circle that day, only nine hundred years of sorrow. Right there, that is the worst side of Hell I will ever know. After those nine hundred years of Mother looking down at me, she said, "Well, there are several ways we could handle this. I think the best way is for you to go back to Mrs. Hogue's house, by yourself. Give her the dime back and you just say what you think is the right thing to say."

I wished that Mother had whipped my bare legs with plaited barbed wire. I wished she had hit me in the head with a heavy stick. I wished she had done anything and everything except send me on that long trip back to Miss Pinkie's house by myself. Mother walked on ahead, toward our house while I made the long, long trip back up Miss Pinkie's sidewalk. I gave the dime back and said something that is not recalled. Mother was waiting for me at the base of the town's water tank. It stood about 100 yards beyond the circle drive. I do not like to think she waited there out of lack of trust that I would take the dime back. I like to think she waited there because she knew I needed to walk home with her. We held hands on the way.

Mother is now dead almost thirty years. After that day, my big life of crime was never mentioned again by either of us. There was no need. We just continued to hold hands.

From The Apple Crate

I am not sure that the little house that we lived in was actually within the town limit of Carrollton, but the half-mile of dirt road that connected the two seemed to make the house a part of the west Alabama town. Mostly mules, wagons, and barefoot boys, like me, traveled that red clay road. Occasionally, during the hot, dry days of summer, a car or truck would rumble up or down it, kicking up the dust as it passed and scattering chickens everyway for Sunday.

Monday was washday and when the freshly washed clothes were all pinned on the clothesline, Mother would caution, "Now you kids watch for a passing car that may be kicking up dust and hurry to get these clothes off the line. We do not want tomorrow to be another washday."

If the occasional car or truck created that hazard, everyone in the family big enough to reach the clothesline and remove the clothespins was expected to give a hand in the clean-clothes rescue. Failing to join in the rescue had its punishment. Water had to be drawn from the well, one bucket at the time, to refill the cast iron boiling pot, plus water to fill three # 2 washtubs. One tub was for the first rinse, and a second tub with "bluing" mixed into the water was for the white clothes. The bluing made the white clothes whiter. (Like today's toothpaste that is supposed to whiten one's teeth. Maybe they use old-fashioned bluing. Who knows about such things?) A third tub was used for the final rinse of the dark clothes. Washday was an all-day affair

By the time I was six years old, there was no daddy in my family, just Mother and us five children. I was the middle child. It was the years of hard times in Alabama. Jobs were hard to come by. Daddy was one of many daddies who simply walked away from their families. At the time, I was too young to give much thought to such things. Now, years later, I sometimes wonder if it was it the shame of not being able to find a job so he could support his family that caused Daddy to disappear for almost fifteen years? Was it anger? Was it desperation? I can understand that desperate people do desperate things. Was it indifference? What was it? I will never know, at least not in this life.

Our house, along with many others, was cold during the winter months of the Great Depression Years. It stood on rock pillars, creating a sizeable crawlspace with no underpinning. The crawlspace was shaped like a wedge, high on the east side of the house and squeezed itself down to nothing on the west side. The chimney foundation, made of rock, occupied the middle of the crawlspace. What a wonderful playground it was!

It was always dry and the dirt was loose and fine as silk. Spoons and knives from Mother's kitchen were wonderful toys, good matches for little hands. No forks were allowed under the house; Mother only had seven of those. I guess Mother wanted to be sure that Daddy would have a fork to eat with, should he come back home. At the end of the day, Mother would call from the kitchen, "You kids get under the house and roundup the spoons and knives, otherwise there will be no supper tonight." The prospect of food for supper was a great inducement for scratching in the dirt to recover a buried knife or spoon. We tried to keep the chickens shooed away from the under-the-house playground. Chicken droppings tended to spoil the wonderful dirt.

Lest it appear that we were "dirt poor," I should add that we had other toys for our under-the-house playground. These were old buckets with holes in the bottom, wooden cigar boxes from the trash of the nearby Carrollton stores (there were eight stores, but only two sold cigars), old tin cups and cans, and Mother's discarded spools from which the sewing machine thread had been used.

No glass was allowed under the house. Mother cautioned it would break and be dangerous; besides, Mother needed to save the glass jars for canning, provided they would accommodate either a small-mouth or large-mouth ring and lid. The canning rings would be saved to use again. The use of a lid in canning was a one-time thing, so we had an abundance of them under the house. With a little effort, the used lids could be stood on end, slightly buried in the dirt, and queued like dominos. Once, I created a domino chain of used lids that completely circled the chimney base. It was a work of art.

The only store-bought toys that I recall ever seeing under the house were a little fire engine, a truck, and two cars. They were made of cast iron and had been once painted red. Time, dirt, and use had worn most of the original paint away. I do not know where these toys came from. They had survived because they were virtually indestructible.

Best of all, we had the imaginations of children and a mother who trusted us not to lose her knives and spoons. Why, we had more toys than we could ever use!

Neither the floor nor the exterior walls of our little house were insulated. Insulation in the attic was virtually unknown, even in the better houses of our little town of six hundred people. Although one could not see daylight through the cracks of the floor and walls, one could clearly hear the wind whistle as it made its way around and under the house, looking for some way to come inside.

Sometimes, on a cold winter night, a neighbor's hogs would get out of their pen and seek the comfort of the warm rocks of the chimney base under the house. Believe me, two or three hogs can really mess up a playground. One cold winter night Frank, my older brother, and I were awakened by the sound of the pigs under the house. They were grunting and squealing around the chimney base. My brother nudged me in the ribs and asked, "Are those hogs keeping you awake?"

"No, but you are."

"I will take care of that," he answered.

He slipped out of our bed, and removed a bucket that sat near the hearth of the fireplace, uncovering a small hole in the floor that had been burned in the floor years before. With the hole uncovered, he gathered some hot coals from the banked fire and carefully dribbled the coals through the hole in the floor, chancing that some might land on a pig's back.

His calculation was good, but bad for the poor pig below. The hot coals obviously found their intended target. The offended pig let out a blood-curdling scream that could be heard a mile away, and all of the other pigs joined in the chorus. It sounded as if they would tear the house down. Quickly, all in the house were wide awake. But, when Mother came running into our room to investigate, she found both Frank and I "fast asleep."

We lived in a four room, frame house. It was rented from Mr. Robinson. The four rooms included two bedrooms, each with an open fireplace, a small eating room (the more pretentious and sophisticated might say a "dining room"), and Mother's kitchen. Today it is fashionable to live in houses that have a great number of square feet of living space. Some boast of such things, as if they were wearing a badge of honor. We were not distracted with such things. I would guess that our house had about seven hundred square feet of living space. But, it had a playground underneath. How many the big houses today are so equipped?

In keeping with the way the rest of the house was furnished, a wood table, with wood benches on each side, and a straight-back, mule-ear chair at each end occupied most of the eating room space. An old pie safe sat against the east wall of this room. I recall no wall decorations in the eating room. Calendars depicting Norman Rockwell's work were the main wall decorations of the two bedrooms.

No upholstered or stuffed chair was in the house. I vaguely recall a rocking chair in Mother's bedroom. Other than this, all other chairs were of the straight-back variety; their bottoms were caned with white oak strips. The only mechanical apparatus in the house was Mother's foot-treadle Singer sewing machine that she kept in her bedroom. I was fascinated with this sewing machine, sneaking every opportunity to play with it.

Once, when about six or seven, I was playing with the sewing machine, standing in front and operating the foot pedal, trying to sew some scraps of cloth together. Mother was in the kitchen. I accidentally got my left index finger under the machine's needle and it completely pierced the tip of that finger. It hurt, but, strangely, not excessively so. I called to mother, telling her, "I have stuck the needle through my finger."

Mother heard my call for help, but the calm manner in which I had called persuaded Mother that I was either playing a prank or not in any danger. I had to call her two or three times before she came to the bedroom. Once there and seeing the needle through my finger, she fainted and fell to the floor beside me, leaving me pinned to the sewing machine. Soon, she rallied, got to her feet, and rescued me.

Tetanus shots for needles through fingers or rusty nails stuck in one's foot were available, but beyond the reach of our family budget. A soaking of the puncture wound in kerosene oil was the common home remedy. My finger was thus soaked. I still have the finger, it has always served me well.

The house and all that was in it was kept clean. The small front and back yards, with hardly any grass, were regularly swept clean with homemade dogwood brush brooms. We kids returning from playing under the house were Mother's greatest challenge to cleanliness.

Bathing was in the kitchen, in a # 3 washtub. With no indoor plumbing, the water was brought inside, a bucket at the time, from the outside well located about twenty-five yards from the back steps at the kitchen door. All water was heated in kettles or pots on Mother's wood-burning kitchen stove. During the hot months, one kettle of hot water mixed with four buckets of cold was usually a good mix. During the winter months, two kettles of hot mixed with three buckets of cold worked better.

Family bathing was a time-consuming affair, what with the drawing, transporting, and heating the water on the stove. Often, the cleanest child would bath first and the dirtier child second, but in the same tub of water.

During the hot summer months there were occasions when my bothers and I would use a fresh water spring located in the pasture behind our house for bathing. We called this method a "Blue Clay Bath" because we used small amounts of blue clay that could be extracted with a sharp object from a nearby bank of red dirt. When this clay was mixed with water and rubbed on the skin it would generate, with the aid of a child's imagination, a small lather. The blue clay and fresh water removed old dirt. The bath was not too gentle on the skin, but it got the imbedded dirt out.

Light in the house came exclusively from either the sun, kerosene lamps, or during the winter months, the open fireplaces. The wick of the kerosene lamp had to be carefully adjusted. If it was too short, there would be little light. If too long, smoke would be generated and the inside of the lamp's globe (chimney) quickly covered with soot. Trips to the barn or necessity house at night were made either in the dark or with the aid of a kerosene lantern. Flashlights were almost unheard of, and completely unknown at our house.

We only had one kerosene lantern, it bore the trade name of "Ezy-Lite." There was much competition among us children, and more than a few fusses, over who would get to use the Ezy-Lite. Like most kids, we would, on occasion, strain our imaginations looking for something to fuss about. My strongest competitor was my older sister, Betty. Once, she and I almost came to blows over whose turn it was to get the next very small piece of pork fat from the next can of pork and beans.

Sometimes Betty and I did come to blows. She was two years older, taller, and stronger than I when we had our last fight in the yard. Mother came out of the house as we fought and said, "I am sick and tired of you two fighting with each other. I am going to just stand back and let you have it out! Now, go to it."

Mother folded her arms and stood back. Betty and I started swinging wildly. Before I knew it, Betty's nose was bleeding and I was devastated. I had not intended to hurt my sister! It was only a little blood, but enough that I never fought her again. Betty was the happy one of the five kids. She too is now gone from my life, but in my mind I can still see the horror of her bloody nose.

Daisy, our wonderful cow, had a small barn for her comfort and use. She was milked there twice a day, but only by Mother. Daisy was our most prized possession. Mother would sometimes say that cow had been sent to us right from heaven. She was actually a gift from Papa, Mother's father.

Just beyond the barn stood the necessary house, an outdoor toilet. By most, it was called a "two-seater." Diagonally across one corner, to the front of the two seats, a catalog was draped across a wire that was tied to opposing nails. At first, I was not old enough to be interested in the catalog pictures of the ladies modeling underwear. (That would come later in life.) When the cold wind was blowing, one's business in the necessary house was brief and quickly attended.

A narrow porch stretched across the front of the house, with a front door that opened into one bedroom. During the warm months, Mother always decorated the front porch with an assortment of flowers growing in a ragtag assortment of rusty pots and pans.

Often we were late paying Mr. Robinson the monthly rent on the house. I believe it was ten dollars. I cannot be sure, but I suspect that many months the rent was never paid. Money seemed nonexistent. It simply was not there. How did Mother manage? I shall never know the complete answer. I do know how she handled the most difficult tasks of taking care of home, cow, garden, washing, ironing, and five children. She handled it with a smile on her lips and a song in her heart. No complaints, no remorse, no bitterness. I have no recollection of ever hearing Mother complain of Daddy being gone or his failure to lend any support for the family over the fifteen years of his absence.

I can yet hear Mother as she sang and whistled her favorite church hymns and songs. "The Old Spinning Wheel" seemed to be her favorite. Her singing of "The Land that is Fairer than Day" and "The Old Rugged Cross" offered promise for tomorrow. And, her Southern Baptist heritage demanded John Newton's "Amazing Grace." In spite of her most difficult life, Mother was a happy person. This is not to say that tears did not sometimes cloud her sight. It is to say that adversity and occasional tears never clouded her vision. She made me the richest kid in town.

I am sure some money for our family came from Papa. Once, Mother had the opportunity of working on the night shift at a cotton mill in Aliceville, ten miles south of Carrollton. She tried it for about a month, getting, at best, three hours of sleep each day. It was simply too much for her. Yet, she kept whistling and singing, her happy face breaking out with a big smile for everyone that came her way.

A large measure of the much needed family income came from my older brother, Frank. Of the kids in our family, he was the very best of us. Daddy had been gone about four or five years when Frank dropped out of school and took a backbreaking job with a section gang for the local railroad. All day he would work handling rails, placing crossties, hammering spikes, and sweating for his family. He was fourteen years old when he started that job, big for his age and strong as an ox. Yet, he was only a kid. Frank gave himself for the rest of us. He put food on the table, and winter shoes on our feet. Frank has been dead many years. I owe him a debt that can never be paid.

Life creates debts. I am indebted to Mr. Robinson for any rent that may have gone unpaid. To his daughter, Virginia, I am most definitely indebted. Like brother Frank, Virginia gave a large measure of herself to me.

Virginia was a young lady when she came into my life. As best recalled, she had recently graduated from college when I first came to know her. She lived with her parents in a large house. A path across the pasture connected our houses. She was tall, slightly thin, and, I thought, very pretty. I always wanted to touch her pretty dark hair, but was afraid to. (I know now that she would have taken no offense if I had.)

I will never know why Virginia took an interest in me, a little boy who stammered badly, but she did. She would have me sit and talk to her for hours on end, never seeming to notice my stammer. Sometimes we would sit in her back porch swing. Often we would sit on her back door steps. Sometimes she would hold my hand. All the time, she would encourage me to just talk. I cannot count the ways in which she encouraged me to just talk.

When I was about nine, I overcame my speech impairment. Who may say what contribution Virginia's effort made in the correction of my speech problem? I suspect a lot. It is wonderful to have a Virginia in one's life. Could she have been another gift from heaven? When I was about age ten, I moved away from my family and went to live with others. Virginia, in helping with my speech, had prepared me for the rest of life.

Now I want to tell you about Mother's warm kitchen on a cold morning. An open fireplace in each of the two bedrooms shared a common brick chimney. These, plus Mother's wood-burning kitchen stove, were the sources of heat during the cold winter days and nights when the wind scratched for a way inside. Sometimes, during the early morning hours when the fires in the open fireplaces had long since died and their ashes had grown cold, I would pull the bedcover to my chin and dread putting my bare feet on the cold flood. Frequently, I would hear the wind talking to me, saying "Get up so I can get you! Get up and I will get you!" That wind had a loud and clear voice. It would make me shiver. Sometimes I thought the wind talked just to me, knowing that I stammered and could not effectively talk back.

But, there was a haven in our small house, a refuge, a place that was warm and safe. Without fail, I knew when my safe place was ready for me. Mother was in the kitchen. She was up! Mother always seemed to be "up." I could hear her either whistling or singing as she fired the kitchen stove, mixed the flour, lard, buttermilk, and baking powder in the dough bowl, and fried the strips of side-meat in the skillet, saving the grease for the making of sawmill gravy. I would also smell the new day and know that it would be warmer soon, and that, for at least today, the outside wind was not going to get me. In was nice to smell the wood smoke of the stove, the meat frying in the skillet, and know the biscuits were baking in the oven. These, plus Mother's whistling and singing, told me that I was safe, that I was home, and all was well. These things scared the ugly wind away, it was overpowered, outgunned. The sounds and smells from the kitchen never failed in rescuing me from the cold, cold wind.

Thus fortified, my feet braved the cold floor and I made my way to my sanctuary, my place of safety and security. It was a box that sat between the kitchen stove and the adjacent wall. The box, a heavy apple crate, fit snuggly between the stove and the north wall of the kitchen. Just the right height, in just the right place, and just the right size for a little boy to back into, take his seat, and enjoy the sounds and smells of Mother and her magic. The fire would crackle and snap as it burned in the stove's firebox on the left side of the stove; my haven was on the right side. In no time, I felt as secure as a kitten snuggling up to a warm brick. The entire arrangement seemed to have been created just for me. Mother whistling and singing, the fire popping, the meat frying, then Mother's spoon stirring the flour into the hot skillet of grease followed by the adding of the buttermilk and more stirring of the soon-to-be gravy.

Now, seventy-five years later, I recall the frustrations of my stammer and not being able to talk back to the cold wind. I recall the safety of my apple crate alcove, the fire popping and the gravy simmering in the skillet. I remember Virginia Robinson sometimes holding my hand as we sat on her back door steps while she encouraged me to talk. I can yet see Frank as he came home tired and dirty from a long, hard day of railroad work. I can yet hear Mother whistling and singing as her fingers kneaded the biscuit dough.

Some may read my story and say, "How sad!" If so, they do not understand, they have missed the beauty of my childhood. I was there, I know. I recall and say, "Mother, Frank, Virginia, and many others in my life that have given so much to me. How wonderful!"

In or Out of the Well

The small four-room house the Berry Family called home was about a half mile from the town of Carrollton, Alabama. Our house stood back from a dirt road that began at the courthouse square of the little town and ran north, past our house, into the sparsely populated rural area of northwest Pickens County.

Motor vehicles on this road during the 1930s were few, possibly less than ten each day. The horse and buggy days of Alabama were virtually over, but the mule and wagon days had grown with each year of the Great Depression. Even so, most of the mule and wagon traffic was limited to Saturdays when the farmers came to town to shop and socialize with friends and relatives.

Our poor family was not of the motor vehicle variety. Not even of the mule and wagon breed. We walked and, as kids, played. Our playground included our yard, the yard of Mr. Tom Burgess that was across the road and up the hill from our house, and a large pasture that belonged to the man from whom we rented our house.

The pasture contained many wonders of life. Hills, valleys, and flat lands were only parts of its whole. There was a sweet water, ever-flowing spring that provided opportunity to build small dams across the path of its water flow and create small ponds. On these small pools, we floated our homemade ships, barges, and boats made of anything that would float. This spring also provided summertime opportunity for my brothers and I to bathe.

A red clay dirt bank fronted the sweet water spring. There were small veins of blue clay that ran through parts of the red clay, much like the veins that run though our bodies. With a sharp object, such as a nail, small portions of this blue clay could be rubbed on a wet boy's butt or other body parts and it would seem to lather. (A child's imagination is a wonderful thing.) I have no idea what the chemical properties of this blue clay were, and as a boy, I did not care. Nor do I know how we discovered that the blue clay would lather when rubbed on a wet butt. Childhood is not for such worries.

The large pasture, more than 100 acres, had many kinds of trees, including two American Chestnuts and three Chinquapins. Gathering and opening the Chestnuts and Chinquapins was a challenge. Muscadine vines that climbed to the top of the highest trees, all fruit producing, were abundant. Another vine that we called "cross vine" grew much larger and stronger. Cross vine swings let all of us be Tarzan long before we saw the "real" Tarzan at a rare Saturday afternoon "picture show."

After repeated swings, the cross vine would sometimes break and the Tarzan swinging on the vine would go sailing through the air with no choice of landing spot. When this happened to my older sister, Betty, she would add to the excitement and mirth by invariably wetting her panties in flight. Too much laughter and unscheduled flights most times brought the water out of Betty.

On one occasion, our neighbor Joe Hogue was in the pasture with us as we tussled with a Muscadine vine, trying to shake the ripe grapes to the ground. Joe, about eighteen years old and a great athlete, took charge of the Muscadine-shaking event, saying, "You kids get out of the way and let me show you how a man does the job."

We stood back and watched Joe climb the tree like a monkey. In just a few moments, he was at the top of the tree, swinging the tree back and forth, and the Musacdines were raining to the ground. And soon, so was Joe.

He had lost his grip and down he came, trying to grab tree limbs to break his fall. He was only successful in part. He hit the ground with a pretty good wallop. We rushed over to where he landed and inquired, "Are you hurt, Joe?"

Jumping to his feet, he answered, "I am not hurt, but I have shit all over myself."

Off to the sweet water spring and blue clay Joe went. Leaving his soiled underwear for future generations, he cleaned himself, and was soon back at the top of the Muscadine vine showing us how a man did the job.

The pasture had a hill with two names: Slide Hill and Hawk Hill. This hill, in the pasture but close to the back of our house, had a growth of tall pine trees with considerable open ground space between the trees. In fall and winter, when the pines shed their needles, this open ground space had a thick, slick carpet. A piece of corrugated tin, with each end slightly curled upward, made for a delightful, fast, and sometimes dangerous slide down that hill. We took turns. One's turn began by lugging the tin back to the hill's top after the previous rider reached the bottom. Sometimes the big pine trees, and smaller trees, got in the path of the daredevil sliding toward the bottom, but such things are damned when one is young. We took our chances. I recall several bumps and bruises, but no broken bones.

Slide Hill became Hawk Hill later when there was an encounter between a Rhode Island Red Hen and a Red Tail Hawk at the back of our house. This confrontation of birds began in our backyard where Betty, Don (my younger brother), and I were playing. The hen and her brood of half-grown chicks were in the backyard, too.

Suddenly, the hawk swooped down from the sky, grabbed one of the half-grown chicks in its talons, and tried to fly away with its prey. Over the pasture fence and down the slope of Slide Hill the hawk sailed with the captured chick. The extra load that the hawk carried impeded its flight ability.

Maternal juices demanded that the mother hen do her best. Across the yard, on the downward slope, she ran. She gained air speed and took to the wing, chasing the hawk that carried her baby. Amazingly, the hen was able to overtake the hawk and collide with it in mid air. With the collision, the hawk dropped its prey and the chick fell to the ground. We went to its rescue.

We picked up the wounded chick. The talons of the hawk had ripped the protective skin away on one side, exposing the intestines. It was time to call on Mother.

In the house, Mother examined the wounded chick and said, "It looks pretty bad. But, let's see what we can do."

While Betty held the wounded bird, Mother first washed the wound with hydrogen peroxide. Then Mother took her sewing needle and, I shall never forget, pink embroidery thread and closed the wound.

Our "patient" was placed in a cardboard box and kept near Mother's kitchen stove until it made a complete recovery. It is hard to recognize one chicken from another, but we all came to recognize that chicken. She never wound up in a pot of chicken and dumplings.

The pasture behind our little house held many treasures and housed many fond memories. It was a time and age when children did not need the close supervision that today's world demands. There was more freedom, more opportunity to explore, learn, and, on occasion, be exposed to danger.

Sometimes, the danger was an unknown one, like the day that my baby sister, Mary, fell into the well and was dead, or so it seemed.

Mary was about age three or four at the time. It was summertime and she was playing in the backyard. Mother was in the house working. (She seemed to be forever working.) Several times, during the hour or so that Mary was in the yard, Mother went to the back door to be sure of Mary's whereabouts and wellbeing.

Each time that Mother checked, except the last, Mary was present. On her last visit to the back steps, Mary was not to be seen and did not answer Mother's call.

Mother went into the yard, calling for Mary. No answer. She became understandably concerned and broadened the circle of her search. Two trips around the house brought Mother to a terrifying sight!

On the backside of the yard, near the barn, Mother found a huge, open hole in the ground. There had never been even a small hole there before. Now it was a huge, open, gaping hole that appeared to be four or five feet in diameter.

Mother rushed to the hole and looked down. What she saw was even more frightening! About twenty feet down in the hole, she could see water. In her mind, she also saw her baby girl!

It was an old, dug well. Years before someone had abandoned its use and covered it first with heavy wood timbers. On top of these timbers, dirt had been piled. Over the intervening years, the forces of nature had left the covered well completely concealed, leaving no surface appearance of the danger below. To say that it was a very dangerous thing is to greatly understate.

On seeing the open hole and the water, Mother knew that her baby was dead! To a parent, there was no room for any other interpretation!

Mother's scream brought men that were working nearby. They examined the situation and sent someone to the county shed, about a half mile away, for a length of rope. Preparation was underway to lower a man into the hole and water to recover the body of the little girl.

Mother bordered on hysteria. Her baby was in that well! Someone went to town to summon a great family friend, Dr. Hugh Hill. (Truly a wonderful man. Rich or poor, night or day, he never failed to answer anyone's call for medical attention.) Dr. Hill came to the house and administered a sedative to Mother.

The man that had gone for the rope returned. The rope was tied around the chest of another and, just before he began his descent into the old well, someone called out, "Look! Coming down the hill!"

It was sister Mary! She had a small bucket in hand. She had gone to Mr. Tom's house for a bucket of sand.

Mother took Mary into her arms and wept. She wept, and wept. I never saw Mother shed so many tears, before or after this frightening event. Her baby was safe. The entire episode probably did not last more than thirty or forty minutes. To my wonderful mother it must have seemed an eternity.

Before this event, when Dr. Hill passed the house and saw Mother working in our vegetable garden, he would stop and call out, "Mary, Mary, Quite contrary. How does your garden grow?"

After this event, Dr. Hill changed his call to, "I am for you Mary, in or out of the well."

Mary, the baby of the family, soon after "falling into the well" acquired the byname of "The Queen." (Most families have one.) This dear sister and I are the only two surviving children today. Mary yet reigns as queen. Just ask her. I remain her obedient servant. A great sister, she!

Looking back at life and family, I marvel at how well Mother managed the hand of life that she had been dealt. Against great odds, she kept her brood of chicks fed, warm, and dry. Among other things, she taught us to laugh. Even when we meet to grieve the death of a loved one, we find it also a time to laugh together.

This happy family spirit now lives not only in Mother's two surviving children, but also in four additional generations. No matter what the occasion that brings us together, we enjoy each other's company and laugh.

Yes, sometimes we cry. But soon, the sun breaks though. Soon the mother hen defies the odds and overtakes the hawk. Soon Mother's spirit takes a needle and pink embroidery thread and closes our wounds, and we laugh.

Miss Heck

I well remember Miss Heck, a small dog of the rat terrier variety that became part of our family in 1939. I was nine years old at the time.

Before Miss Heck came to our house, we were a family of six—Mother and us five children (seven if Daisy, our cow, was included in the count). For several years prior to the arrival of Miss Heck we kids had made bids for a family dog. But it was the Great Depression Years and Mother was compelled to meet our pleas with sadness in her voice, explaining that we simply could not afford one.

In these statements Mother spoke truthfully. The 1930s were truly hard times in all of the United States. Carrollton, Alabama, my hometown, was no exception. Aside from Mother and the children, there was only one other mouth my family could afford to feed. This was a mouth that my family was compelled to feed, it belonged to Daisy.

Papa Mills, my maternal grandfather, had given Daisy, a Jersey milk cow, to our family shortly after Daddy had left us. Mother would say, "Papa brought Daisy to us, but she came from heaven." Mother would also say, "We must feed Daisy, because she feeds us."

In truth, Daisy seemed a gift from heaven. She produced enough milk and butter for a family of six, sometimes with extra milk to sell or barter. Mother would sometimes say, "Daisy keeps us alive. Without her, I do not know what we would do." As a child, I took these words literally. I thought that Daisy had to live for our family to live.

We kept Daisy in Mr. Robinson's pasture, behind the house that we rented from him. As long as the grass in the pasture lasted, Daisy was fed only enough cow feed to keep her standing still while she was being milked. During the late months of summer the pasture grass withered and died, increasing Daisy's need for cow feed. At these times we looked for grass outside the pasture.

Often, during these late months of summer, the grass grew tall alongside the public roads. The mowing of and spraying of the road right-of-ways with herbicides was a thing of the future. My family took advantage of this grass by tying Daisy with a chain attached to a metal pin alongside the road. We called the procedure "staking Daisy out."

My older brother, Frank, was the family member in charge staking Daisy out. He would find a grassy spot, snap the chain to Daisy's halter, and lead her to the selected site. There, he would hammer a metal pin into the ground and control the radius of the circle in which Daisy could graze with the length of the chain between the halter and the metal pin. Many times I heard Mother caution Frank, "Be sure and not let Daisy get too close to the road. Be sure that Daisy is not too close to a ditch, we do not want to lose our cow." The importance of Daisy to my family was well understood.

About the same time that Miss Heck came to live with us, I thought that my carelessness might cause my entire family to die. I thought I had killed Daisy and that would be the end of our family as well.

For at least a year before this traumatic event, I had been pestering Mother to allow me to "stake Daisy out." My repeated requests were met with such things as "Joe, you are not big enough to do that; Joe, I am afraid that something may happen to Daisy." With statements of real concern, and for good reason, Mother denied my requests.

Finally, my perseverance paid off and Mother gave in to my request, but with the admonition, "Son, be very careful now. We cannot let anything happen to Daisy."

"Mother," I assured her, "I can do it." (I have never been plagued with a lack of confidence.)

With the metal pin and hammer in one hand, and the chain in the other, I led Daisy to a spot I had already selected. The grass was growing tall in front of our neighbor's house, Mr. Tom Burgess. I called him, "Mr. Tom."

After Daddy left our family, Mr. Tom had become a surrogate father for me. I was sure that my staking Daisy on that part of his property that fronted the road was permissible, even without asking him.

The spot I had selected was on a high bank, with the roadway being some five or six feet below. I knew that the length of Daisy's chain had to be carefully calculated so as to not let her get too close to the high bank. After all, Daisy was a gift from heaven that kept my family alive.

Leading Daisy to the spot I had chosen, I released her chain and she started eating the tall grass as I drove the pin into the ground. I had watched my bother do this many times before. Once the pin was set, I calculated the length of the needed chain and looped it over the pin. I thought I had Daisy well situated to come back home late that afternoon with a full stomach.

From a distance, all seemed well when I went back to retrieve the cow that was keeping my family alive. Daisy had eaten all the tall grass within her circle and she was patiently waiting to be led back to our barn. As I came closer, she seemed too close to the edge of the tall bank, but that was no cause of immediate concern.

When I reached her, things looked different. Daisy was too close to the bank's edge. Worse yet, I had given her too much chain and it was wrapped around her back feet. The little boy in me had made a mistake, and I did not know what to do.

I decided that if I could remove the looped chain from the pin, I could lead Daisy away from her position of danger. As I lifted the chain from the pin, Daisy tried to come forward, toward me. She stumbled and fell, going backwards over the tall bank.

The last thing I saw of her, before she went out of sight, were her beautiful, big, brown eyes. She was looking right at me, as if to say, "Why did you let this happen?"

I rushed to the edge of the bank, and there, in the ditch below, lay Daisy.

Several times, she attempted to get back onto her feet, and failed. I slid down the dirt bank, scared almost to death and crying, "Get up Daisy! Get up Daisy!"

Our faithful cow struggled again, and with great difficulty, got back onto three legs. Her right back hip and leg seemed not to work. I cried. I prayed. I cried some more, "Please don't die Daisy. Please don't die!"

I was so afraid that Daisy would die and her death would mean the death of my entire family. I was afraid to attempt to get Daisy back to the barn. I was afraid not to. I was simply fearful of everything I thought I should do.

With many tears, I started leading Daisy back home. I did not know what to do, but getting her back to the barn seemed best. I did not want Mother to know that she was hurt. I did not want Mother to know that I thought Daisy was going to die.

Waking slowly, Daisy hobbled on three legs, barely putting her right back foot on the ground as I led her home. I cried and I prayed all the way.

I was glad that no one was outside our house as I led Daisy past. I was filled with shame and sorrow. I was simply lost, not knowing what to do or which way to turn.

I managed to get Daisy past the house and into the barn without being seen. I put her in her stall and went into the house. I was afraid to tell anyone what had happened. I was very much a little boy that knew not what to do or say. In my shame and guilt, I said nothing.

With great dread, I waited for Mother to go to the barn at milking time. I knew that she would find a dead cow. After what seemed an eternity, Mother went to the barn with milk bucket in hand and I waited. And I waited some more. It seemed as if Mother would never return. I both wanted her to return to the house and I was afraid for her to.

Finally, after what seemed a year, Mother returned with a worried look on her face. That was so unlike her; she was usually a happy person. I was waiting in the kitchen when she came through the backdoor. She looked at me and gently asked, "Joe, what happened to Daisy?"

"Is she dead?"

"No son, I think she will be all right. Tell me what happened."

My emotional dam burst. I cried and I cried, sobbing out what I had done and what had happened. Mother took me in her arms and held me close.

In a few days, Daisy's limp disappeared and she continued to provide more milk and butter than the Berry Family could use. Possibly Mother was right. Possibly Daisy did come from heaven.

Shortly after I thought that I had killed Daisy, a tornado came through our part of the state, causing great damage and nine deaths. I shall never forget that violent storm. It brought midnight darkness at midday. In addition to the violence of the whirling wind, it brought the heaviest rain that I have ever known. Proving that every storm has a silver lining, the storm apparently brought something else to our house.

My hometown was a small one with about 150 houses and a population of less than 600 people. We not only knew every person in town, but also every cat and dog and who they belonged to. Before the storm, we were painfully aware that none of the dogs belonged to us. In vain, we had tried to get Mother to let us have a dog.

But with the passing of that terrible storm came the clearing of the sky, the lightness of day, and a silver lining: a small, mostly white, Rat Terrier dog mysteriously appeared on our front porch. She was not a local dog. We knew them all. We always thought that she was brought to our house on the wings of the storm.

Immediately, on finding the dog, our five young voices, in unison, began the pleas of, *"Please mother, please! May we keep the dog? She has no home! If we do not keep her, where will she go?"*

Mother was outnumbered and trapped. We knew that we had won the battle when Mother said, *"Heck, another mouth to feed."*

Our pleas and prayers had been answered. Now, at last, we had a dog! To commemorate our victory, we decided to name the new member of our family *"Miss Heck."*

Immediately we opened a training school for Miss Heck and she proved an excellent student. Soon Miss Heck was retrieving balls and sticks, rolling over on command, walking on her hind legs for a bite of biscuit, and sitting when told. She was always so happy to please. Best of all, she learned to play hide and seek. On command, Miss Heck would stay in place while we hid. When someone shouted *"ready,"* Miss Heck would follow her nose and search out everyone in hiding.

It appeared that Christmas of 1939 would be a special one. We were now a family of eight, including Daisy and Miss Heck. We had a dog, and not just any dog. We had Miss Heck. And, Daisy was alive and well. Both cow and dog had become family.

The anticipated happy holiday took a bad turn. About two weeks before Christmas, Miss Heck disappeared!

We searched the town over, knocking on every door, asking every person we met. We cried, and prayed, and searched, but Miss Heck was not to be found. We searched, prayed, and cried some more. Miss Heck could not be found. We walked all the streets, searched all the ditches, fearful that Miss Heck had been hit by a car or truck. We even walked the railroad track, fearful that a train had hit Miss Heck. To no avail, Miss Heck was gone.

Christmas Day was not cheerful that year. Miss Heck's mysterious disappearance had stolen the joy of Christmas. The family gathered around our fresh cut and hand decorated cedar Christmas tree and opened our few presents. Our stockings contained some fruit and nuts, plus a candy cane. But our hearts were not in tune with the joy of Christmas. Miss Heck was gone!

It was a long, sad day. At bedtime, Mother banked the open fires and blew out our two kerosene lamps. All was quiet and sad at the Berry House. That was not the way Christmas should be, but that was the way it was.

Thereafter, a family dispute developed. A dispute that was never resolved. As with most family disputes, it was over a silly thing. Our unresolved dispute was over the question of *"Who heard her first."*

All five of us children insisted, *" I heard her first. "*

The unsettled family fuss notwithstanding, we were always happy that before the end of Christmas Day, we heard a scratching at the front door.

Miss Heck was back! She had come home for Christmas!

Me and Mr. Tom

I saw Tom Burgess ("Mr. Tom") through the eyes of a child and I remember him that way. Those who were inclined to view things this way would have considered the two of us as a social mismatch. In any case, he was a great influence on my life.

Mr. Tom lived in a large frame house across a dirt road and up the hill from our small, four-room, unpainted frame house. His house, in its fresh painted whiteness, was framed in the summer months by the greenness of the large surrounding oak trees. A large front porch, with its swing and rocking chairs, all in matching white, greeted those who approached.

As a boy, Mr. Tom's front porch swing seemed to talk to me with its squeaking, telling wonderful stories, and taking me to places I had never seen before. His home was my home, a place of ease, security, and comfort. Mr. Tom made it that way. In his company, I was safe.

Up the front steps and across the porch of his house led me to a beautiful oak door with stained glass panels that opened into a long hallway. Three bedrooms were to the right of the hall, large living and dining rooms were to the left. Mr. Tom's bedroom was at the end of the hall and a large kitchen was off to the left.

By the standards of Carrollton, Alabama, the "Burgess Place," as it was commonly known, was one of the town's finest. Mr. Tom and his wife, "Miss Flo" to me, and his two spinster sisters lived in the big house on top of the hill. I do not know how long the house, barn, and surrounding farm land had been owned by the Burgess family; it is safe to assume several generations.

A hundred yards down the hill and across the gravel road was the small rental house in which my mother and us five children lived. It too had a front porch that spanned the length of the house. Two small bedrooms were in back of the porch and a small kitchen and eating room in back of the bedrooms. Our entire house, front porch and all, could have been placed inside Mr. Tom's living and dining rooms, likely with room to spare.

Mr. Tom's house was lighted with electricity, ours with kerosene lamps. His house had indoor plumbing, ours an outdoor toilet. His had a good roof, ours sometimes required placing pots and pans on the floor and beds to catch the leaks from rain. His house, I am quite sure, was free of mortgage indebtedness. Ours was rented;

fortunately from a kind man who did not evict when the rent was past due. Mr. Tom always drove a nice car. Unless someone gave us a ride, our family walked.

As a child, I did not see the Burgess Place or my house as I now describe them. Then, they were simply the places where we lived. As a child, social inequality had no meaning, it was neither part of my vocabulary nor of my thinking. For this, much credit goes to Mr. Tom. In many ways he was like a daddy, standing in the place of a daddy who was missing. He had no children of his own, so possibly I stood in the shoes of the child who was missing in his life. However it may have been, we became close friends.

Our relationship began when I was about six and he was about thirty-five and grew in importance to me over the next three or four years.

Mr. Tom helped to open the windows of my world. As a child, when we did things together, it was me and Mr. Tom. As we walked the fields behind his house, as we rode in his car on his rural mail route, as we sat on his front porch and talked, as we did so many things together, it was me and Mr. Tom doing it. The fancy, formal language of "Mr. Tom and I" would come much later in life. Back then it was the other way around.

Mr. Tom and my mother were about the same age. Mother was the daughter of James Morgan Mills, "Papa" to me. The Burgess and Mills families had known each other for several generations. We were living in the small rental house, down the hill from Mr. Tom's house when my daddy, in 1936, walked away from our family. Daddy was there one day, and gone the next—no one knew where. It was after daddy left that I sort of became Mr. Tom's son, at least for three or four years.

In all the hours that I spent with him after daddy left, I recall no mention of daddy being made by Mr. Tom. Instead, he just seemed to have stepped into daddy's shoes. I did not, at the time, think of Mr. Tom being a stabilizing influence on my life, this realization came later. Mr. Tom, as steady as a rock, stepped into my life and filled a void. I can see that now.

I recall being concerned only three times about what Mr. Tom was doing, or not doing. The first of these concerns arose as he and I drove his car on the sometimes muddy, slick, dirt roads of his rural mail route. Most people would have said that he was a rural mail carrier. I did not see him that way. To me, as a child, he was simply the man who carried the mail, the man who often took me on his mail route, the man who made me feel that he and I drove the car together, the man who made me a part of his magic life. In all ways, it seemed a joint venture.

At the time, Pickens County, Alabama, where we lived, had only one paved road and it was ten miles to the north of Mr. Tom's mail route. Sometimes, when we were carrying the mail and his car got to skidding and fishtailing on the muddy roads, he would say, "Turn into the skid, Joe, turn into the skid." Once he got the car going straight again, he would add, "Joe, we can't go straight in life when we are in a skid." Those words, coming from Mr. Tom, were important to me, they made me feel that I was actually driving the car.

Many times, on the muddy roads, the car would lose traction and go into a slide. As the car would start a skid to the right, Mr. Tom would laugh and call out, "Turn her to the right, Joe, turn her to the right." If the skid were to the left, he would reverse his directions to me, but always furnish the laughter.

I was very concerned the first time the car skidded completely into the ditch. In spite of all that Mr. Tom and I could do, and no matter how quickly we turned the steering wheel into the skid, the car went completely into the ditch. And it would not come out.

On that occasion, Mr. Tom looked at me and said, "Joe, I know the farmer that lives at the foot of the hill. I am going to his place to get him to bring his team of mules. As soon as I get back, we will be out of the ditch and on our way. Will that be all right with you?"

"Yes sir, Mr. Tom."

"Son, while I am gone, I am leaving you in charge of the United States mail. Don't let any highway robbers take it away from you."

Several times, when I was ages seven through nine, Mr. Tom's car got stuck in a ditch. If no one came along to help get us out, Mr. Tom would go looking for someone with a team of mules to pull us out, saying, "Joe, I am going for help. You take care of the mail."

Do you not see how much Mr. Tom trusted me? He left me in charge of the United States mail. And, I am pleased to say, not once did any highway robber take the mail from me, or even try.

Mr. Tom and I both attended the First Baptist Church of Carrollton. Sometimes in church I became a little concerned about Mr. Tom.

He sang in choir. I sat with the congregation, but in a place that I could see and watch Mr. Tom. When he sang, he would twist his mouth to the side of his face, and I found that funny. I never laughed at my friend doing this, but I liked to watch him sing. So his singing in church did not give me concern. It was his praying.

Mr. Tom was chairman of the church deacons, and the superintendent of the Sunday school. Often, during the Sunday worship service, the preacher would call on Mr. Tom to lead the congregation in prayer. That was when I got concerned.

I was not concerned about Mr. Tom; I was mildly worried about God. To me, Mr. Tom would take too much of God's time with his prayers, he seemed to have too much to talk to God about. But my worries about this were not too great. I thought that God was big enough to take care of himself.

My childlike concerns for Mr. Tom were demonstrated one day as he and I carried the mail. I must have been about nine at the time, old enough to take notice of Mr. Tom's lifestyle as compared with others that I had come to know or hear of. We were riding together that day on the Speed's Mill Route and I decided to ask him some questions that, in a child's way, seemed important. (The road must have been dry and I was not worried about sliding into the ditch.) I opened with, "Mr. Tom, you do not smoke, do you?"

"No, Joe, I do not smoke."

I did not think he smoked, and that did not seem right. I had gotten old enough to know that smoking seemed important. My older brother and some of his friends had been smoking. They were smoking rabbit tobacco and sections of cross vine. The cross vine grew up into the trees.

My brother and his friends would cut short sections, cigar length, from the dead, dry cross vine and set one end on fire. Then, they would draw the smoke though this porous vine and complain about the "bite" of the smoke on their tongue. I had seen them do it! The rabbit tobacco came from the leaves of a dead weed. It was stripped from the dead stalk and rolled, cigarette fashion, in pieces of brown paper cut from old grocery sacks. It seemed like they were having fun smoking and Mr. Tom was missing out.

Well, that answered one on my concerns about Mr. Tom, but there were others of a more serious nature.

"Mr. Tom, you do not chew tobacco do you?"

"No, Joe, I do not chew."

That was another mark against him. I guess I was just in a faultfinding mood. My Papa Mills chewed tobacco. He chewed Beechnut, and it seemed important for a man to chew tobacco. It seemed that if Papa did it, every man should do it. I knew that Papa was a good man, and that Mr. Tom also considered him a good man. I was getting really concerned about Mr. Tom as we carried the mail that day.

"Mr. Tom, I don't reckon you drink whiskey, do you?"

"No Joe, that is something I have never done."

See how that conversation was going? Every time I asked Mr. Tom an important question he seemed to fail the test. No one in my immediate family drank whiskey, but I had heard my older brother talk about the behavior of Carrollton's three town drunks and how they acted when they were drinking whiskey. To me, it sounded as if whiskey drinking was fun and Mr. Tom was missing out.

I thought I would give Mr. Tom another chance. That seemed a fair thing to do.

"Mr. Tom, do you ever cuss?"

"Well Joe, I try not to," he replied.

That pretty well wrapped it up. I had thrown all my best pitches and Mr. Tom had struck out. I had heard some cussing and I thought I understood its value.

Joe Hogue, our neighbor, was about eighteen and his cussing ability seemed almost as good as that of Mr. "Goat" Adams. (I never knew the true first name of Mr. Adams.) In many ways, Joe Hogue was my hero. He could climb a tree quicker than a monkey. He rode his horse, Old Maude, with neither saddle nor bridle, and his cussing ability seemed to increase each time I was around him and out of the hearing of adults.

Other than Joe Hogue, and to a lesser extent my older brother, I had no reference point from which to gauge the cussing ability of Mr. Adams. A few weeks before my questions to Mr. Tom, Mr. Adams had drilled a well close to where I lived and for several days I had witnessed some of his cussing ability.

Compared to Joe Hogue and my brother, Mr. Goat Adams seemed to have far above average, everlasting cussing ability. He could go on with steady, nonstop cussing for more than five minutes without drawing a breath. His gasoline engine on his well-drilling rig was hard to crank. Mr. Adams, even before trying to crank that engine, would warm it up with a good cussing. He would walk around and around that engine, cuss it from all four sides and then walk around in the opposite direction and cuss it some more. Even at my young age, I thought that in Mr. Goat Adams I was hearing a cussing master at work.

We rode in quietness some distance that day after I had put my questions to Mr. Tom. We stopped at mailboxes, leaving letters and small packages.

As we rode on following my questions, I thought about his answers. He was truly my friend and he seemed to be missing out on some things that looked like fun for others. I did not want my friend to miss anything that might bring pleasure to his life. Such were my concerns.

After riding some distance in silence and with genuine love, I said, "Mr. Tom, I reckon you don't do anything except carry the mail."

"Joe," he laughed and answered, "you are right. About all I do is carry the mail."

Shortly thereafter, I moved away. I went to live with Papa, and then others. After I moved away, I saw little of Mr. Tom, but the memory of this kind man went with me and yet remains, now more than seventy years later.

I moved away, grew up and did many things that I knew that Mr. Tom would not approve of, many things I never wanted my children and grandchildren to do. But, I remembered that I could not go straight if my life were in a skid. I remembered that Mr. Tom had taught me that some skids in life are beyond control. And with those, we can only do our best.

Fifty years later, I went back to see Mr. Tom. We sat on the front porch of the house that I had been given the run of when I was a boy. His wife, "Miss Flo," was with us. His two spinster sisters that had lived with him were now gone.

We talked that day. We talked about things past, present, and things yet to be. We talked about Papa Mills, Mother, and the days of my youth. As we talked, I relived some of my experiences and the things this wonderful man had taught me.

I figured it would be my last visit with Mr. Tom, and it was. If his belief that there is a life beyond this one is correct, I hope he and I share that next life together. I hope I see him singing in a choir someday. If that happens, I hope he will twist his mouth around to the right and sing out of the side of his face while I am sitting where I can see.

As I was leaving the nice shade of Mr. Tom's porch for the last time that day, he asked, "Joe, do you remember those things you asked me about my lifestyle that day when we were on the Speed's Mill route?"

"Yes sir, I remember."

"Well, Joe," he laughed, "I have some bad news for you. I have long since retired from the post office. Now I do not even carry the mail."

In the days of my childhood, it was me and Mr. Tom. We did not smoke, chew tobacco, drink whiskey, or curse. But together we went to church, drove the '32 Chevrolet, tried to correct the skids of life, and carried the mail.

Entrepreneur

If one keeps good health, aging can be a wonderful time of life. A time to think, reflect, and recall some of the good things one has done, stupid ones too. Awareness of aging, for me at least, is a new experience. It is something that has been happening to me for all of life without my awareness. I had to approach the end of the row to even know there is a row. I suspect it happens to most old folk this way.

With age, my world seems to shrink. It is a good feeling, giving me opportunity to see enough of the trees so I may understand the forest. "Things" now are for the garbage heap. I do not pray very often, but I know that when I get into a real bind, prayer comes to mind. When I pray, I keep it simple. Mostly, I ask God to rid me of the oppressive burden of owning too many "things." At my age, I want to travel light. Sometimes I pray that God will spare me the long prayers of too many preachers, the shallow talk of too many politicians, and the grace of too much society. Also, I pray that God will grant me the company of honest people, the love of little children, and the ability to express myself with the fewest possible words.

Often now, I wonder how many of my eighty years of life has been the product of some plan of mine and how many has been the result of pure chance. It seems that chance has prevailed. Some of my old friends contend that God has planned and directed their lives. Not so with me. I do not believe for a moment that God has had a hand in some of my stupid activities, like doing those things I never wanted my children and grandchildren to do. (Aging has made me a little more open and honest about some of the skeletons in my closet, but not completely so. Even if I live 500 years, I will never be prepared to "tell it all.")

My wonderful wife, Linda, asked me to list all my work experiences and the places where I have worked, and things I have done. I will tell you some of it, but not nearly all. There are some things that are best left unsaid.

The last fifty years are easy to reconstruct, I have practiced law in Huntsville, Alabama; mostly trial work involving cases that spanned a wide variety of issues. My trial practice was a general one. I never developed a specialty of litigation. I tried issues ranging from the life cycle of the subterranean termite, the germination qualities of cottonseed, the toxic threat of chemotherapy that will lead to death unless the antidote is properly given, and murder. Had I developed a trial specialty, I could have been a better lawyer in a narrow manner. But I enjoyed the broader walk of getting into things I knew nothing about and trying to learn something new. With many of my clients, I laughed. With more than a few, I cried. It was a wonderful journey for which I carry no burden of regret.

The last twelve years of my life have been walked free of the burden of serving that jealous mistress called "law." I have been what some call "retired." That is not a good word; it suggests that I am now secluded, remote, or lonesome. Not so. It is the time of life for me to attempt repayment of many old debts.

Either chance or God, I know not which, placed many people in the path of my life who gave me a helping hand. Sometimes a huge helping hand. These supporting hands are now long since dead and buried. The only way I know to attempt repayment of what I owe to the dead is for me do something for the living.

To some extent, this unpaid debt is a burden. Not a heavy burden, not one that keeps me awake at night, but one that keeps me looking for a way to repay. Sometimes I ask myself *if I do not pay this debt now, when?* At eighty, the "when" part of that question stirs old legs and arms to action.

With awareness of an unpaid debt, and awareness that "when" is now or never, I now look for ways to give back to my community. I regularly engage in visiting classes ranging from kindergarten to the college level, sharing my interest in storytelling, writing, and American History. I give talks to church and civic groups and teach in the continuing education program at the University of Alabama in Huntsville.

Most exciting of all, each fall I dress in ragged overalls, a tin-pot hat, mismatched shoes, no socks, a shirt made from a burlap coffee sack, and, with a hiking stick, I become John Chapman of Leominster Colony of Massachusetts and walk into various elementary schools, presenting Johnny Appleseed to the little people. Typically the teachers have the kids arranged for the appearance of this wonderful and interesting man. When Johnny Appleseed walks into the classroom, eyes of those beautiful children become as large as watermelons and my spirit for life is renewed. But these things are the fun things of life and not part of my wife's assignment to write of the places I have been and my work experiences.

The experiences during the first twenty-nine years of my life were many. I will not include such things as drawing water from the well and filling the outdoor wash pot and tubs for Mother's weekly washday, or bringing fire and stove wood into the house and other routine household chores that were a regular part of the lives of most kids who experienced the hard years of the 1930s in rural Alabama. Rather, I will start by telling about my little hometown and my first work where earning money was my objective. As best recalled, this began when I was about seven, maybe eight, years old in Carrollton, Alabama.

Carrollton was a sleepy little place, with no street lights, no traffic lights, and only one traffic stop sign which seldom demanded obedience. The cars and trucks were few and the stop sign had no meaning for the mules pulling the wagons. The town went to bed early and was called awake at dawn each following morning. It was impossible to sneak the sunrise past the town's numerous roosters.

Maybe only half the homes were wired for electricity. Wash pots and tubs in the back yards and clothes hanging on the clotheslines were common affairs. Mondays, for most, were "wash days." The town had no movie theatre, arts council, or Chamber of Commerce. The closest thing to drama was the annual high school play, directed by Mrs. Clemons, an English teacher.

The town's fire department was of the volunteer variety. The fire truck, with its 500-gallon water tank, was always parked in back of Dr. Hill's office, with the keys in the ignition. On occasion the older boys would take the fire truck for a joy ride, adding a little spice and excitement to the quietness of the night. No harm was done, and the truck was always left close to where it had been parked.

The town sponsored no civic clubs, but it did have three churches—Baptist, Methodist, and Presbyterian. No organized temperance group pestered our three local town drunks. The more remote sinners were prayed for monthly when the Ladies Missionary Society met in the basement of the Baptist Church. About one-third of the local families had their own milk cow. Ice boxes kept the milk and butter fresh in most of the homes without refrigeration.

If my little hometown had its share of marital infidelity, which is likely, I was not aware of it. I remember no divorce action being discussed by the adults during the first fifteen years of my life. Catholics and Jews were nonexistent in my small world, as were people of Asian extraction. I was thirteen years old before I saw an Asian. He was wearing a uniform of the United States Army, guarding a German prisoner-of-war.

Some adults would have seen the small town of Carrollton as a place that was both economically and culturally deprived. At the time, that was not my view, nor is it now. I saw it simply as the place where I lived. My world was a very small one, largely limited to the distance that my maternal grandfather's 1927, four-door, Model T Ford could travel in one day, with enough time saved to get back home before supper.

Carrollton, the seat of government for Pickens County, had a population of not more than 600 people. The county courthouse, centered in a roadway circle, but called a "Square," was the town's centerpiece. At the time of my first effort to earn money, all roads in the area, except the one that circled the courthouse, were dirt with enough river gravel mixed in to add some stability during wet weather. Four dirt roads, like the spokes of a wagon wheel, ran north, south, east, and west away from the courthouse.

A one-half mile walk north from the courthouse would lead to a small, four-room, frame house that Mother and us five children called home. It would be from this little house that I would launch my first venture in the free enterprise system.

Before telling of my first business venture, I will attempt the painting of a word-picture of my hometown, giving a verbal walking tour around the courthouse and identifying the buildings and their occupants. Starting at the dirt road that ran north from the courthouse and traveling in a clockwise direction, the northeast corner of the Court Square was occupied by the Phoenix Hotel. It was a frame building, now faded, but once painted white, with a wide front porch and enough rocking chairs to accommodate as many as fifteen guests. Two or three were the most hotel guests I remember seeing in those chairs, and these occasions were only four times each year when court was in session. In its better days, the Phoenix Hotel would have been a very impressive and stately facility, but that was before my time.

The hotel was owned and operated by the Lyles family. Though having seen its better days and now in decay, the hotel was still Carrollton's most impressive commercial building. It had a large dining room and grand piano in the sitting room (I suspect it was the only grand piano in town). To a boy who lived on the edge of poverty, the Phoenix Hotel was most impressive.

I do not recall working inside the hotel, but I do remember working in the large barn/shop that stood in back and to the north of the hotel. The barn had been originally built to stable the horses and house the buggies of the hotel guests. Under the same roof was a large shop. When I was about fifteen, I worked in this shop for several weeks under the supervision of an experienced carpenter helping repair some of the hotel chairs.

Next, in the clockwise journey around the Court Square, in the northeast corner of the circle was a small building divided like a duplex into two offices. The same lawyer, Mr. Dare Patton, regularly occupied one office. Mr. Patton was said to have played football for the University of Alabama in the late 1800s. To a little boy, this too was most impressive.

In the office adjoining that of Mr. Patton other lawyers seemed to come and go. It is said a town that cannot support one lawyer can always support two. In accord with this adage there was a second regularly occupied lawyer's office in town, but it did not front the Court Square.

The Dew Drop Inn Café came next in this clockwise circle. It sat on the east side of the square, north of and adjacent to the dirt road that fed off the Court Square to the east. The Dew Drop Inn, with a gas pump in front and an icehouse in back, sold hamburgers, hot dogs, and snacks. This café and Owen Ferguson's Café that was located to the east of town, next to the railroad track, were the only two places in town that served food. The Dew Drop Inn catered to the whites, Owen Ferguson's to the blacks. At the time I worked at the Dew Drop Inn, it sold little of anything. Gross daily sale receipts in excess of fifty dollars were rare.

When I was sixteen I had the sole responsibility of the management and operation of the Dew Drop Inn for a full summer. In the spring of that year, at the close of school, the owner of the business hired me in less than three hours and gave me a crash-course lesson in how to run the business. Then he left me, went home and got drunk, and I did not see him again until it was time for school to begin that fall. I have been truly frightened for my life on two occasions, the first was at The Dew Drop Inn that summer.

I was alone at the Dew Drop one Sunday afternoon when a local businessman came into the café highly intoxicated, drew a pistol from his pocket and threatened to shoot me for allegedly mistreating his son. I had no idea what the man was talking about, but I was introduced to the fear of immediate death. (A few weeks later, I saw this man standing on the porch of the Probate Office in the presence of other businessmen. I mustered all the courage that I could find, walked up to the man and, in the presence of the other gentlemen, confronted him with his drunken activity. I concluded my statement by telling him that he should be ashamed for acting like a jackass. My knees shook all the way back to The Dew Drop Inn, which I had left unattended.)

Going south from The Dew Drop Inn, across the dirt road that went east, was a small store that had no official name I can recall. It was commonly called "Miss Alice's" after the name of the widowed lady, Alice Jones, who owned and operated the business. The store's inventory, a very modest one, was a mixture of dry goods, groceries, and bagged cow feed that was delivered to the few purchasers from a loading platform at the store's backdoor.

Later, I would sometimes work for Miss Alice in this store as a sales clerk, errand boy, and janitor combination. I would also work at her house, or more accurately behind her house, when I was nine and ten years of age. In this employment, I would go to her house each morning, milk her three cows, take the milk into the kitchen, and then drive the cows east down the road, past Owen Ferguson's Café and the depot, to the pasture. At the close of the day, I would reverse the order of things, retrieve and milk the cows, and leave them overnight in the small barnyard behind Miss Alice's large home. For this work, I earned the amazing sum of twenty-five cents each week. That is not a mistake, I said "week." I was glad to get it.

Adjacent to Miss Alice's, still on the east side of the Court Square was a sometimes grocery store, first known to me as the Jitney Jungle. When open, its inventory was largely groceries, fresh and canned. This store also sold cow food, as well as chicken feed and had a loading dock at the rear. The owner of this business was something of a mystery to me. I thought it belonged to a Mr. J. T. Phillips, who was the man who hired me from time to time to work there stocking shelves, sweeping the store and front sidewalk, arranging the storage room, and other odd jobs.

Completing the businesses on the east side of the square was the dry goods store of Mr. Lloyd Beasley. The name of this store escapes my memory. I had a particularly warm relation with Mr. Beasley. He was a man with a ready smile who kept and hunted quail with his trained dogs. I worked in his store for the entire winter of my junior year of high school. In addition to the principal inventory of dry goods, the store carried a small line of canned goods. One day of that winter, a somewhat prissy young lady approached me as I worked and asked, "Do you have any cock fruit tail." The devil that has always resided within me took control, and I yelled out across the store, purposely loud enough that everyone could hear, "Mr. Beasley, do we have any cock fruit tail?" Mr. Beasley laughed and directed me to the location of the fruit cocktail. When I graduated from Carrollton High School, Mr. Beasley gave me a new pair of very nice dress shoes. They were the first pair of high quality shoes that I remember having.

Keeping shoes on one's feet during the depression years was, in several ways, a challenge. The first challenge was to accumulate enough money to buy them and get them on your feet before the severe winter weather arrived. The second challenge was keeping the shoes in one workable piece until the weather moderated the next spring. Most of the maintenance problem was keeping the soles of these shoes attached to the upper part.

After a few weeks use of cheap shoes, the only kind we could afford, the soles at the very tip would start separating from the upper part of the shoe. Slowly the sole released its grip and the separation increased. When the separated part of the sole measured about an inch or two it would start to "flap" with each step. Once the flapping started, the separation rapidly increased. After about a month of flapping with each step, the sole was completely separated back to the heel. Sneaking up on someone while flapping was out of the question. Flapping while walking was embarrassing; it was like advertising *I am the poorest kid in town.*

I have no recollection of personally doing it, but some kids I knew would walk barefoot with their new, cheap shoes tied around their neck until they got within sight school. There, they would stop and put their shoes on before going into the school. This practice was motivated by the desire to preserve the "new" appearance of the cheap shoes and to delay the start of the flapping as the soles separated.

There were at least two home remedies for the flapping ailment. If one had the money, a "half-sole kit" could be purchased, the flapping part cut from the shoe, and with a cheap glue included in the kit, effort could be made to glue the new half-sole onto the upper. After about a month, the new half-sole would start to separate and the flapping began anew.

The second method of "curing the flap" was to take a pair of pliers and several metal "hog rings" and attempt a reattachment of the separated sole. The hog rings were made to attach to a pig's nose to keep them from rooting under the fence. The rings were made of metal, staple-like in design, and applied to the pig's nose with pliers by squeezing the staple closed in the desired location. Once closed, the staple formed a "ring," thus the name of hog-rings. The same principle was used by holding the flap part of the shoe sole in place and squeezing the hog rings in a manner that would reattach the sole to the upper part of the shoe. The hog ring remedy for the flaps was better than the half-soles. But with the hog rings in place the flapping sound was replaced with a distinct metallic "ring" as the wire rings impacted the floor. If walking on concrete, the metallic ringing sound was greatly increased into a full symphony of clicks and clacks. These many years later, I well remember the "barefoot" days of youth, the flapping of the soles, and the clicking of the hog rings. From these experiences I have an aversion to being barefoot again.

Moving around the courthouse circle, away from Mr. Beasley's store, to the south side of the square would lead to Housel Hardware, the only hardware store in town, one of only four in the entire county. Mr. Bill Huffman, a wonderful man, and later a surrogate father, managed this store.

I have had several "second families" during my life, the Huffman Family being one. I lived with them during my last two years of high school. During this time, I regularly worked in the hardware store, learning many things that added to my mechanical, electrical, plumbing, and carpentry skills. I also milked the Huffman Family cow, and almost killed her one time with my experiment that was calculated to break her of the habit of urinating while I was milking.

I always sat on a milking stool, allowing me to milk with both hands with the milk bucket sitting on the ground beneath the "faucets." Without fail, this cow needed to relieve her bladder about midway through the milking process. When this happened, I had the option of either getting an unwanted splatter-shower or grabbing the milk bucket and vacating the milking-stool. There was only one good choice, I would grab the bucket and give the cow the barn stall until the bladder emptied. Not to be outdone by a cow, I concocted a remedy. I decided a good dose of electricity would break that old heifer of a bad habit.

Finding an old generator from a crank telephone and some small gauge copper wire, I attached one wire to the generator's positive pole and a second wire to the negative pole. These respective wires were wrapped one around the cow's back leg, the other around the upper part of her tail. The generator, with its crank handle, was on the ground to the left of my milking stool. I waited for the magic moment. Just as Old Faithful started doing her thing, I reached down and gave the crank a quick twist.

First, I got a live demonstration of how quickly electricity travels. Next, the cow went through the north wall of the barn, then though the first fence, and over the second fence that led to the pasture. The milk bucket was badly bent, just how is unknown. It was weeks before I could get the cow to come back to the barn. Mrs. Huffman asked, "Joe, what has happened to our cow?"

I lied with, "Mrs. Huffman, I do not know. I have read that out in Texas there is a plant called a locoweed. I understand that it makes cows go crazy. Maybe some of that weed is now growing in Alabama." (My apology Mrs. Huffman, at the time a lie seemed better than truth.)

Going back to the hardware store to continue the walking tour around the courthouse and from there going west across the dirt road that ran south from the Court Square brings to view a frame building whose use defies description. Various, small businesses quickly opened and, just as quickly, died. No occupant stayed long enough to establish an identity. I have a vague recollection of doing some kind of work in this building, but I cannot recall what is was or for whom it was performed.

Completing the southwest side of the Court Square was another small clothing and dry goods store owned and operated by Cornelia Timmons and her mother, Mrs. Elliot. The business name seems to have been "Elliots." This store carried more ladies clothing than men's and displayed many bolts of cloth and various sewing materials. It was the day and age of home sewing and Elliots Store was Carrollton's sewing center. Many, if not most, cow and chicken feeds were sold in printed cotton sacks that could be converted into dresses and shirts by skillful hands and sewing machines.

I never worked in this store, but I did occasional work around the Elliot home, mostly yard work. Mr. George Valentine Timmons, the husband of Cornelia Timmons, was, for lack of a better description, my high school history teacher. Whatever teaching skills he may have once had were lost long before I reached his class. The man simply did not teach, he gave us silly "busy work" to keep us occupied. I developed a strong dislike of even going to his classroom. Years later, in college, I discovered my great love for the history of our country.

West of Elliots Store, and before reaching the next building, was a large open area that extended to the south and west. This was Carrollton's parking lot—not for the few motor vehicles of the town and county, but for the mules and wagons. Of course, there were no parking meters and Carrollton did not have a city police department. (The Pickens County Sheriff provided law enforcement.) I am sure this vacant lot was privately owned, but no parking fee was paid. Parking the mules and wagons was on a first come, first serve basis. The mules would stand hitched to the wagon stomping their feet and swishing their tails in effort to ward off the biting horse flies. Saturdays, the busy shopping day, would sometimes find fifteen or twenty mule-drawn wagons parked there. The shade of about ten trees on this vacant lot provided the choice parking spots for the wagons. An occasional run-away team of mules was one of Carrollton's main sources of entertainment.

On the south side of this vacant lot, away from the Court Square, stood a frame building that housed *The Pickens County Herald*, a weekly newspaper published and edited by Mr. Jack Pratt. Mr. Pratt would sometimes create mild controversy with his editorial comments. I recall the occasion of a local Baptist preacher seeking election to the office of county superintendent of schools. The prevailing school of thought was that preachers should not become involved in politics. To overcome this notion, the preacher announced that he had prayed about running for the office and the Lord had spoken to him during a night of prayer, telling him to seek the office. Mr. Pratt caused quite a stir with an editorial comment that, "Instead of hearing the Lord speak to him in the middle of the night as he claims, he may have simply heard a jackass bray."

Standing in the southwest corner of the square stood a building that was divided in its use. The front quarter was used as a men's Domino Club. I never knew what the rules of membership for this club were. During cool, rainy weather, and during all winter months, some of the unemployed men, of which there was an abundance, would gather in this room and play dominoes for hours without end. Neither the Domino Club nor any other building or house in town was air-conditioned. So during the hot months the men of the Domino Club would move to a more comfortable setting under the shade of the trees on the Court Square.

Even without the members of the Domino Club being there, the shaded lawn of the Court Square had its regular visitors. These were the unemployed men of the area. Daily, weather permitting, Monday through Saturday, they would congregate under the shade trees in the southeast corner of the square. Some would sit on the Civil War Monument on the east side of the square, across the street from The Dew Drop Inn and the store of Miss Alice. The unemployed men, seated in these locations, had the best opportunity to see the few north-south motor vehicles that passed through town.

Sometimes, but not often, a driver of a motor vehicle would stop, looking for someone to hire for a few hours, or even a day. The hungry men wanted to be able to quickly respond to a nod or call for someone to work. Sometimes the stopped driver would call out the name of a particular man who was wanted. At other times, the driver would simply hold up a finger, or two, indicating the number of men needed.

Although in great need for a job, civility was not uncommon among these hungry men. Often one man would yield his "turn" to respond to the driver's signal to another man who was believed to have greater need for a job. These men, usually ten to twenty in number, would sit in caned-bottom mule-ear chairs, whittle strips of red cedar with their pocketknives, and talk. Storytelling was a main pastime. Some would fashion a checkerboard from a piece of heavy cardboard and engage in checker games, using bottle tops as their checker pieces. Most wore patched overalls and cotton shirts whose collars had worn out, then detached, turned over and sewn back onto the shirt. A patch sewn on top of an old patch was not uncommon. Some men were barefoot, and only a few wore socks.

They were friendly men who carried a faraway look in their eyes. They, most times, seemed to be looking beyond the moment, beyond the day for something else. As a little boy I would sometimes sit with them and listen to their talk. In spite the lost look in the eyes of most, they joked and laughed. They told funny stories. I seldom heard profanity. Once a man took a piece of cane and whittled me a whistle from it. I got to know these men and counted them as my friends.

The Court Square was the place of choice for political talk and campaign speeches. When I was sixteen (1946), James "Big Jim" E. Folsom stood on the south steps of the courthouse, making his bid for the Governorship of Alabama. Big Jim was a tall, hansom man with a head full of dark hair. As he finished his talk to the twenty or thirty men that made his audience, he got a good laugh, and likely some votes, by adding, "Fellows, my opponent is spreading the rumor that Big Jim is a woman chaser. I ain't gonna lie to you. If you bait that trap the right way, you will catch Ole Jim most every time." The crowd loved it, and he was elected.

Going back to complete the circle of businesses fronting the Court Square, the back three-fourths of the Domino Club building was used as a distribution point for the "commodities" (flour, cornmeal, dried beans and peas, sugar, and cheese being distributed by the Federal Government to hungry families, like mine).

Thursday was commodity distribution day. Mostly women stood in line to receive the commodities. (I did not think about it as a child; as an adult, I suspect the male ego and the feelings of shame of not being able to feed their families made the men hesitant to stand in line for food. The mothers, with their mother's urge to feed their young, did not enjoy standing in line for food, a higher calling drove them.)

North of and adjacent to the Domino Club stood another store where I worked, the Yellow Front Store. This store, one of a small chain of stores of like kind that operated in two or three adjacent counties, might be compared to today's "Dollar" stores. Larger wholesale purchases of inventory gave the storeowner, The Sumter Farm Company, a financial advantage of purchasing and then selling for less. As one might suspect, the fronts of all stores in this small chain were painted a bright yellow, in keeping with their name. This store was managed by another Mr. Phillips (no relation to the Mr. Phillips who ran the Jitney Jungle Store on the opposite side of the square). I worked at The Yellow Front Store mostly on Saturdays, the longest trade day of the week.

The Yellow Front carried groceries, dry goods, and had the best cow, mule, and chicken food trade in town. The regular hours of store operation were easily understood. The doors were opened for business at sunrise and stayed open until the last customer left the store that night. Sometimes, particularly on Saturday, this would be midnight. But, for the employees, the day was not over when the last customer left. In preparation for early opening the next business day (closed on Sunday), after the last customer was out the door, shelves had to be restocked and the floors swept clean.

Several memories from The Yellow Front Store follow me, three of which I share. First was the custom of endorsing paychecks held by people who could not sign their name. The customers who did not know how to write, when their bill of goods had been tallied and payment was due, would hand the clerk their check and say, "You sign for me and I will tech [touch] the pen." The clerk would take their check, sign their name on the back, and then extend the pen that had been used toward the customer and they would physically "tech" it. At the time I thought it a silly thing. After I studied law, I learned it was legally significant. Their touching the pen that had just written their name was an overt manifestation that they were adopting that writing as being their own. I suspect the custom came to our country as part of the English Common Law.

The second of my Yellow Front memories now resides on a cabinet top in my kitchen. It is an ugly looking, yellow jar and lid that I have always called a cookie jar. When I was nine years old, I resolved to save enough money to purchase my mother a Christmas present. I had no memory of her ever having received one before. I worked and saved enough money so that, with the discounted price Mr. Phillips gave me, I was able to purchase that cookie jar for Mother's Christmas. Mother, for the remainder of her life, kept that cookie jar in her kitchen. Now, for the remainder of my life, it belongs in my kitchen. It is, after all is said, not such an ugly, yellow jar. (It seems much of life is like that; understanding something often removes its ugly.)

The third memory is one that would greatly excite modern-day public health departments. The area farmers would raise sugarcane, cook the cane juice into syrup, place the syrup in one-gallon tin buckets, and sell it to the local merchants to retail. This canned syrup was frequently referred to in the plural as "them syrups." Some farmers were more skilled in cooking them syrups than others. If the fire under the large syrup-cooking pan was too hot, the syrup would develop a "burned" taste. If the fire was not hot enough, the syrup would be too thin and not adhere to the buttered biscuit properly. At the point of consumer purchase, the taste and consistency of the syrup was sampled in this manner: A strip of heavy, brown wrapping paper would be torn from the big roll of paper, then folded two or three times, making a semi-rigid "tasting spoon." The lid would be pried from the top of the gallon bucket, the customer would dip about one inch of this "spoon" into the syrup and transfer the sample that adhered to the spoon to his mouth. The lid would be replaced on the bucket and the taster had the option of accepting or rejecting them syrups that had been tasted. Would not such an arrangement today cause excitement?

Just north of The Yellow Front Store, before the town's only bank building, stood the Quality Shop, a retail clothing store owned and operated by Mrs. Hazel Curry. Her husband, Judge Curry, would sometimes hire me to handle some of the janitorial services for this store. This duty led me to the awareness that, for reasons I will never know, an old coffin and burial shroud were kept in the back storeroom of the Quality Shop. This was information that the devil in me needed for survival.

When I was seventeen and working in the hardware store, Walter, an older member of the Huffman family by marriage, kept complaining of his ill health. For several months this alleged bad health was made manifest only by his verbal complaints. The members of the Huffman family thought the complainer was lazy, not sick. I concurred in this belief.

With the aid of the hardware store's flatbed truck, an older friend, and my internal devil, the coffin and shroud were borrowed from the Quality Shop and transported to Walter's home. I knew all doors would be unlocked—no one locked their doors—and I knew that Walter would be sound asleep. The coffin was quietly carried into his bedroom and placed on the floor beside the bed. I opened the coffin lid, carefully folding the old, dirty shroud over the open lid, and sat down on the bed beside Walter. Shaking him awake, I told him how sorry I was that he had been feeling sick for the past few months, and that I did not think he had long to live. I told him that I had something I wanted him to try on for size. I pointed to the floor and the open coffin. We seized Walter and tried to put him in the box. My friend and I, even with the devil's aide, were simply not equal to the task. Walter made his escape from the house in his underwear. I was well pleased that my first lesson in applied psychology was not only designed but also executed by me. I never heard Walter complain again.

The First State Bank of Carrollton stood adjacent to and north of the Quality Shop. As I kid, I simply knew it was there, but I had no occasion to do business with it. Later in life, when I was twenty-one, I opened my first account with this bank. Until then, I had no need of a bank account.

Leaving the bank building and crossing the dirt road that led to the west from the Court Square, stood the United States Post Office Building. The more affluent citizens had a rented post office box and the combination numbers that opened its lock. The occasional mail for my family came via general delivery, meaning we could receive mail only when the post office business window was open. With the little mail that we received this was no handicap.

From the Post Office, going north and rounding the curve to the right, was another county building that housed the Probate Office, and the offices of Tax Assessor and Tax Collector. The Office of the County Commission was also in this building along with offices of the County Health Department on the second floor. Further east from this building, across the dirt road that ran north to my house, completed the circle around the courthouse and brings one back to the Phoenix Hotel and all the empty rocking chairs on its front porch.

The Court House building is not without its own charm and memory. In many ways, Carrollton's only claim to fame centers on "The Face in the Window" of the courthouse. If one stands near the Probate Office (that I just described) and looks up to the attic window on the north side of the courthouse, the likeness of a human face can be seen in one of the four windowpanes. It is said to be the face of Henry Wells, a black man who was accused of burning the old courthouse building. ("The Thirteen Ghost Stories of Alabama" carries one account of how the face in the window came to be. But I have created a different version.)

The large courtroom on the second floor of the courthouse brings to mind another youthful caper that I attribute to, in a jocular manner, the devil within me. One Halloween night several of my peers and I found that an exterior door of the courthouse had been left unlocked. This seemed a sign from on high to "come in and do something."

A new two-horse red wagon, displayed for sale, sat behind the hardware store just across the street from the courthouse. Leading my four friends, across the street we went. We disassembled the wagon and carried it piece by piece into the courthouse, up the stairs to the second floor, through the courtroom and out onto a balcony attached to the south side of the building. There we put the wagon back together and left it fully assembled on the balcony. Leaving the courthouse, we were careful to see that all exterior doors were locked behind us. The next day, there was considerable speculation among the town folk as to "How did those kids get that wagon on that balcony?"

My little hometown had two businesses that serviced motor vehicles with oil changes and grease jobs, both with a gasoline pump standing in front. These pumps were literally hand-operated. A twenty-gallon glass reservoir sat on top of the pump with calibrated markings on its side. The markings, reading from bottom to top, indicated "one gallon," two gallons," etc., up to "twenty gallons." When the attached pump lever was hand-rocked back and forth, the pump would deliver the gasoline from the underground storage tank to the glass reservoir on top of the pump, filling the calibrated glass container from bottom to top. If the customer wanted five gallons, the gasoline was pumped up to the five-gallon mark, at which time the nozzle of the delivery hose would be inserted into the mouth of the vehicle gas tank. When the lever on the nozzle was squeezed to its open position, gravity would take control, delivering the gasoline from the glass reservoir above to the vehicle's tank below. No electricity was involved.

These businesses were sometimes called "service stations," or more frequently, "filling stations." It was a fixed custom that the operator not only pumped the amount of gasoline that was requested, carefully filling the reservoir "up to the mark," but also checked the oil, the air pressure of the tires, and cleaned the windshield. In fact, they were a service station. As best recalled, sixteen cents per gallon was the lowest gasoline price I knew.

The little town had no dentist, but a wonderful medical doctor, Hugh Hill. Dr. Hill, a very short, somewhat portly man, was a special friend, not only to my family, but to all who knew him. At the time, he was the third generation of "Hill Doctors" in Carrollton. He never withheld his professional care from those who could not pay for his service. He never sent anyone a bill for prior unpaid service. He always responded when there was need for a house call. (His son, William Hill, became the fourth generation of Hill physicians in Carrollton. William was selected as rural doctor of the year for the United States. In the article announcing this wonderful distinction, William was quoted as saying that he never looked at his list of accounts receivable because he never wanted to know who owed him money when he rendered a medical service. When I read that, I immediately thought of his father who was such an inspiration to me.)

Carrollton was strongly segregated, as was the entire South, and most of the Nation. The public toilets and the water fountain in the courthouse all bore the signs that read "WHITES ONLY." Black people in town needing to relieve either bladder or bowel had to either go to their homes or resort to the plumb thickets or bushes on the outskirts of town.

The public school, for the Caucasians, was located two blocks south of the courthouse. Grades one through twelve (there were no kindergartens) were all housed under the same roof. The total enrollment was approximately 250 students. Aside from the classroom teachers, the remaining administrative staff was one principal, one full-time janitor, and one part-time janitor. (The full-time janitor became another special friend. He was a black man named Tucker Lee. He was badly crippled and walked with considerable difficulty. Each day, he would ride to school in his one-mule wagon and tie his mule under the nearby trees during the day. Many times, Tucker Lee would see that devil in me trying to cause trouble. When seeing this, he would quietly take me aside and offer words of advice and caution. Schools today need more Tucker Lees.)

About five blocks to the east of the courthouse was Owen Ferguson's Café, the only black business in town. It served food and had, in an adjoining room, the only pool table in town. Most of the church going white people in town seemed to think there was something sinful about a pool table, and a deck of cards was often referred to as "fifty-two tickets to hell."

Diagonally across the intersection of two dirt roads from Owen Ferguson's Café was the depot for the AT&N (Alabama, Tennessee, and Northern) Railroad. The "Tennessee and Northern" part of the name was a misnomer, the rail track ran only ten miles north of Carrollton, stopping almost 150 miles south of Tennessee, but it did stretch to Mobile, Alabama, at the south end of the State.

Although the AT&N was a small railway, passenger service once each day, north and south was offered. Freight service, separate from the passenger service, was the main source of revenue for the rail company, and that had to be meager. This railroad no longer exists. (Several times I played hobo and stole a ride on the freight train to

Aliceville, ten miles south of Carrollton. These were the rare occasions when I had the necessary nickel price of admission to a Saturday afternoon double feature cowboy "picture show." Carrollton had no movie theatre, but Aliceville did.)

One day, Carrollton's local alcoholic (I will call him "Tom") was seated on the bench in front of the depot when the northbound passenger trail stopped at the station. A fancy dressed gentleman stepped off the train to stretch his legs during the stop and looked at the sign on the front of the station that read "CARROLLTON, ALABAMA." It was summertime and the trees between the courthouse and the depot were in full foliage. From the depot, all that could be seen of Carrollton was Owen Ferguson's Café some 100 feet from the depot. The fancy dressed traveling man who Tom called a "Dandy" looked at the sign on the depot, looked around and not seeing the town, addressed Tom, "My good man, is this Carrollton, Alabama?"

"Sure is," Tom hiccupped.

"My good man, where is the town?" the dandy asked.

Raising his hand above his shoulder, with his thumb pointed west and in the direction of the foliage-concealed town, Tom said, "It is that away."

"My good man," the dandy responded, "why did they not put the depot closer to the town?"

By this time, Tom had had enough of this "My good man" business and he put the dandy back on the train by saying, "I guess they did not put the depot close to the town because they wanted it down here next to the damn railroad track."

Across the rail track, to the east, was Pate Lumber Company. It operated a small sawmill and engaged in both the retail and wholesale of lumber. This lumber company was Carrollton's only industrial employer and the number of non-family employees probably did not exceed twenty-five. (Most of the paychecks that were presented to me that I had to endorse for the payee and let them "tech the pen" came from Pate Lumber Company.)

Most of Carrollton's homes for the whites were located to the north, east and south of the Court Square. Most of the homes for the blacks were to the west in an area called "West Highland." Few people ever locked their exterior doors, even at night. Many residents did not have keys to their doors. The only "controlled substances" that were available were alcoholic beverages called "home brew" and "white-lightening." These two, of the homemade variety, rarely caused a problem. I recall seeing few physical confrontations during my years there, and these were not of a serious nature.

Thus, my world as a boy was a very small one. It was a court square with a few surrounding businesses connected by a half-mile of dirt road to the small house in which I lived. As one may see, I had work experiences with most of the businesses that fronted the Court Square. In large, even great, measure this was all I knew of planet Earth. Our home had no electricity, plumbing, or radio, and the remainder of the world did not reach us by newspaper or magazine.

The various jobs that I have thus far described were not my first. I started out with plans of being an independent businessman. I was about seven, possibly eight, years old. There is nothing unique about my starting work when I was so young. During those desperate financial years, starting young was a common experience.

In some unknown manner, I concluded that I might get rich in the roasted peanut business. I called them "parched peanuts." Equally often, peanuts were called "goobers." My plan was to parch the peanuts in the oven of Mother's wood-burning cook stove. We already had some stove wood, split and dry, in the wood shed.

I had no concept of one part of the oven being hotter than other parts. The firebox of the stove opened with a front door through which the split sticks of wood could be inserted. The stove's single oven was adjacent and to the right of the firebox. A large front door opened into the oven with its single, adjustable height rack.

Even before making my investment of capital in raw peanuts and brown paper bags, Mother tried to explain how difficult it would be to properly roast peanuts in that oven, how some parts of the oven were much hotter than other parts, and how the peanuts would have to be turned over in the pan to keep the top parts from burning while the bottom parts remained uncooked.

Mother tried to explain such things to me, but I had a problem. I could hear, but I did not know how to listen. (Age has presented a role reversal, now that I am old enough to listen, I cannot hear.)

Mother's good advice notwithstanding, I had a plan and a determination that matched it.

My initial investment capitol was a dime, possibly a gift from Mother, or possibly money earned by running errands for our neighbor, Mr. Tom Burgess. For a nickel, I purchased a peck of raw, dry peanuts. (For those who have been loosely educated and deprived the finer things of life, a peck is a dry measure that equals eight quarts.) With the other nickel, Mr. Phillips at The Yellow Front Store sold me twenty-five small brown paper bags, parched peanut size. I foresaw generating three bags of parched peanuts from each of the eight quarts and selling each bag for a nickel. Thus, if my plan worked, I would gain a dollar twenty on a dime investment. At the time, having more than a dollar seemed an unreal dream, and it turned out that way.

Mother had also told me of the labor that would be required in bringing stove wood into the kitchen, building the fire and keeping it burning. She had explained that the raw peanuts had to be evenly distributed over the cookie pan in which they were roasted. They could not be stacked on top of each other. She had explained that too many peanuts in the pan would not leave room to properly turn them in the roasting process. I had heard, but, as said, my listening was grossly defective. (Even as a little boy, my determination was great.)

I had the stove, the raw peanuts, the bags, and dry stove wood in the shed and I was ready to test the free enterprise system. To give myself a little credit, I did listen to Mother about not putting too many peanuts in the pan. A quart seemed to work nicely. This meant eight pans, one at the time in the oven. It was a time consuming process.

I fired up the stove, got it hot, and placed my first pan in the oven. In almost no time, it seemed, smoke was puffing its way from both sides and the top of the oven door. Using a towel, I opened the door about the time that Mother came into the kitchen. Inspecting my problem, she said, "Joe, the oven was too hot, these peanuts have been burned up. Feed them to the chickens and try again."

As soon as the pan cooled enough for me to handle, I went to the small back porch off the kitchen, threw the burned peanuts in the yard and called the chickens. By the time I arranged another quart of peanuts in my pan, the stove had cooled considerably. That, I thought, was a good sign. On first try the stove had gotten too hot.

With the second pan in the oven, I waited and then looked. Everything seemed in order; no smoke came from the oven. I waited some more, and again looked. The peanuts had not changed in complexion; at least they had not burned. After several "looks," Mother came to the kitchen, took a look, and said, "Joe, the oven is too cool, you need to put more wood in the fire." She suggested two sticks. Hearing, but not listening, I thought four sticks would do a better job.

I followed my superior judgment and soon the smoke was again puffing out all sides of the oven. Soon, I carried my second pan of burned nuts to the back porch and called the chickens. The day turned into a series of trials and failures. The peanuts in some pans were burned on one side and not cooked on the other. In some pans, the peanuts in one end of the pan seemed to be well roasted, but the nuts in the other end of the pan were either roasted too much or not enough, and the exterior shells did not indicate which was which. The chickens quickly adapted to the calamity. When they heard the hinge of the kitchen's screen door squeak, they came running to the edge of the porch.

At the end of four, five, maybe even six hours, I had six bags of roasted peanuts that I felt would pass muster. These bags of nuts were placed in an open Mr. Goodbar candy box and I carried my inventory of parched peanuts to town. (Mr. Marion Johnson, County Tax Assessor, made my picture that day. I was standing on the top steps of the county building, across the street from the Phoenix Hotel. The picture depicts a pitiful looking little waif.)

My burning and feeding most of my peanuts to the chickens had been a painful experience. My first effort to sell my parched peanuts was even more painful. I had visualized the men in the Domino Club and the men sitting under the shade trees on the courthouse lawn as the best potential market for my peanuts. I knew all these men by sight and more than a few by name. They had always been friendly and they seemed to have plenty of time to spare.

I started with the Domino Club, and then moved across the street to the shade trees. At each place, my reception was the same and it hurt. These men that I had seen so often, these men who had always been friendly, sometimes even jovial, seemed ashamed that they knew me. My approach was, "Would you like to buy a big bag of fresh parched peanuts? They are only a nickel."

In my mind, I had practiced that sales pitch, and it sounded good to me. As I approached and walked away from each man, without a single sale being made, I was dumbfounded, puzzled, and deeply hurt. These men I had counted as friends would not even talk to me. Some would mutter, "Not today." Some would say nothing and shake their head, "No." Some would look either down or away, as if I did not exist.

I made my way back home with my Mr. Goodbar box containing the six bags I had gone to town with. I simply could not understand where I had gone wrong. I thought I had a good plan and I had completely failed. It was a sad day for a little boy.

Mother was sitting on the front steps when I arrived back home, waiting for me. She made no effort to count the bags of peanuts I had returned with. There was no necessity, it was written on my face. Mother, not saying a word, listened as I related my experience in town. Most of what I said centered around the hurt I felt when my friends acted as if they did not know me, their turning away when I tried to talk to them. I sobbed out my tale of woe.

When I finished Mother spoke, saying something like this, "Joe, there is something you need to understand. Those men are your friends, but they were ashamed to tell you that they did not have a nickel in their pocket, or if they had one it was needed to buy bread for their children. Those men do not have jobs. They cannot find jobs. They did not talk or they looked away because they were ashamed that they couldn't feed their own families. They were not looking away from you, they were looking away from where they found themselves."

Mother suggested that I take my six bags of parched nuts back to town and go into the county offices and attempt to sell them to the people who had jobs. This time, I both heard and listened. I took my parched peanuts back to town (at which time Mr. Johnson made my picture) and sold all six bags.

I have attempted to relate what Mother told me on our front steps that day as best as long memory allows. The words I attribute to her cannot be precisely correct, that was a long time ago. I am very sure of one brief thing that she said when talking about the men in the Domino Club and under the shade trees. She said, "Joe, you have to understand that those men are poor."

In spite of the desperate financial condition of our family, I had never known before what a poor person was. I say this as great tribute to my mother! She managed, in spite of great adversity, to instill a positive self image in the minds of her poor brood. (Mother, you did a great job.)

This story began with my desire to comply with my dear wife's request to list my life's work experiences and the places I have been. I have gone astray and not gotten very far with my assignment. Such is the way of an old storyteller.

Ruby-Throats

He enjoyed changes in his routine that gave him opportunity to stop, look, and listen. Too much of life had already rushed by his door. A recent encounter with a surgeon's knife had not been pleasant, but it was followed with pleasing instructions to "take it easy for a week, no lifting, and walk as much as you like."

The butterfly bushes at the deck were in full bloom, letting him see more butterflies, both in number and variety, than ever before. He found the shade of the carport, his book, and the butterfly bushes good company. From there he could also watch the humming birds dart to and from one of their nearby feeders.

Twice before, when much younger and quicker, he had been able to catch and hold hummingbirds for a few moments, admire their smallness and beauty, listen to their feint chirp, share them with a child, and then set them free. Now he sometimes cut a small piece of red tape and stuck it on the tip of his nose, lured the hummingbird within a few inches of his face, watched them hover there, and watched for which one would be the first to blink.

Before his surgery he had planned his days of rest and filled the hummingbird feeders. It was late August, time for some of these wonderful little birds to begin their trip south. His plan for recovery was simple. It consisted of a chair in the shade close enough to watch the butterflies, the Ruby-throated hummingbirds, and a good book to read. He toyed with the red-tape-on-nose trick, but decided to save that for another day when he was again steady on his feet.

He had been told the plastic-like patches left to cover the incisions along his mid-stomach line would wash away as he showered, and he followed the advice of taking it easy for a few days. He had seen butterflies and hummingbirds over his seventy-five years, but never like now. As he watched, he realized that seeing was a function of watching and waiting. He resolved to do more of that on his own, not waiting for another encounter with a doctor and his knife.

Using the special hiking stick he had carved for the occasion, he walked his driveway down to the road two times each day, fetching the morning paper and, later in the day, the mail. The stick was handy, masking his now-and-then stagger. He did not want to stagger, much less to be seen that way. The fig bush was doing its part, along with the prunes, to cleanse his system and get him back "on track." Old systems like regularity; they look with horror on disruptive influences.

With his handy stick, he watered his flowers, gathered his paper and mail, plucked a few fresh figs, and was grateful that his recent surgery was relatively minor. Mostly, while the sun was still shining, he watched the butterflies and hummingbirds.

Hurricane Katrina was making her way towards New Orleans that Saturday morning as the he, stick in hand, made his way toward the sprinkler that spewed its watery breath on the dry August ground. Surgical wounds or not, he was determined to save those hydrangeas along the backyard fence. One of his hummingbird feeders hung from a Maple tree in that part of the yard. Possibly, he thought, some of his feathered friends would be there to greet him.

As his hiking stick guided him that way, at first he did not see the flash of silvery green, nor hear the faint high whistle of the male's call or the quiet whir of little wings. No sooner than he saw one, that he saw the other. Male and female hummingbirds. But what were they doing? He had never seen them dance this way before. Many years he had watched these birds, but this was something exciting and new. Leaning on his hiking stick, he quietly stood and watched.

The dark patch under the male's chin flashed black, then red as he swung from the maple's shade into the bright sun and back to the shade again. He seemed to swing a steady arc of 180 degrees. An invisible wire seemed to have turned him into a pendulum.

The male hummingbird had become a metronome. Back and forth, back and forth, throat black, then red, then black again. And his lady friend danced in step. She did not swing in his large arc, but she

kept in step. She never lost eye contact. Her body, midair, swiveled
to and fro, keeping time and twisting in harmony with the traverses of
his fanciful arc.

Two pairs of tiny wings, beating seventy-five times each
minute, offset the forces of gravity. Two tiny hearts beat 450 times each
minute, stirred by the forces of love. His swinging arcs and flashes of
black and then red seemed to say, "See! See! Grand am I!" Maintaining
her steady distance of about eighteen inches and twitching tail feathers
as she swiveled and turned in time with his swings, she seemed to
answer, "Yes! Yes! I see. Grand you are, I see!"

Time stood still. He had never seen the wedding ritual of the
Ruby-throat before. Time is an awesome thing standing still. He leaned
on his oak hiking stick and received a refresher course in the art of
wooing. He wanted to take his watch from his pocket and time the
event. This he did not do, thinking that it would have seemed obscene.
One should not time a sacred moment, and sacred it was. Later he
could not recall the elapsed time of this male on his flying trapeze with
his lady friend dancing in perfect step. Trying to reconstruct, he
thought the initial encounter lasted possibly twenty seconds. It is
impossible to gauge time that stands still.

The swinging stopped. He hovered in place and she
approached. It is difficult to describe her approach, *violently* first comes
to mind. But such a word seems out-of-place, too harsh. Face-to-face
she approached, aggressively and quickly so. Their bodies collided in
midair. Many times over the years he had seen the aggressive nature of

the hummingbird. But this approach was different. Many times he had see the male turn tail and run from a more aggressive female, but today it was different.

Face-to-face, he accepted her almost violent approach and five feet above the ground, face-to-face, they coupled. Their bodies seemed to lock. In a most un-hummingbird-flight manner their interlocked bodies staggered through the air. They still seemed face-to-face, but he could not be sure. They half-flew, they half-staggered, they half-hovered. The old man had never seen this before and time continued suspended. All of creation stood still.

The clock was not ticking. How long did this midair, locked-in-love coupling continue? Again, later, he estimated five to ten seconds. And then the two bodies, still coupled as one, fell into the grass. They fell, oblivious to his presence, within three feet of where he stood leaning on his stick. The day, the beautiful tiny birds, the occasion, all had become a special gift from God. It seemed a day that God had kissed, ending all fighting, war, sorrow, and hunger. Night and day had merged. All was dark and all was light. The birds and the old man were all suspended in time and space. All God's kingdom was at peace.

His first impression was that both had died. He could barely see the bodies in the grass that stood two inches high. Then he did see a body, or was it two? He knew that, just a moment before, two had fallen there. But, even in the grass, the bodies seemed one and lifeless.

For the second time he was tempted to reach for his watch, to time the moment. Yet, that would seem profane—indecent, uncivilized, or unchristian. There are occasions in life when time has no place. He decided to mentally calculate their time of rest.

Or, was it their time of death? Not a feather was moving in the grass. Death seemed the master, but something told him it was a time of rest. Resting on his stick, he patiently waited and estimated the elapsed time.

For at least a minute they rested, or slept, or did whatever hummingbirds do on such occasions. Then they stirred. It was impossible to know the position from which she first stirred, but the female was first out of the grass. She flew toward the feeder hanging from the Maple limb close to where this four act drama had begun. She stayed on the wing, hovering close to the feeder.

Soon the male followed, taking his rest on the feeder and thrusting his long beak into the red liquid. The old man smiled in memory, thinking, "That fellow needs a drink and some rest." She would have none of that foolishness. This was her wedding day. The eating and drinking could wait. She darted back and forth in his face, almost physically forcing him from the feeder perch. She was not to be denied.

Before, it had been him. He had been the one swinging the steady arc on an invisible wire. Before he was the one that was so grand. Now the roles were swapped. She never adopted his fanciful, regular swinging-arc style. Her movement was more of a bob-and-a-weave, a here-I-am, here-I-am-not style. What she lacked in grace and style was fully compensated by perseverance. She was not to be ignored. Forced from his feeder perch, again they coupled in midair. Again the half-flight, half-fall, drunken-like stagger of bodies mating in the air. Again, bodies interlocked, they fell to the ground. This time, ten to fifteen feet from where the old man stood.

Again, God was in his Kingdom, and there was peace on Earth. The old man was tempted to step closer. It was a beautiful, unforgettable moment. He wanted to see more, but intruding would not be respectful. His mind took him back to yesteryear. He recalled times and places where privacy had been demanded. No, stepping closer was out of the question. It simply could not be done.

Twice more, they played the same score. Twice more the male was the last to stagger from the grass and the one eager to partake of the nectar in the feeder. Twice more, they ended in the grass.

But, the last time down ended differently. This last time, after a long interlude in the grass, the two arose as one, their bodies still coupled. For a few moments in midair they continued mating and then parted. The male sought his feeder perch and a much needed long drink of sweet water. The female flew away around the house and out of the old man's sight.

Many times thereafter, the old man tried to capture in words the magic, mystery, and splendor of the few moments he had witnessed. He always found words inadequate. There was no way to describe the kiss of God.

Miss Fannie's Gift

As an exhibit at the state fair in Birmingham it would have attracted no attention. The judge would have glanced its way and then quickly passed it by. Most people would consider its design and workmanship inferior. That would have been understandable. Miss Fannie's gift had all the earmarks of unsteady hands guided by eyes that were dimmed by age. Had it ever been shown at the state fair, or the Madison County Fair in Huntsville, even the passersby might have been embarrassed by what appeared to be poor handiwork. Products of life are sometimes that way. We see another's work and say, "I do not think I would want others to know I made that." Opinions of this kind sometimes spring from only looking with the eyes and not seeing with the heart.

I first met Miss Fannie on a pleasant Sunday in upper Paint Rock Valley in Jackson County, Alabama. I never knew her husband, he had been dead several years before I met her in 1960. Earlier on during that day I first met Miss Fannie, I had gone to the Huntsville

Airport to meet my great-uncle, Bunyon Bouldin. Uncle Bun was age ninety-four. He had called, requesting that I meet him and carry him to a Bouldin family reunion in Paint Rock Valley, the place of his birth. My paternal grandmother, Mattie Bouldin, was born there too. (This valley, named by the Native Americans, is said to have gotten its name from a colored rock cliff where the Paint Rock River empties into the Tennessee River.)

Uncle Bun napped as I drove from the airport to the Valley. He stirred from his nap when we reached the upper part of the Valley. At Princeton Community he asked, "Is this Princeton?"

"Yes it is Uncle Bun," I answered.

He gave a feint smile and said, "Just fourteen miles from home." He then closed his eyes to continue his nap and his dreams of yesteryear. It had been more than seventy years since he last lived there, but he remembered that Princeton was just "fourteen miles from home."

For that family reunion we met at the home of Varnie Robinson; he too was a relative. I have many relatives that live in that area, most of whom I do not really know. On the day that I first met Miss Fannie, I probably met twenty-five kinfolk that I had never seen before.

Uncle George Bouldin and his wonderful wife, Maggie, were present. I had met them before. Uncle George and Uncle Bun were younger brothers to my grandmother, Mattie. They both told me that Mattie had given them financial assistance when they were in college.

She had already graduated from Winchester Normal College in Winchester, Tennessee and was teaching school. My kinfolk in the Valley seemed to have all helped each other. Uncle Bun had spent most of his adult life in Argentina. Uncle George worked for many years as a missionary in Japan.

Over the next few years after first meeting Miss Fannie, I enjoyed other trips to Paint Rock Valley, seeing relative old and new, sharing the food, and being told of things past and hopes of things to be. During those intervening years and my attendance at other family reunions, Miss Fannie always brought a coconut cake made with fresh grated coconut! I do not think she would have approved of coconut from a can or a freezer bag.

Before breaking bread together at these reunions, Uncle George, one of several family theologians, always offered thanks to God. Uncle George was a tall man that carried himself with quiet dignity. He used plain and simple words in his prayers of thanks, making no effort to impress either God or family members with his splendid vocabulary. He was fluent in several languages, and a recognized expert in Japanese language, having spent forty years of his life in that country. (Uncle George and Aunt Maggie returned to the United States from Japan at the eve of World War II. When the war started, our War Department sought his help as a teacher of the Japanese language. He and Aunt Maggie dearly loved the people of Japan. Because of this love, he reluctantly consented to the request of the War Department. He also loved the United States.) The way Uncle

George spoke with God in his prayers of thanks, one would have thought God was seated at the same table. I knew only a few of my great aunts and uncles. Uncle George was my favorite.

Miss Fannie must have been about seventy years old when I first met her. She was quiet in her speech, but most folks listened when she spoke. She dressed in plain cotton of subdued colors. I recall no striking features, except her dark eyes. They appeared almost black, but they were interesting and happy eyes. They seemed to sparkle and dance when she talked. She seemed not to mind that some of the men chewed tobacco, but she strongly opposed any woman's use of snuff. Most of the relatives used neither. When we first met, she was steady in her walk; her use of a walking cane would come later.

At these reunions, Miss Fannie not only brought her delicious coconut cake, she also brought memories. Memories of her childhood in that area, of walking two and a half miles—one way—to the public school north of her home, of the six-week recess from school each fall for cotton picking, of the Indian Peach trees on her father's farm and the wonderful pickled peaches made from the fruit, of her mother's hot kitchen during the summer months at canning time, and the Great Depression Years when many lived mostly on cornbread, potatoes, greens, and turnips.

At these meetings, I sought Miss Fannie's company. I loved her knowledge of the family history, going back to the first Bouldin taking the sailing ship "Swan" from England and sailing to Jamestown, Virginia in the year of 1610. Shortly before this meeting, Uncle Bun had published and distributed a history of the Bouldin family. Miss Fannie discussed the determined effort of John Bouldin, a man of very modest means and the family patriarch in the Valley, to educate his twelve children, which included my grandmother. I agreed with her that it was most remarkable that all twelve of the Bouldin children had earned at least one college degree, and a total of twenty-three degrees among the twelve.

On another occasion, Miss Fannie had told me of nearby Freedom Baptist Church where Uncle George Bouldin had been first ordained as a minister when he was twenty years old and his pursuit of education that led to a PhD in Theology at the Louisville Seminary. She also knew of several other relatives that had served as pastor of Freedom Church and how the church would delay the baptizing of its converts until the hot months of July and August. And even then the water of the Estill Fork of the Paint Rock River where the baptizing took place was, in her words, "so cold it would almost make one lose their religion when baptized in it." (She laughed when she said that.) She spoke of the cold water of the Estill Fork from personal experience; she and many of my relatives had been baptized there.

She knew of the devastation of the Valley when the Paint Rock River would flood and cover the crop lands, sometimes taking barns, cribs, and even houses with it. For many years the residents of the Valley had tried to get either the county, state, or federal government to dredge the river canal, clear the debris, and improve its flood control. Their efforts had been futile. Sometimes, she said, the individual property owners along the Paint Rock would attempt to remove trees and logs that blocked the flow of the water. Sometimes organized community efforts attempted the clearing of the waterway. This river ran north to south, twisting itself, snake-like, from the northern end of the Valley to the Tennessee River some thirty miles south, according to a straight-line measure. If one followed the serpentine course of the river, it would likely measure almost twice as long. When talking of the Paint Rock floods, Miss Fannie would sadly shake her head and say, "The men did not have the equipment to clear the trash and trees, and the job was just too much." After Miss Fannie died, the river channel was partially cleared, and the flooding problem, though still present, was somewhat reduced.

She told me of the frequent community efforts to make life better for all. As a young girl she had attended more than one barn raising on neighboring farms. The neighboring men would do the advance work of clearing the building site, preparing the foundation, and having the lumber and roofing shingles on location. Then, on the appointed day, the women and children, traveling in their wagons, carrying food and all that was needed for "dinner-on-the-ground" would go to the site and make the barn raising a happy, semi-social affair. By sunset, the frame of the barn would be standing, skeleton-like, in place. The neighboring men would return the following day, or so, to complete the building. The gathering of the women and children at the construction site was a one-day affair, always on the day that the framing would reach into the sky. Miss Fannie said that as she watched the structural timbers being put in place, it seemed as if fingers of a large hand were reaching into heaven. She told this as if it were a special memory.

Miss Fannie said the same pattern would be followed in the re-building of homes after a loss from fire, flood, or storm. Frequently new homes would be built with neighboring help for newlyweds. More often than not, a building site for the new house would merely be selected on the "home place" and the house was built for the newlywed couple without any deed to the land being given. This poorly planned arrangement frequently led to later confusion, particularly if the parents died leaving no will that designated how their property was to be disposed of. With equal frequency, deeds were prepared using legal descriptions such as "Beginning at the foot of the big oak tree across the road from the mailbox, thence going about 700 feet south to a persimmon tree, thence going about 200 feet west to the corner fence post, thence about 600 feet northeast to the big rock by the creek, thence going back to the big oak tree." Over the following years, trees would die, fences would be moved, and when the original owner died, family feuds would begin. For most of Miss Fannie's life, things were done a little differently in the Valley than most other places.

She laughed when she related watching her grandfather and my great-grandfather drive the hogs down the public road of the Valley, taking them to the flatboats on the Tennessee River and on to market. At the time, the Valley road was no more than a wagon trail following a path made by the Native Americans many years earlier. (The road had been paved at the time of my first meeting Miss Fannie.) Until ready for market, our forefathers would attempt to keep their hog herds on their own land, separate from their neighbor's. Sometimes, she said, during the winter months, the pigs would be turned into the woods to root for the acorns. Once each year, the shoats (young pigs) would be separated from the more mature hogs that were ready to be either butchered on the farm or sold.

Miss Fannie said she never liked the deathly squeals of the hogs as they were killed for family use. However, the tasty eating of fresh pork was a welcomed change from the salted pork the family had eaten during the preceding eleven months.

It seemed her favorite memory on this subject were the pig drives down the dirt road on their way to market. She placed the date of the last of these events as being when she was a teenager, "before I married." (This would have been the late 1800s.) She related, "Our forefathers would count their respective hog herds before they were combined for the pig drive. This count of pigs would establish the ratio for the division of the proceeds of the sale. The value of a particular pig had no bearing on the division of the total money received. Each owner had one or more herding dogs that would accompany the drive down the Valley. En route to the river flatboat, some pigs would be lost or sold. Equally often, additional pigs would be purchased and added to the drive. Sometimes, the herd would be sold to a broker when delivered to the landing on the bank of the Tennessee River. At other times, the herd would be delivered on consignment to the owner/operator of the flatboat to be sold on reaching the ultimate market." She was not sure, but she thought the pigs were sold at either Paducah, Kentucky or New Orleans.

I have fond memories of the things that Miss Fannie shared with me during the few times I met with her and other family members in Upper Paint Rock Valley. Prior to 1972, all of our meetings had been within three miles of Freedom Baptist Church and the nearby Bouldin home place.

Notwithstanding my pleasant and interesting encounters with this delightful lady, I had no reason to expect her to come to my law office in Huntsville, Alabama.

I was very busy with the work already stacked on my desk that summer day of 1972 when my office receptionist called me on the intercom saying, "Mr. Berry, there is a Mrs. Green here to see you." I had no idea who Mrs. Green was and I told the receptionist that she would have to talk with someone else. The receptionist whispered back, "Mr. Berry, I think you need to see this lady. She says that she is a distant relative." With impatience and some irritation, I agreed to see her.

Moments later, Mrs. Green, with the aide of a heavy walking cane, made her way up the stairs to my office. I immediately recognized her. I knew her as "Miss Fannie," not as Mrs. Green. No sooner than I recognized her than I was pleased that I had taken the time to see her in spite of the unfinished work that sat on my desk.

By this time, she was close to ninety years old and had aged considerably since I had last seen her. Her back had become slightly bowed and she appeared thin. But, her dark eyes still sparkled and danced when she talked. She seemed worried. I immediately regretted that she had had to walk up the interior stairs to reach my office. Had I known that it was Miss Fannie and that she now had need of a walking cane, I would have met her in a first floor office.

We engaged in light talk about family, weather, and health for a few moments. After which, Miss Fannie explained that she had gotten a neighbor to drive her to Huntsville and that she needed my advice.

It quickly became apparent that not only had Miss Fannie aged in body, but that she was also confused. Her confusion related to the war bonds she and her deceased husband had purchased thirty years before. On this subject, she was seeking my help and advice.

Along with millions of people, Miss Fannie and her husband had saved all the money they could during WWII and purchased government savings bonds. This was a popular method for the public to help finance the war effort. As she recalled, they had purchased the $25 variety for $17.50 each. They would be worth $25 ten years after purchase. Miss Fannie had been a good citizen and purchased all the war bonds she could; she did not recall how many. She said there might have been fifteen or twenty. She simply did not know the number, but she did know the bonds had been purchased and at maturity they would be worth $25 each.

She explained that her husband had tended to business matters, and he was long dead. She recalled that some of the bonds had matured while her husband was living and they cashed them at the post office. She was sure about that, but she thought there might be some bonds missing, un-cashed. She could not find any bonds at home. She explained that they always kept the bonds in the big trunk at the foot of the bed. She had searched the trunk and other places in the house, but no bonds could be found. She hastened to add that possibly all bonds had been redeemed and that none were missing. (The dear lady was simply confused.)

Miss Fannie did not put it that way, but I sensed that she likely had need for a little money and a few bonds worth at least $25 each would come in handy. I was not sure how to find out about such matters, but I knew I was better equipped to inquire than Miss Fannie. She was pleased when I told her I would see what I could do and get back in touch with her as soon as I had some answers. I obtained the full names of both she and her deceased husband, together with their social security numbers, and walked Miss Fannie down the stairs and out the front door. I did not take her arm; it seemed she wanted to manage on her own. I walked along side her, just in case.

A letter to the Treasury Department led me to a data center in St. Louis and the exchange of two or three other letters. A search lasting several weeks led to the determination that war bonds had in fact been purchased by this family. It was also determined that all bonds had been redeemed.

I wrote Miss Fannie, trying to let her down kind of gentle-like, and gave her a report of my search. I really did not want to write her that letter, it was painful to do so. I had that feeling in the bottom of my stomach that Miss Fannie needed some cash. It was just a feeling, but I could not pry into her personal affairs. I mailed her a report of my futile search. She needed to know.

Within a week, the reliable walking cane delivered Miss Fannie back to my office. With gentle dignity, she thanked me for my search and told me that my letter had been received. She called it a "nice letter." If she was disappointed in not finding any bonds, she did not let it show.

"I came by to pay you for your service, Joe," she said.

I explained that I did not intend to charge a fee. I told her that very little of my time had been spent and that she had received no benefit from my effort.

Miss Fannie immediately countered: "Joe, Abraham Lincoln said that a lawyer's time and advice was his stock in trade, I must pay you for your service."

I told Miss Fannie that I simply could not charge her. I appealed to her emotions by saying, "Miss Fannie, it would give me pleasure if you allowed me to do this as a courtesy to you."

She pondered my request and countered, "Well, if that is the way you want to trade, it would give me pleasure if you allowed me to make something and bring it to you."

I immediately thought about Miss Fannie's wonderful coconut cake that I had sampled several times before and agreed to the arrangement. Again, I saw Miss Fannie out the front door of my office and onto the sidewalk.

A year or more went by and I gave little thought to Miss Fannie or the cake that I had visualized. She was a distant relative and mostly out-of-mind. When recalled, I thought mostly about the things Miss Fannie had told me about Paint Rock Valley, our common ancestors and the pig drives to the market. I assumed Miss Fannie had forgotten about my cake or pie, or whatever she had intended to make for me, just as she had forgotten about cashing in all the war bonds. The truth is, I almost forgot about Miss Fannie. She was a relative that I had seldom seen. She became pretty much a forgotten old lady who walked with a cane and had dreams of finding some lost war bonds. Once or twice, I had thought she may have had fried peach pies in mind instead of a coconut cake and she was waiting for the peach crop to mature. But with the passage of time, I lost that thought too.

It was a hot August day, many months after Miss Fannie's last visit, when I returned to my office from the courthouse. The receptionist told me Miss Fannie had been by. It was further explained that Miss Fannie had said she was afraid she could not make it back up those stairs to the second floor and had requested that someone leave her gift in my office. "I put it on your sofa," the receptionist added.

There I found it. Wrapped in used, wrinkled Christmas paper and tied around the middle with a used, wide red ribbon. The faded

Christmas paper was not large enough to cover the content, the gift protruded out both ends.

No, Miss Fannie's gift was never entered as an exhibit at any fair. Had it been, it would not have won any prize. It was the product of old hands and old eyes. Most would have found it poorly designed and poorly made. It was a "patchwork" quilt. But unlike most patchwork quilts, the patches were largely irregular in size and the patterns of the patches lacked uniformity. Most quilt makers take pride in the smallness of their stitches; Miss Fannie's were large and irregular. Even an impartial critic would have found much fault in her labor of love.

But others were not the ones looking. The gift was for me, made with old, wrinkled hands and carried to my office with legs that now depended on a helping cane. Other eyes would never see the beauty that I saw in Miss Fannie's handmade quilt. To see its beauty, it had to be seen with both eyes and heart.

Mouth That was True

Roosevelt and his two hunting buddies turned north on Spragins Road and continued to the foot of Wade Mountain. Spragins hollow was bathed in darkness, a good night for the raccoons to be on the move.

Stopping his truck, Roosevelt slipped out of the driver's seat, went to the back of the pickup and lowered its battered tailgate. Lifting the rusty bolt that held the clasp on the front of the wooden box, he opened the hinged door of the dog box and said, "Come on Trace, show these men that your mouth speaks only the truth."

Trace, a black and tan coon dog, did not need the instruction. He always told the truth and knew by first name every coon that lived on that mountain. Quickly he vanished into the darkness. Roosevelt and his two buddies waited for thirty minutes by the truck. They spoke of hard times, a failed cotton crop, and children in need of clothes, shoes, and sometimes food. It was 1939 and Alabama was still in the grip of the Great Depression. The hunters understood hard times; they did not think in those terms, but they could have written a book on the subject. Tonight they thought in terms of coon hunting.

They stood at the base of Wade Mountain quietly talking and listening until their conversation was interrupted. "I hear him boys. He is trailing. That one yelp now and then means I may have a coon to fatten up before the night is done," Roosevelt told his friends. Roosevelt often fed his family a raccoon that had been caught and corn-fed for several weeks. After chicken and rabbit, it was the next best meat his family could afford.

Trace continuing his occasional yelping and ten minutes later Roosevelt announced, "He is warming up. He backtracked for a while, but he has him turned around now. Let's kind of move on up the hill in that direction. Sounds like that coon he is chasing is pretty smart. Trace might have a good time tonight, he likes the smart ones."

A quarter of a mile up an old logging road, they crossed over the fence of the McGee Place and sat on the stumps of the oak trees that had been sold and cut six years before. Roosevelt fished a metal can from the bib of his overalls and emptied loose tobacco out of his Prince Albert can into a cigarette paper. He paused to listen for Trace and then expertly rolled a cigarette in the darkness. His friends, realizing that was likely the only can of tobacco that Roosevelt owned, refused his offer of the can and suggestion that they "roll their own."

Meanwhile, Trace was moving more rapidly across, up, and down Wade Mountain. His vocal output changed, too. His yelp was courser and more frequent. Roosevelt knew the sound. The darkness hid his smile. It was a smile of pride. Pride of a dog that knew his work and was always steady in the chase. Pride of a dog whose mouth never lied. Pride of a companion that was always faithful. Pride that Trace was part of his family. Although Roosevelt never thought of it in those terms, there was pride of ownership too.

Trace was considered by most as the finest coon dog in the area. From the small cotton mill town of Huntsville, Alabama, his reputation spanned more than 200 miles in every direction. This good reputation was the result of Roosevelt, on the five occasions that he could afford the contest entrance fee, having entered Trace in coon dog competitions. Once each in Georgia and Tennessee, and three times in the National Tree Competition at Corinth, Mississippi. Five times he had called on Trace to speak truthfully to the competition judges that did not know him and five times Trace had answered the call, winning the blue ribbon.

Roosevelt had pride of ownership. But, there was more to it than that. The reasons for pride went much deeper. Trace was both his child and brother. Best of all, Trace was his companion. They understood and respected each other; there was never any misunderstanding between them. Trace was family. The bond defied definition, but it enjoyed complete understanding and acceptance by both dog and man.

There were many times when other coon hunters with money to spend tried to buy Trace. There were many offers of purchase. Roosevelt always needed the money that was offered. Trying to provide for his wife and nine children was a big assignment, even in good times. Trying to make ends meet as a sharecropper near a small cotton mill town of Alabama during the Great Depression years was far removed from what one would consider "good times." There was an ever-present need for more money at his home; the life of a sharecropper was not easy. The offer of others to purchase were frequent, but there was never a time when Roosevelt wanted to sell Trace.

The Prince Albert cigarette almost finished, Roosevelt ground it out beneath his shoe and said, "Boys, he's moving him now. He has got him going, he has carried him to the Bonner Place on the north side of the mountain. It won't be too long now. Let's move on up a bit. That coon is looking for a Sweet Gum with a hole in it. He is looking for a place to hide."

In a few minutes there was a noticeable change coming from the faithful dog. From a yelp the sound changed to a long, mournful, wailing call. A call that ended almost with a gurgle. A call that seemed to say, "I have done my work, now it is up to you."

"He's got him fellows. He's got him. That mouth doesn't lie. Come on boys, that coon is up a tree."

In keeping with the language of all coon hunters, Roosevelt always referred to Trace's "mouth." It was never "bark" or "voice," it was mouth, and Trace's mouth always spoke true. From the time that the dog was thirteen months old, he had never lied about the location of the coon.

Crossing the crest of the mountain onto the Bonner land, they found Trace at the base of a large white oak tree, his eyes sparkling in the beam of Roosevelt's flashlight. Roosevelt knelt beside his dog to say, "Fellow, you don't tell nothing except truth." Trace seemed to understand.

Three days after the Wade Mountain hunt a doctor from Atlanta, driving an expensive Packard automobile with a fancy two-wheel dog trailer towed behind, drove into Roosevelt's yard. Roosevelt, splitting stove wood behind the house, came around the house to greet the visitor. The doctor got right to the point, "I am Dr. Horace Abbott from Atlanta. I heard you have a pretty good black and tan, and I came over here to buy him." The statement was in the manner of a wealthy man speaking to a sharecropper. Rather than an inquiry, it was almost a command. Most of his life, Roosevelt had heard such language. He took no offense.

"Yes sir, I have a good dog, but I am not trying to sell him. Come on in the house sir, you'll catch cold standing here in the yard."

The doctor was escorted across a low front porch and into the small, six-room, frame tenant house. The "sitting room" held five straight-back chairs placed in a semicircle around an open fireplace. There was a double bed against the back wall and a small chest-of-drawers beside it. The only wall decoration was a current calendar bearing the name of Thompson's Seed and Feed at the bottom. The calendar depicted a Norman Rockwell scene. A Bible lay on a small table beside the bed. A single window, to the left of the entrance door, provided the only light during the day. At night, a kerosene lamp on the table illuminated the Bible that Mary, Roosevelt's wife, read aloud to the family at bedtime. Roosevelt could neither read nor write.

Roosevelt placed two hickory logs on the existing fire and suggested the center chair for his visitor, it was closest to the fireplace, the seat of honor. No sooner than seated, the impatient doctor pulled nine one hundred dollar bills from his pocket and said, "Here is $900. That is a big price to pay for a dog, but I understand he is very good one. My offer is more than fair."

Roosevelt had never seen that much money at one time, and was tempted. He thought about his near barefoot children and the tattered, patched clothes they wore. He thought about the poor cotton crop that had been gathered, but not yet ginned and sold. His one-third of that crop might equate $400. He thought about his unpaid bill at Smith's Store, as best he recalled it was more than $300. He thought about the tires on his old truck, two of them with "boots' in them that would not last through the winter. There were many things to think about, including a talk with Mary.

"Excuse me just a minute Dr. Abbott. I need to talk to my wife."

Excusing himself, he went to the kitchen. Mary and five of the nine children were gathered around the wood-burning stove for warmth. A wash pan sat beside the water bucket on a shelf next to the back door. The family dining table, with a wooden bench on each side and a mule-ear chair at each end occupied much of the kitchen. The stove wood box, filled to overflowing, was between the door and stove. The kitchen was filled with the strong smell of the "souse meat" that Mary was making from the trimmings of the hog that Roosevelt had killed the previous day. Roosevelt would sometimes laugh and say, "At this house, we eat all the pig except the squeal, and if Mary could catch it, she would cook that, too."

Hanging on a nail, just outside the kitchen door, was a number three washtub. It served as the family bathtub when brought into the kitchen and filled with water brought in from the well that stood twenty yards to the back of the house. Mary would heat water on the kitchen stove to moderate the chill of the cool well water. Mary and the kids had heard the doctor's offer of $900 through the un-insulated wall that separated the kitchen from the sitting room.

Roosevelt walked over to the stove where Mary stood cooking the souse meat saying, "Honey, that is a lot of money and we sure could use it."

"Yes, Roosevelt, that is a lot of money."

Roosevelt knew the decision was his and that he had his faithful wife's support no matter what he decided. Roosevelt looked at the five younger children, the youngest a toddler. He looked at the worn shoes on their feet, shoes that had already been handed down from an older child. Some had been handed down two times. "Honey, we sure need the money," he repeated as he walked toward the back door.

As he was leaving the kitchen, heading toward the dog pen that stood in back of the smoke house, Mary patted his shoulder, saying, "Baby, I know how you love that dog. Go talk to Trace about it. That's what you need to do. Talk to your friend about it. Whatever you and Trace decide will be the right thing." Mary understood the relation.

Roosevelt walked past the lean-to shed on the side of the smoke house. In passing, he placed the seventy-five pound anvil on the top lid of the wooden saltbox where the freshly killed hams and shoulders of the hog had been placed and covered with salt. In five weeks, he would hang that meat in the smokehouse and start the slow burning hickory fire in the pit that had been dug in the dirt floor. The ashes of last year's fire would have to be first removed. He had already spoken to his sixteen-year-old son, Henry, about cleaning out the ashes. Remembering that Henry was old enough to have girls on his mind, Roosevelt smiled, recalling his youth. He would have to remind Henry that the job was not yet done. The anvil on top of the saltbox would hold the lid down tight and keep the barn rats away from the fresh meat that was being cured.

With Mary's soft pat on his shoulder and the doctor's $900 in mind, he walked to the dog pen. As he walked, he again thought of his desperate financial situation and was saddened by his thoughts. Often, he had told Mary, "Honey, our dog is worth more than all else that we own, including my old truck. How are we going to make it?"

"We will do it, Roosevelt. We have done it before and we will do it again," was always her supportive answer.

In spite of Mary's constant support, sometimes Roosevelt had serious doubts. As he approached the dog pen, the many needs of his family and the $900 offer weighed on his mind. Trace had heard him coming, but did not rise to greet him. It was not the time of day to head for the hunt, the coons prowl and leave the fresh scent on the ground at night. If Trace was puzzled by Roosevelt's approach, he did not show it. He had already eaten his cornbread that morning and the sun was noonday high. Trace, knowing this was a social visit and no serious business was at hand, hardly raised an eye toward his master. Now if it had been early evening and getting dark, it would have been a different matter. Trace was a night operator and his belly had already been filled in his earlier once-a-day feeding. Midday visits by his master were no cause of excitement.

Roosevelt stood at the gate, looked at his dog, and thought about the many good times he and the dog had enjoyed before going back in the house to talk to the doctor. He had received large offers for Trace before, but never one approaching $900. The offer seemed one that he could not refuse. Making his way back into the house, he bypassed the kitchen, going to the front porch to enter the sitting room where the doctor was warming his feet before the fire that had been made lively by the two added sticks of wood.

Once inside, Roosevelt looked at his guest and asked, "If I sell Trace to you, how are you going to feed him?"

The doctor's reply led Roosevelt to understand the doctor did not think it right for a sharecropper to ask a wealthy man how he would feed his dog. "I consider how I feed my dog is my business," the doctor answered. No offense was intended by the question and Roosevelt was sorry that offense had been taken.

Roosevelt understood Trace's eating habit and, like the remainder of his family, he wanted his dog to be properly fed. In his mind, he saw Trace being fed with "store bought" food and knew that his companion would not like that.

"I feed my dog with cornbread," Roosevelt replied.

"If you want me to, I will feed him cornbread," the irritated doctor responded.

"How do you make your cornbread?"

"I have someone else make it for me."

"Dr. Abbott, I thank you for coming all this way and your offer is generous. But, I just can't bring it about to part with Trace. I just can't do that."

Dr. Abbott drove back to Atlanta, his fancy dog trailer empty.

Later others tried to buy Trace, some when times were even harder than when the doctor came. Many times Roosevelt looked at the great needs of his wife and children. Many times he walked to the dog pen and looked at Trace. Many times he asked how the intending purchaser would feed Trace. Some prospective buyers would give the magic answer of "cornbread." This answer would lead to more questions of how the cornbread would be made and cooked. Roosevelt knew that Trace liked his cornbread cooked with an egg in it, with a pinch of soda and a tablespoon of sugar. He knew that Trace liked his bread cooked in a cast iron skillet, on top of the stove, with the bottom side crusty brown and the topside soft and white. He knew that Trace wanted only pure lard used to grease the cornbread skillet. He never found a man who indicated that he would cook cornbread for Trace the way that Mary did. In spite of the often-crying need for money, Roosevelt's final answer always came down to, "I just can't do it. I just can't do it." Trace was family, and family could not be sold. His ancestors had been bought and sold. No matter how difficult times might be, he could never bring himself to sell a family member.

In 1948, Trace suffered what was likely a light stroke. For two weeks, he staggered to his left and often lost his balance and fell. Slowly, with Mary's cornbread in his belly, he partially recovered. Several times thereafter, Roosevelt took him to the base of Wade Mountain and turned him loose. He still had the nose, but his movements were uncertain. He tilted to the left as he tracked the coons that he knew by first name. His disability slowed him, but his mouth still spoke only the truth. When he gave that long, wailing, gurgling call, the coon was up the tree.

In late December that year, Roosevelt and Trace returned to the mountain they knew so well. They left the dog pen and six-room house in the same truck, with the same wooden dog box in back, its door held secure with the same hasp and rusty bolt. The baby that had been a toddler when the doctor called was now almost eleven years old and knew how to read and write. Henry had cleaned the ashes from the smoke pit regularly until he took a job at the cotton mill and moved to

Huntsville. Mary still knew how to make cornbread that was pleasing to Trace.

On that last hunt, Roosevelt turned Trace loose near the corner of the McGee place. In the darkness he sat for a while on the tailgate of his old truck, rolled a Prince Albert cigarette, placed the tobacco can in the bib of his overalls and waited to hear the mouth of his faithful friend. For most coon dogs the wait would have been considered a short one. For Trace it was far longer than usual.

But the wait was not in vain. Roosevelt, hunting alone that night, heard the familiar sound. The coon was in the tree and that reliable mouth seemed to say, "Here he is. I have done my part, come and get him." Roosevelt gauged the distance to be about a half mile and headed that way. In route, the faithful mouth fell silent and spoke no more.

Roosevelt searched all night. It was past the break of day when he found Trace at the base of a tall Tulip Poplar tree. Trace's hunting days would be no more. Roosevelt went back home for his shovel and buried Trace where his mouth had fallen silent. A large limestone rock was used to mark his grave.

****

A charitable organization has purchased part of Wade Mountain with the intent of preserving the woods for future generations. Hiking trails have been established, one passing within a few hundred yards of a large Tulip Poplar. Those who know of Trace sometimes pass that way. Those that knew of this member of

Roosevelt's family sometimes pause nearby and listen for the mouth that always spoke true. Should you pass that way, pause for a while and listen.

(Writer's note: I had the great pleasure of becoming Roosevelt's friend, and lawyer. Several times, after Trace had died, I was invited to go coon hunting with Roosevelt. The hurry and push of making a living and meeting my obligations always got in my way, or so it seemed. I never heard the mouth that spoke only truth. The loss is mine.)

Mushing

Judge Thomas Greene was tired. Too tired. Too many years of hearing people vent their anger and frustrations in divorce cases, too many questions for which there were no answers, too many problems for which there were no good solutions (often not even poor ones) had made him that way. At age sixty-three he sometimes felt that he was eighty.

The idealism of youth that Judge Greene had brought to the court bench thirty years ago was gone. Now all the problems looked alike, even the parties and witnesses often looked the same. In private conversation he told family and friends there was nothing new under the sun, just a different crowd doing it.

The judge's years on the trial bench had given him an overdose of human misery and problems. He had recently written in his diary, "There are no surprises left for me in what people do. Sometimes

I am grieved, sometimes disappointed. But, it is sad to say that I have seen and heard so much of peoples' problems that life no longer has any surprises. This realization takes away some of the quality of life. Life without surprise is less than life."

The judge had reached the sad realization that in a divorce case there were no winners. At best, there were survivors. The adults were always unhappy with his final decision. This he could live with, realizing that if either of the adults were happy he had probably made a poor decision. In an adult game, he could still cope with the notion that a divorce was a contest without a winner.

The children were a different matter. Too many nights were sleepless ones as he wrestled with the decision of which parent a child should live with. Many times he had seen a small child lock his arms around the legs of the noncustodial parent as he was tugged away by the mother or father who was given primary custody. Now, when these things happened, he would go to the toilet and vomit.

Judge Greene had told no one, except his wife, that he intended to resign from his office when the present case was concluded. He had been drinking from a cup of sorrow too long. His spirit cried for fresh air, sunshine, mockingbirds, and buttercups.

The judge looked over the field of players in the current case. The lawyers were his friends and good at their game, but they too looked the same as all lawyers in all divorce cases. The husband in the case presently before him, Harvey Adams, was a local surgeon with a busy practice and a good golf game, shooting in the mid seventies each

Thursday afternoon. The wife, Helen Stowe Adams, was well educated and fashionably groomed. She had a busy social life and belonged to all the right clubs and societies. The judge knew they were both good people, cursed only with too many of the so-called blessings of life.

The doctor and his wife were not angry at each other, just distant. Growth together had eluded them, instead they had simply, and sadly, grown apart. Separating this couple and dividing their considerable assets would be no problem. The judge had a formula that he had devised for that purpose.

But what of the little girl born of this marriage he was asked to dissolve? Cases like the present one, where he had to make a decision about the present and future of a small child, were always difficult ones. Both parents wanted the child and the judge was sure the child wanted and needed both parents. The little girl was almost three.

The tired judge well understood the way the legal game called "divorce" was played. It was an ugly, sometimes vicious, affair of each side trying to make the other side look bad. The objective was to gain favorable consideration of the trial judge.

The skills of the lawyers were a large factor in the frightening and dangerous legal tug-of-war that regularly occurred before Judge Greene's eyes. In the struggle to make his wife look "bad" for the judge, and little realizing he was describing his own life, the doctor had testified about his wife's busy social schedule and her many outside activities that took her away from Anna, their small child.

Before the trial had begun the doctor's lawyer had explained to his client how there was small chance of the judge granting primary custody of Anna to the father. The lawyer understood Judge Greene and his philosophy about such things. But the doctor wanted to try. Maybe the doctor was sincere; maybe he wanted to soothe his conscience. "I want Mrs. Simmons called as a witness," the doctor insisted.

Clients need to be placated and Mrs. Simmons was called to the witness chair. Mrs. Simmons may be fairly described as plain, uneducated, and unsophisticated. She was also badly frightened. Additionally, she was given the impossible task of telling the truth, the whole truth, and nothing but the truth. Truth is too often a shade of gray, the whole truth a will-of-the-wisp. But the doctor thought she would help his claim for custody of Anna.

Mrs. Simmons had worked for Helen Adams for nineteen years, eleven of which were before she married Dr. Adams. Mrs. Simmons still worked in the Adams's home and hoped to work there after the divorce was granted.

Mrs. Simmons was at the home when little Anna was born and brought home from the hospital, and she had been there six days each week for all the child's short life. In many ways little Anna belonged to Mrs. Simmons, and she to Anna. The witness, though lacking formal education, was not lacking in understanding. She knew the doctor wanted her to say something negative about the mother, that is the way such battles are fought. Mrs. Simmons had a real dilemma, and the judge understood that.

The doctor's lawyer had informed his client that it would take shocking testimony to persuade this judge to separate the mother and child and, from all appearances, Mrs. Simmons had nothing shocking to tell.

"Yes," Mrs. Simmons testified, "Yes, Mrs. Adams is gone from home quite a bit. But she always sees to it that I will be there to take care of Anna." The witness explained that the mother "was out of town frequently, leaving me to take care of Anna." But she added, "Dr. Adams is usually with her when she goes out of town."

And so Mrs. Simmons's testimony went. The lawyers understood that her testimony neither hurt nor helped either party. The essence of what she testified to was that both parents were busy people, engaged in many things that took both away from home and Anna.

The judge, recognizing Mrs. Simmons's difficult position in testifying in the presence of the lady she worked for, decided to intervene. Possibly he sensed there was something this witness wanted to say, but was reluctant to do so.

"Mrs. Simmons," the judge said, "I have a very difficult job to do. I have the great responsibility of making a decision about which parent little Anna is to live with. It is an important decision, one that will likely affect the little girl for the rest of her life. Do you see how difficult my job will be?"

"Yes sir, Judge. I know that you have a very hard job. I pray for you."

"What a nice thing for you to say, and I know you mean it. I will gladly accept all the help that prayer can bring, Mrs. Simmons. I could not sleep last night, I woke up about 2 o'clock this morning and never got back to sleep. I was worried about this little girl. Do you see how important it is that I have the best possible information to work with when I decide about this baby?"

"Yes Judge I am sure you need all possible help that you can get. That's for sure. Judge, I do not see how you can make such hard decisions."

"Well, to tell you the truth, I never know if I am making the right decision. I can never be sure I am doing the right thing. I too pray about these decisions, but even then I am never sure. Mrs. Simmons, I need your help, I need you to help me make the right decision about Anna."

Mrs. Simmons seemed to have forgotten about the mother and father and others in the courtroom, but she was puzzled by the judge's request for her personal help. After a moment she responded, "Judge, I will help in any way that I can. But praying for you is all that I know to do."

"Mrs. Simmons, I know you are honest both in your prayers and wanting to help me with a difficult decision." The judge looked away for a long time, staring out the window to his left. He then continued, "Maybe there is no additional help that you can give. Maybe you have done all that you can do to help me with this. You are a very nice lady and I am glad that little Anna has you in her life. Both of you are richer because you have each other."

The judge seemed, for a few moments, that he was through with the witness, but the lawyers were not quite sure and said nothing. After a long silence that became uncomfortable for all, the judge continued, "Mrs. Simmons, you have worked in the home with this child for all her life, you have been with her six days each week, sometimes more. You have seen the child with her parents more than anyone alive. Before I release you from the witness stand, I would like to ask you a final question. Is there anything else that you know about these parents and this child that you have not told me? Is there anything else that you know that will help me make the right decision about this child? Is there anything about either of the parents that you think I need to know? I need any help that you can give."

The witness looked to her left at the lady she worked for; it was difficult to gauge the nature of her inquiring look. In a few moments she turned her attention back to the kind and tired judge.

"Judge," she said, "I hope this does not cost me my job, but there is one thing I need to say."

"Mrs. Simmons", the judge responded, " I have put you in this position by my question. Please forgive me for that. I too hope you will not lose your job, I would feel very bad if you did. But you and I both know that Anna is more important than my job, or your job. Please help me in any way that you can."

The witness sat silently, looking down at her hands. She twisted a handkerchief between her thumb and fingers of her left hand. Then she seemed at peace, oblivious to all except the judge. She wiped her cheek and nose and spoke from her heart. One not knowing better might have thought she was talking to herself.

"Judge, I'm the oldest person in this room. I've lived a long time and raised four children of my own. They are all now grown, and have children of their own. They are all good children that have never had any real trouble in life. I think I had a lot to do with their being such good children."

Mrs. Simmons broke the reverie of her children and their lives and refocused on little Anna.

"Judge, there is one thing that Anna's mother does not do that I think she ought to."

"What is that Mrs. Simmons?"

"Judge, Mrs. Adams does not mush on that baby the way she ought to."

The old judge knew what was meant, but he wanted to be sure. More to the point, he wanted both the mother and father to know what was meant.

"What do you mean by 'mush on'?" he asked.

"Why Judge," the witness answered, "I mean to love on. I mean to hug on. To kiss on and hold on. That's what I mean by mushing. Judge, everyone needs a lot of mushing."

The judge continued, not only for the benefit of the parents, but also for himself, "Mrs. Simmons, what happens to us if we do not get the mushing we all need?"

"Judge, most everyone knows that mushing feeds your spirit. It feeds the good angel that looks after your spirit. You need both the angel and the spirit to be healthy and happy. That is what mushing does for you."

With a wry sense of humor, the witness added, again as if speaking to herself, "I bet even judges need a lot of mushing."

A silence covered the courtroom as everyone present reflected on what had been said. The judge thought of his own tired spirit and the things this good lady had said, and finally he broke the quietude. "Mrs. Simmons, you can never know how much mushing a judge needs. I want to thank you for what you have done personally for me and for the insights that you brought to this courtroom. You brought more wisdom into this room than the combined good sense of all the expert witnesses who have testified in my court during the last thirty years."

The judge paused for more reflection. "Mrs. Simmons, this court is in your debt. I personally am in your debt. It is beyond my power to control, but somehow I feel that your job is secure for as long as you want it. Mrs. Simmons, I thank you. You are excused from the courtroom."

Mrs. Simmons made her exit past the table of the mother and her attorney, stopping long enough to give both hugs. Next, she stopped at the doctor's table and gave both the doctor and his lawyer a hug.

The doctor's lawyer made preparation to call his next witness. The judge held up both his hands, palms open to the lawyers and clients, a clear signal that the case was at a stop.

"I will not take further testimony in this case at this time. In fact, I will not take testimony in any case for the next six months and all of you are entitled to know why," the judge stated.

The judge continued, "I have grown weary of my work, for too long I have had an overdose of human misery. For too long, I have drunk from a bitter cup. I have not announced it, but I had planned to retire from the bench when this case was concluded."

He again looked out the courtroom window a long time before he resumed, "Mrs. Simmons has explained some things about life that I did not fully understand before. She has caused me to see some things differently. As I stated, I am tired and I plan to use six months of my accrued vacation time that I have never found the time to use before. I will use this time to reflect on what this good lady has said to me. Maybe there are others in this courtroom that would like to do the same thing. I will notify the attorneys when this case is rescheduled. Court is adjourned."

Six months and one week elapsed before the judge saw the lawyers again; they appeared in his chambers without their clients. The judge apologized for the delay and indicated that his rest had been beneficial. "I guess I can go for another year or two. I will place this case first on my next trial docket," he explained.

The older of the two lawyers spoke, "Judge, the parties jointly move the court for a dismissal of this case and as grounds for the motion advise the court that, with Mrs. Simmons's help, the parties are learning to mush."

(Writer's note: This story is based on a trial experience of the writer. To spare feelings, all names have been changed. The doctor and his wife, both now dead, lived together as husband and wife for the remainder of their days. I saw "Mrs. Simmons" a few times after the trial. When meeting, we always gave each other a hug.)

Runaway Mules

Even before I could get my overalls on, I heard Papa calling, "Go hitch 'em up to the wagon and take the corn to the mill."

Heck, I had fishing on my mind. Who wants to take corn to the mill when you could be fishing? Fooling with mules wuz enough to make anyone ill of mind. A single mule can be an ornery critter. Two skittish mules to a wagon can just about aggravate you to death.

The day got off to a bad start with me wanting to go fishing and all. I tried to forget fishing and went to the barn to harness up Jump and Scat (that's the names of the mules I had to hitch to the wagon). Everything's got to have a name, especially a mule. Mules resent not having a name, everybody knows that.

Josh McGeehee once had a mule without a name. That no-name mule wuz a whiz at kicking, one of the best in the county. That mule kicked what little brains Josh had over half the county and part of

Mississippi. 'Course, Josh didn't have much brains to begin with, so there wuz no great loss of brains. Josh kept on going and living. Loos'en half of nothing didn't seem to make much difference to Josh.

Some said they thought Josh even acted smarter after that mule kicked his brains out. They said he seemed to talk a little smarter. 'Course, Josh didn't have far to go to talk a little smarter. Couldn't no one understand what Josh said before that mule wailed him upside the head, and the number wuz about the same after that mule got him.

That mule got all Josh's teeth, 'cept one. Yes sir, that mule's foot got all eight of Josh's teeth, 'cept that one on top. The one that survived the kicking wuz moved a smite. It wuz kind of shoved to the middle of that upper gum, kind of centered 'neath his nose. Josh wuz proud he had a tooth left. He got it gold capped and had three little diamonds set in it. That tooth wuz the original "Smiley Face." Josh loved to grin and show off that smiley tooth.

He kept that tooth clean, rubbing baking soda on it to make that gold just sparkle. The one tooth, smack in the middle of that upper gum, and them three little diamonds grinning at you like a cat wuz right strange to see. It scared the wits out of little babies and most grown folks, too. Just about every time that one smiley-face tooth would make the babies cry and old women pee their britches.

The circus folks come to town and saw Josh and his smiley face tooth. They wanted him to join up and travel with them. They said he wuz a "natural." Now I don't know what a natural is, but they said Josh wuz one, so I guess he wuz. Josh said he weren't cut out for no circus. Besides, he wuz sparking Miss Hattie right regular like and didn't want to leave town.

At first, Miss Hattie said she did not like that gold, smiley face tooth. But she said it growed on her. I never did see no difference in the size of that tooth and it stayed in Josh's mouth. But Miss Hattie claimed it growed on her. I never did understand how it wuz growing on Miss Hattie when it wuz still sett'n right 'neath Josh's nose.

I'm sorry. When I get to telling a story sometimes I jump off the track. I didn't mean to tell you about the circus and that tooth growing on Miss Hattie. Just forget that part. I guess I'm like an ornery mule, sometimes I kind of kick out of the traces and jump the fence.

Even though Josh didn't have no brains left, thanks to that no-name mule, he did know how to use that one tooth to good 'vantage. He could scare a dog out of his skin with that tooth, not to mention what he could do to a pregnant woman. Josh, with no help at all, 'cept that tooth, caused eighteen miscarriages, and marked more babies than any one could count.

Old Doc Murphy kind of got rich off that tooth. Doc made up a special tonic what he would give to the pregnant women that had unintentionally looked at Josh's shiny tooth. He said his tonic made the woman big with child hold her own, said it gave her a better grip. Doc did not talk it 'round town, but he would give Josh twenty-five cents a day just to sit on the bench outside the courthouse and grin at the pregnant women. No sooner than a swell'n woman saw the gold tooth, she would head to Doc's office for a bottle of his special grip tonic.

Yes sir, Doc would sell that special tonic for five dollars a bottle. Old Doc said he guaranteed his product, said he would give the money back if any pregnant woman over sixty-five years who dropped her baby early after taking his tonic. Doc never had a claim made, never had to pay out a dime on his tonic guarantee.

But Doc had a decent streak in him. Even though he wuz making money off that one gold smiley tooth, Doc told Josh that for fifteen dollars he could move that tooth back in place. Josh kind of liked the tooth where it wuz, but once that kicking mule moved it to the middle of the gum, he never could catch his dog.

He had a fine blue tick hound that wuz a jim dandy coon dog. Having only one tooth and it being right in the middle of his pucker, Josh could not whistle for his dog. And every time he opened his mouth to call that dog, that gold tooth would shine like a new dime and that smiley face just jump out at the dog. That blue tick would see that tooth, tuck its tail, and run for the next county. Other dogs scatted when they saw that tooth, too. I didn't see it happen, but it wuz said that Josh's tooth could make a cast iron bulldog get up and run off the porch. Several folks said they saw that. Some said that tooth could even make a bobtailed dog grow a tail just so it would have something to tuck 'tween his legs as he tried to escape that smiley tooth. 'Course some folks will spread the truth 'kinda thin.

Anyway, Josh could not whistle for his dog on account of his tooth being smack in the middle of his whistle pucker and Josh asked Doc if he could fix his pucker so he could whistle for his dog. Doc

looked him over and allowed the proper way to fix his pucker wuz
to move the tooth back where it come from 'fore that kicking no-name
mule got hold of Josh. Doc said he had a fool proof plan for sending
that smiley tooth away from its present pucker block'n position.

Josh talked to Miss Hattie about letting Doc move that tooth
back where it come from. I think I already told you that Josh wuz kind
of trying to do some sparking with Miss Hattie. He knowed Miss Hattie
had said that tooth had growed on her. I never did understand that, the
tooth wuz in Josh's mouth and I did not see how it wuz growing on
Miss Hattie. But I think I done told you that already. Anyhow, Miss
Hattie wanted Josh to be able to catch his hound dog, so she agreed
that Josh could let Doc undertake the tooth-moving job.

Doc took Josh out behind the barn and put some blinders on
him. Now some of you city folks don't know what blinders is. Blinders
is things they put on the sides of a mule's head, fixing the mule where
he can look north without seeing to the east and west at the same time.
It is kind of hard to explain blinders to city folks. I hope you get my
drift.

Anyhow, Doc put the blinders on Josh and told him to stand
real still. Weren't no need to tell Josh to be still. He saw Doc's mule
standing there and knowed that mule wuz bad to kick at anything that
moved. Doc put them blinders on Josh and got everything lined up just
the way it should be. Josh stood real still, just as pretty as you please.
Like I said, Josh weren't too smart. He wuz a whole bunch of bricks
shy of having a wagon load.

Now Doc ain't always had the same mule he had Josh lined up with for putt'n that tooth back where it come from. Maybe you would better understand to know that Doc traveled in a buggy. That new doctor down the road had one of them Model T's. Doc said that it weren't professional riding in one of those things.

Before he got that kicking mule, Doc had a small red mule, but lost that red mule in a crap game with the Baptist preacher. Doc said he should of knowed better than to shoot crap with a Baptist preacher, 'specially when the preacher wanted to use his own dice. Anyhow, when the new doctor got his ModelT, Doc decided he needed to spruce up a bit and got himself a buggy horse. He got him a fine buggy horse that stood about fifteen hands high, and wuz sound of wind and limb. At that time, Doc also got a new buggy, too. I mean Doc had a jim dandy horse and buggy rig.

Doc went over the river one night in that new buggy, over to the Mississippi side. He had a new harness on that fine horse. Doc wuz all spruced up, wearing a new suit. I mean both Doc and his rig wuz a sight to see. He rode over to Mississippi on the ferry down at Pickensville.

Doc said he wuz going over there to make a house call on a pregnant woman. 'Course Doc had no license to doctor a woman in Mississippi, but he wuz a kindly and caring man. I guess it wuz a little more than that. To tell the truth, Doc kind of fancied himself up to be a ladies' man. Later on, Doc said he knowed the woman wuz not pregnant, but he felt like she wanted to be. He said he just liked to be around when a woman wanted to get pregnant, that he liked to be there when things like that happened. Doc said his oath of office required making house calls on women that wanted to get in a family way. He called it a hippopotamus oath, or some such oath. Doc could use some big words now and then.

While Doc wuz making that Mississippi house call, the woman's husband got home a little early. The husband coming in unexpected kind of disrupted Doc's house calling business. Doc thought it best not to try to hitch no horse to a buggy before heading back to Alabama. You might say Doc kind of gave that fine horse and buggy to that woman's husband.

Doc left that man's house in some kind of a hurry. I mean he wuz picking them up and putting them down. When he got to the river, the ferry wuz on the Alabama side. Doc said he did not know how to swim, but he learned in a hurry.

I don't know if it is true or not, but they said Doc never did no more house calling in Mississippi. Doc said he had kind of surrendered Mississippi, said he had more house calling business on the Alabama side of the river than he could tend to.

There I go again. I done fouled the ball off into the weeds again. Done jumped off the track about gett'n Josh's tooth moved back to where it come from. But that's how Doc come to own his kicking mule. When he lost his buggy horse, he got a mule. That's the mule Doc had Josh lined up with out back of his barn, the one Doc wuz going to use to put that tooth back in the right socket.

Now, I am back on track. Just stay with me and I will get this story told. It will take a while longer, but if you will just stick with me, I will get it finished.

You see, Doc wuz a scientificated man and he reckoned a mule had knocked that tooth out of socket and it would take a mule to get it back in place. Doc wuz smart like that. Now like I said, Doc had a decent streak in him and he wuz willing to lose his tonic selling business and put that tooth back in the right socket. He wuz going to do all that for just fifteen dollars. Now you must admit, that shows a decent streak in Doc. Not many doctors would give up a good tonic business for just fifteen dollars.

Now I am getting this thing together. I apologize for getting off key and hitting all the foul balls. But now we have it. Josh is dressed up with his blinders on and Doc has him lined up with that kicking mule. Hold on now. Now we get to the good part.

Doc had bought that kicking mule he had Josh lined up with for just five dollars. If you don't know your mules, that's a mighty good price for a mule, even in hard times. I guess the reason Doc got that mule so cheap wuz that mule didn't have no name.

Now if you want to make a kicking machine out of hybrid animal, just let him grow up without a name. The hybrid is naturally already upset about not being a genuine article. He is naturally embarrassed about being half horse and half jackass. That's enough to make anybody upset. But when you refuse to give something that is half jackass a name, that's about like slapp'n a grizziling bear upside the face.

You had better listen to what I tell you, if you ever see a mule that ain't got no name, you better give him plenty of room. He will kick you clean across Alabama and halfway across Mississippi. Getting ready to put Josh's tooth back in the right socket, Doc had both Josh and that kicking mule lined up proper. Ain't no doubt about that. He had Josh in blinders and that mule backed up just right. Doc wuz good about alignment. He could take good aim.

When he came out that window of that woman's house in Mississippi, he hit it dead center. He did not hit sash or frame. As he went out, he hardly ruffled the curtains. He hit the ground on his feet, running like a rabbit. In addition to the fine horse and buggy, Doc left all of his personal belongings over the river. That man over in Mississippi wuz too fat to wear Doc's suit of clothes, but he shore wuz proud of that buggy and horse, he said that Doc had 'willed' them to him.

I'm sorry, I done told you about all that. I keep drifting off. The ball keeps curving to the left.

You might say that mule Doc had Josh lined up with for that tooth mov'n job wuz a 'two footer'. He liked to come up on his front feet, so he could get elevation in the back. That mule wuz one of the best I have ever seen. Sometimes he looked like he wuz learning a new way for a mule to get around. He could almost stand, well I started to say stand up straight, but that's not right. Maybe saying that mule could stand up backwards would be better. Any way you say it, it wuz again nature the way that mule could get up on those two front legs.

As that mule went up on his front toes, he could hide those back legs and feet. He could make them go clean out of sight. As he elevated his rear end, that mule could tuck those back legs up under his belly. He would tuck 'em so tight they couldn't be seen. It wuz just again nature what that mule could do.

Once up on those front feet, that mule could just stay there. Looked like he would just freeze. I'm telling you, it just weren't natural. Once up like that, back feet tucked in belly tight and cocked like a pistol with a hair trigger, that mule would grin.

Unlike Josh, that mule had some pretty teeth. It wuz a sight to see that mule all grinned up, toe dancing, back drivers cocked and in place. I know you don't believe this, but that mule's grin could have sold toothpaste. I mean a ton of toothpaste. I wonder why Doc did not think of that?

There I go, getting my foul balls lost in the weeds. You want to know about the relocation of Josh's tooth, about its homecoming and I keep on hitting balls over the pasture fence.

After that mule had showed his pretty teeth to all that would look his way, he would look around for more audience. He wuz a regular ballaranner, or whatever you call them folks, proud of his toe dancing and his mouth crammed full of teeth. All this time while he wuz doing his toe dancing, he kept them back feet set on ready. I mean he kept the gun loaded and the hammer cocked. Do you catch my pitch? That mule liked to show out.

That day, out back of Doc's barn when the tooth moving business wuz underway, finding no clapping and shouting for his toe dancing and grinning, that mule turned his head back toward Josh. Course that mule didn't see too good. That's another reason why Doc got him so cheap. There they were. Josh with them blinders on. That mule tip toeing around, looking for a target. Not seeing too good, but looking.

Doc had had that mule long enough to know his ways. Doc knowed that mule's volume wuz turned up by a good goose in the flank. If you really wanted to rile that mule what ain't got no name, just give him a good goose in his ribs. 'Course, Doc wuz drunk. No shame bout that. Doc wuz that way most of the time. He had made a call on Homer Simms the night before. He went to collect a fee. Homer always paid in corn whiskey. You could say Doc wuz carrying a little heavier load than normal as he lined that kicking mule up with Josh, ready to gouge that mule in the short ribs at the right time and let that no-name mule's back feet put that smiley tooth back where it come from.

'Bout the time Doc went to give that mule a goose in the ribs, that guinea hen ran under his feet. Kind of tripped Doc up and he missed the flank. In fact, he missed the entire mule. Doc kind of fell into what you might call the danger zone.

Now the only thing that mule liked better than a sett'n duck wuz a moving target. That mule did not have any strong affection for

Doc anyhow. That mule lowered the hammer on his gun and sent Doc flying. As different parts of Doc flew by Josh, Doc's left hand slapped the blinders off Josh. They never did find Doc's right leg and foot.

When the blinders come off, Josh saw that mule's back legs were sticking straight out and Doc, in small pieces, wuz flying by. Doc wuz gone with the wind.

Since that tooth had kind of growed on Miss Hattie and since Doc wuz all broken up, Josh decided to just leave that tooth where it wuz.

I don't know how I got so far off base, I didn't set out to say anything about Josh. I wuz wanting to go fishing and shore didn't want to fool with no mules. But when Papa say something, best do it, and Papa done said, "Boy, go hitch 'em up and take the corn to the mill."

Jump and Scat, that wuz the names of Papa's mules, 'case you done forgot, knowed I wuz in ugly mind that day. They knowed I had fishing on my mind. Mules are smart like that. I got 'em all hitched up and put four turns of shelled corn in the wagon. Corn all sacked up, like it ought to be.

Got to admit I wuz slapping at them mules with the lines, me being all riled up like I wuz 'bout not going fishing. But there weren't no call for them mules to run away. That is 'til they ran over that yellow jacket nest. Them yellow jackets just covered them mules and me up. They covered us like the dew covers Dixie.

Instead of sticking to the road like a regular mule, they took to the ditch. Runaway mules is more irregular than Bill Clinton trying to tell you what sex is and what sex ain't.

First, they run through Miss Hattie's backyard and gathered up 'bout a half mile of Miss Hattie's clothesline. Got her bloomers and petty coats that wuz hanging on the line, too. 'Shor did. Got a whole week's washing. Got six petty coats and seven bloomers. Miss Hattie wuz always regular about her bloomers. Some days she might miss a petty coat. But she never went without bloomers. Them crazy mules and wagon pretty much undid the clothesline. We went through the yard and around the house, pull'n the clothesline behind the wagon, them bloomers just waving in the wind.

Josh and Miss Hattie wuz sitting on the front porch when we went 'round to the front of her house. When he saw all Hattie's bloomers flapping in the breeze, Josh cackled like a hen over a fresh egg. Miss Hattie hit Josh up side his head with a hoe and moved that tooth 'bout halfway back in proper place. When them mules saw Josh's solid gold, smiley face tooth they caught their second wind and things got kind of testy.

Scared them kids half to death as we came across the playground. Caused what you might call a squeeze play at home base. But them kids were quick enough to scatter. Seemed like they enjoyed seeing Miss Hattie's bloomers flapping in back of the wagon.

It wuz mighty early in the day for a tent revival meeting. Them drink-no-whiskey workers get going early. The preacher must have heard us coming. I heard him yell, "Praise the lord, judgment day is here." All the saints fell to their knees and the sinners come pouring out of that tent like a covey of quail. Team and wagon made a clean sweep of all the saints. The sinners didn't get a scratch. All kinds of bottles fell out of the pockets and purses of all the sinners as they jumped the fence and ditches. Sheriff said me and them mules busted up more whiskey in two minutes with a run away wagon than he had in the last two years.

Down about Glover's store, them mules decided to swap the remains of Miss Hattie's clothesline and bloomers for 3 miles of barbwire fence. We left them bloomers hanging on a fence post smack dab in front to that store. Miss Hattie wuz mortified when Old Man Glover told folks he thought he recognized them bloomers.

By that time, we done lost most of the corn. I did not have time to look, but I'm certain that all the corn wuz gone when we joined up with that funeral procession. We caught up to it from the rear and we pretty much visited all the mourners and family 'fore we got to the front end. Some of the young, the ones with good hearing and quick feet, made it to the ditches and got out of the way. The old folks in the funeral procession, well, they wuz old anyway.

You might say Old Man Henry Adams had called that funeral meeting. He wuz riding in the front wagon. His hearing wuz not good at all. Matter of fact, I don't guess you can say anything about his wuz good. I don't know the proper word; I guess you might call him the

honoree. He wuz the one what had called that meeting. He had
been laid out more than a week.

Some of Old Man Adam's kinfolks had to come over from
Georgia for the funeral. He had been laid out long enough to be fully
ripe. He wuz rank enough that nobody wuz a'mind to spend much time
looking for him after me and the mules came through. You could still
smell Mr. Adams right enough. He was just scattered so bad he would
have been mighty hard to gather up and bag. Everybody though it best
just to let him rest in peace.

Nobody being a'mind to look for the old man, they just called
the funeral off. Some of them Adams folks got upset. Don't know why.
Them mules, wagon and me left plenty material for several more
funerals and the collective remains wuz much fresher. There ain't
nothing more contrary than a run away team of mules, in particular
when you'd rather be fishing.

The Christmas Cookie Jar

It sits on the cabinet above the kitchen sink of my home gathering dust. On seeing it, friends and guests may sometimes under their breath say, "What a hideous thing."

If said, these words would give no offense. It is an ugly thing. It almost defies description with its repulsive pale yellow color and nondescript flower design of blue and orange. It is also a thing that defies definition of its intended use. As a little boy, I called it a "cookie jar." As an old man, I still call it the same.

That cookie jar became a part of my family many years ago. Possibly in my story you will find some beauty in that ugly cookie jar. Such is my wish.

I turned nine in October 1939. Daddy was gone, we knew not where. Pennies were a rarity at our house, dimes mostly unseen.

Twenty-five cent pieces? Well, that was a different matter. I got one
of those each week for milking Ms. Jones's three cows twice each day,
seven days each week. That rate of pay likely translated to less than a
penny for each hour's work, but time was not a factor. Time was all
that I had. At nine years old, one has no concern with the ticking of a
clock, nor did I have a watch with which to measure the moments.

That quarter each week opened new worlds for me. A nickel
got me a seat each Saturday afternoon in the Princess Theatre and a
bird's eye view of a "picture show" (that is what a movie was called
then). Not just any ordinary picture show, but I'd get to see a double
feature western picture show. In addition, there was always a newsreel
sandwiched in between Hop-Along Cassidy and Lash LaRue, or
whoever was shooting the Indians that day.

A nickel bought many bullets, barrels of gunpowder, and the
loud, never-ending pounding of galloping horse feet. The cowboys
always won the fights, killing all the Indians. The only good Indian was
the one who aligned himself with the cowboy, but even the good
Indian was expected to always defer to the cowboy, riding behind him
and shooting the bad Indians. Another nickel would buy a large bag of
hot, freshly popped popcorn. I have no recall of how the remaining
fifteen cents of my weekly income was spent; for less essential things of
life, I would think.

But, it is not my intent to tell you about picture shows and
popcorn. I want you to know about that ugly, in the eyes of strangers,
cookie jar and how it came to rest on the shelf in my kitchen. I want

you to know about an event of more than seventy years ago that tested my will, an event that taught me that doing the right thing is sometimes doing the hard thing.

One might call this a Christmas story. It took place during the Christmas season and centered on my desire to make my mother happy and my wish to please myself, but not being able to do both. So, if you wish, call it a Christmas story. To me, it is not a story at all, it is simply an old event of life that remains a fresh memory.

That year, I knew Christmas was coming and times were lean around our house. But lean times were of no concern, it had been that way for as long as I could remember. Having never known what many would call "good times," how could I know such times? That would be like missing someone I had never met.

At the time, I was growing old enough to take notice of Mother; it seems that is the way it began. I was beginning to notice how hard she worked and how tired she sometimes became. Mother was a daily presence in my life, but I was beginning to see her in a new way. It is easy to overlook something that is always there. At nine, I started to see her as a person.

I began to notice that she was a human being, that she was like other people. I did not think of it in terms of her having "needs" like others. But looking back I realize that was what I had started to see and understand. Likely for the first time, I felt an urge to really please my mother, to do something on my own that would be special for her.

I was beginning to think of some way that I might make her happy. It takes boys a few years to begin to think like that, but I was catching on. Possibly I had given Mother gifts before, but none are recalled.

Lean times or not, we always had a Christmas tree, one decorated with homemade paper rope and popcorn. At the time, I had no recall of Mother ever having had a present under the Christmas tree. I thought to myself *how happy Mother would be to find a present under the tree.* I guess it was just my time to think of Mother. It happened that way.

I do not want you to believe my getting the cookie jar for mother was an easy choice. It was a mighty tough call on my part. For a few days, I had been thinking about placing a gift under the tree for Mother, but thus far, that was all there was to it. Just thinking.

Long before I noticed that Mother never had a present under the Christmas tree, I had wished for a Tinker Toy set. My friend, Mike, had Tinker Toys and I had the strongest possible taste in my mouth for the same. Mike always let me play with his Tinker Toys, but that was not the same as having your own. But some way that fall I had worked my way past the desire for Tinker Toys and entertained thoughts of getting Mother something for Christmas. At least I thought I had gotten beyond the Tinker Toy crave.

At nine, I was not real strong in advance planning. Besides, my regular income was limited to the twenty-five cents each week that Ms.

Jones paid for milking the cows, and the shoot-em-up double
feature and popcorn each Saturday took a large slice of my budget. One
might say that I was just sort of toying with the notion that Mother
needed something under the Christmas tree. I sort of knew the need
was there, but that is as far as my thinking and planning had gone.

Before Christmas Day, there would be a test of wills. The
problem was the contesting wills belonged to me. I do not want you to
think that at age nine I was suddenly overcome with human kindness,
love, and compassion for Mother. I loved my Mother, but there is a
limit to how much a nine-year-old boy can love his mother or anyone
else, particularly if that boy has other loves like popcorn, picture shows,
Tinker Toys, and self.

The first testing of my metal started on a Friday late in
October, the day that I helped Mr. Phillips sweep his store and stock its
shelves for the next day's business. Saturday always brought the mules
and wagons to town, wagons filled with farmers and sharecroppers that
lived within a ten-mile radius of my small hometown. Saturdays were
social days for friends to meet in town and talk of the hard times of the
Great Depression and speculate if cotton would ever again sell for ten
cents a pound.

As I finished stocking the shelves on the left side of the store,
that's where the canned goods were kept, Mr. Phillips called me over to
the cash register on the other side of the store where the dry goods
were kept for sale. I knew he was going to give me some money for my
help. Boys come to understand such things. As I thanked Mr. Phillips

for the nickel, I noticed it on the shelf behind him. I saw it through the eyes of a boy that was beginning to understand the need of his mother for a present under the tree.

I saw it as a way to let her know that I was beginning to understand that her life was difficult, trying to feed and care for five children with no father around. I look at the cookie jar today and realize most, if not all, would consider it an ugly thing. But I saw it differently then. That now ugly cookie jar was then a thing of great beauty and I saw it as a way that I might reach and touch one that had need of being reached and touched. I did not think of it that way; I saw it that way. I guess my vision was better than my thinking.

My eyes told me that Mother would be excited to find that jar under the Christmas tree. For a while, my eyes made me forget about the important things in my life, like cowboys riding fast horses and shooting the Indians. I asked Mr. Phillips about the price?

He looked at the marking on the bottom of the jar, and then looked at me. He was an understanding man, a man that gave me some chores now and then around his store. He knew I had the regular job of milking Ms. Jones's cows each day. Maybe he remembered when he was nine and beginning to think about a mother's needs. It seemed he understood.

He looked at the marking on the jar's bottom a second time before he answered my question, then saying, "Joe, one dollar and seventy-five cents is the best I can do." I shook my head, "No." Mr. Phillips understood and placed the jar back on the shelf.

I made several stops that day as I walked the half-mile home. Under the large Magnolia tree in front of Dr. Hill's house, I sat on the rock wall between the yard and sidewalk thinking of the cookie jar and imagined Mother's excitement of finding it Christmas morning. At the base of the town water tank, I stopped a second time. Maybe, I thought, I can skip the Saturday shoot-em-up and popcorn. I had another six or seven weeks before Christmas.

It was almost November and I had thirty-five cents. But thirty-five cents was a long way from a dollar and seventy-five. As I made my way home, I made my last stop at the foot of the tall dirt bank, down from Mr. Tom's house. It seemed such a beautiful cookie jar, and it seemed my mother needed it in a bad kind of way. For the moment, putting Tinker Toys, cowboys, horses, and Indians aside, a boy's love of his mother took control. I knew she had need of that cookie jar that sat on the third shelf, mid way of Mr. Phillip's store. (It was many years before I understood the need was more mine than hers.) In this manner, I resolved to do whatever it took to get Mother that cookie jar.

I worked hard the next few weeks. I stacked firewood for Mr. Timmons. I told Mr. Tom that I would like to fill his box with wood for his kitchen stove each day. I knew that was a safe bet; Mr. Tom, like Mr. Phillips, was always fair. Three times I was able to help Mr. Eubanks get his cow—the one that was bad about jumping the fence—back in the pasture. Once a passerby had a flat tire on his car just outside of town. Getting him some help to fix that flat was worth a dime. For the next few weeks, I missed all the shooting, riding, war whoops, and Indian killing at the Princess Theatre.

All the while, I kept an eye on that cookie jar. Each time I checked Mr. Phillip's store, it was still there. I was fearful that someone else was looking at that thing of beauty. Every chance found me going by and talking to Mr. Phillips, eyeing to be sure the jar was still on the shelf.

Plans of life, whether one is young or old, sometimes hit a bump in the road. My problem started in the second week of that December. Up until then, there was no problem. Up until then, my mind was on Mother, the cookie jar, and trying to save the fortune that was needed to give her a happy Christmas morning. Until that time, I never gave Tinker Toys a serious thought.

Oh, I knew the box of new Tinker Toys were there in the hardware store, just a few doors away from Mr. Phillips's store. It was natural that a boy would take notice of things. Several times I had gone into the hardware store and looked at the box with its bold letters proclaiming, "*JUMBO SET, 550 PIECES.*" I knew how much I would like to have it, not even my friend Mike has a *JUMBO SET*. But I knew the price of $3.25 was beyond my reach. No matter how much I worked, that *JUMBO SET* was an impossible dream.

So, the bump in the road was not knowing the *JUMBO SET* was on the shelf in the hardware store. The price of $3.25 was more than a bump, it was a mountain. One I could never climb. The bump would come later. The bump would come when I could feel the bump the most, when it would hurt the most.

The bump in the road of my cookie-jar-plan was not really in the road. It was in the front window of the hardware store. It appeared there the second week of December. When I hit that bump, things changed in a bad kind of way. Mr. Huffman managed the hardware store and he caused the problem. He meant no harm, but he sure caused a big problem, and he did it with a piece of brown cardboard and a logging pencil. Not only did he make up that sign, he placed it in the store's front show window and at a level that would catch the eye of a boy who was saving his money for a special Christmas present. To add to my misery, the *JUMBO SET* of Tinker Toys had been moved from the store's toy section to the hardware's front show window. The fresh made cardboard sign was leaning against the Tinker Toy box. That was the bump!

That is when the infighting of my wills started. That is when I started losing my love of Mother and licking my lips for eternal, positive happiness and life ever after by owning a *JUMBO SET* of Tinker Toys. Seeing that box moved to the show window and the hand-made sign leaning against it started my understanding that one's love is greatly influenced by one's reach.

The moving of the big box and placement of the sign right where I was sure to see it gave me understanding of what my preacher grandfather was talking about when he spoke of Daniel wrestling with the lion.

Except, now I was Daniel and the lion was that big sign that read:

"Jumbo Tinker-Toy Set, Reduced to $1.99"

That sign leaning against that box gave a lion-like roar! And that's when my real problem began. Western movies and the trimmings that go with the galloping horses and gunpowder, I could handle. My love of mother could handle some things, but Tinker-Toys were a completely different matter. Love of Mother had its limits.

Those Tinker Toys were no longer hidden on the back shelf of the hardware; they were now in full view. I could stand on the sidewalk and see the hardware store off to my left and Mr. Phillip's store on my right. From this position, and that is where I stood that day, I could see the big box of Tinker Toys to my left and trying to look into Mr. Phillip's store from that vantage brought only darkness to view. It seemed almost as if God was speaking to me, giving me a sure sign.

Mike Mullins had his Tinker Toy set. He had gotten it for Christmas the year before, but is was not the *JUMBO SET!* It seemed this love of Mother business was much younger than the love of Tinker Toys. Love of Mother being immature seemed to yield to senior love of Tinker Toys. I had a problem in the making, a major problem.

My milking and chasing the cows, stacking the firewood, and filling the wood box had worked magic. I now had one dollar and seventy-five cents. Unless one of Ms. Jones's cows died in another week, I would have the most money I had ever had in my entire life, two dollars.

The Tinker Toy taste seemed to overpower my shopping taste. But something else took hold. Call it what you wish. Call it decency, compassion, understanding, the beginning of maturity, or love of Mother; something inside the little freckled-face boy took hold.

Later in life, I would read Lincoln's words about the better angels of one's nature. Possibly I have a better angel within me and it stepped forward that day; a newfound emotion conquered. My desire to see my mother's smile on Christmas morning proved even stronger in my heart than the Tinker Toy taste in my mouth.

Mr. Phillips personally wrapped the jar for me. My mother was pleased with her cookie jar. So pleased, in fact, that she kept it for the remainder of her life. She not only kept it, she kept it in a prominent place on a kitchen shelf, a place where all friends and guests could see. Just as today I keep the cookie jar on a shelf in my kitchen, a place where my guests and friends may see.

Others will never see the beauty in that ugly jar that Mother saw those many years ago. I was pleased to see Mother's smile that Christmas morning, just as she was pleased to see my smile that same day as I unwrapped my wonderful *JUMBO SET* of Tinker Toys. Merry Christmas!

Papa, the Smartest Man in the World

Papa's house was originally called a "dogtrot". A long center hallway, standing open on both ends, separated its rooms, with the bedrooms on the north side of the open hallway, the kitchen and family room were south of the "dog run", as the open hall was sometimes called. To find Papa's house, one would leave the dirt road that connected the towns of Carrollton and Reform (Alabama) at the Stansel Baptist Church and follow a narrow dirt road about one-half mile west to the two large oak trees standing at the end of the road. Papa's house was just beyond the trees. (The house and trees were still there in 2003.)

I was born at Papa's house when it was still a dogtrot. Before I was seven, both ends of the open hallway had been closed and additional rooms were added on both sides of the hallway. In this conversion, a large storeroom with its wonderful collection of tools, chests, boxes, a mule harness, cowbells, and a broken spinning wheel was created south of the hallway, across from the room where Mother said I was born. When I was twelve, the large storeroom was converted into a large living/dining room and all the treasures of the storeroom were lost. But, Papa was still there.

Papa's name was James Morgan Mills. He was a small farmer, for fifty-five years a Baptist Minister, and my maternal grandfather. He was also a large part of my life (and even though now dead, he so remains). His house is the scene of my first memory of life. At the time, I was less than four years old, playing outside his kitchen door at the southwest corner of house. This scene of memory is yet most vivid. It was summertime, and I was playing in the yard just west of the steps that led to the kitchen. The baby chicks on the ground around me were fuzzy little things. I had no idea that the mother hen was watching as I picked up one of her babies. With the first "peep" from the distressed chick in my hands, the mother hen made her presence felt. In less than a moment, the hen seemed to use her wings, legs, feet, and beak to thrash every part of my body. That mother hen seemed to be all over me. I no longer hear the peep, but my mind retains the thrashing of a protective mother hen.

My family lived, for a few years after I was born, in a small house on Papa's land. This house was on the north side of the one lane dirt road, about midway between the mailbox on the main road and Papa's house. My daddy was still with the family at this time. My only memory of Daddy participating in a family outing is when he took us fifteen miles south of where Papa lived to a movie theatre in Aliceville, Alabama. The movie, or picture show, called *State Fair* featured Will Rogers. The only part of the movie that I remember is the hog calling contest, of course won by Will Rogers. When Roger opened his mouth widely and gave his championship hog call, the pigs came running straight toward where I was seated, it seemed as if they would run right out of the movie screen and onto my lap. I almost died from fright! It was 1934, and I was age four. I have no recollection of ever sharing any other outing or event with Daddy. In many ways, Papa stepped into his shoes and I got the better part of the swap.

Papa's modest farming was on forty acres of land with a team of mules, a wagon, and an assortment of plows sufficient to cultivate about half his property. The remainder of his land was in pasture. He would sometimes laugh and say, "I farm on an eight-hour system. Eight hours before dinner (the noonday meal) and eight hours after dinner." (For the uninformed, "supper" was the last meal of the day.)

I spent much of my youth at Papa's house. The footprint of his left foot in the newly plowed earth always turned outward a bit more than did the right one, as if his left foot were determined to take in a little more of the world than his right one. When I was age ten, he shortened the handles of a plow, called a "Georgia Stock," cutting it down to my size, enabling me to plow alongside Papa instead of following his footprints. I never felt like a bigger man than the day Papa customized the Georgia Stock just for me. For the next eight years after Papa modified the plow, I lived about half the time with him, plowing, planting, and harvesting. Like the newly plowed ground, I bear his footprint.

From the time that his watermelons first ripened in July, he usually managed to place one in the shade of a tree, or if we were plowing in the bottomland he would put the melon in the small creek that ran through the pasture next to the field where we worked. Workdays garnished with a cool watermelon! Wonderful days! Wonderful memories!

Most people in the community knew Papa as "Preacher Mills," and he married many young couples. Life was much simpler then. Seldom were weddings planned, organized affairs. It was not uncommon for Papa to be plowing in the field when some young man, wearing his "best," would come across the field and say, "Preacher Mills, my girlfriend and I would like for you to marry us."

Sometimes the groom-to-be would add, "You married Mama and Daddy, and I would like for you to marry me." No matter how busy he was, Papa would answer the unexpected request by saying, "Let me put the mules in the shade and I will meet you at the house."

Back at the house, Papa always delayed the ceremony until he could wash his hands and face. If too dirty, he would bathe. He would put on a clean, white shirt. The young couple would wait nervously in the living/dining room until Papa came in and asked for their license to marry. Satisfied that all was in order, Papa offered a brief prayer and performed the ceremony. He would close the brief wedding ceremony with another prayer, and say, "You may kiss your bride."

Sometimes, the nervous young groom, after the ceremony, would shift from one foot to the other and ask, "Preacher Mills, how much do I owe you?" To this inquiry, Papa would smile and say, "Oh, whatever you think she is worth." Today, many would consider such a good-natured comment as being male chauvinistic. This was not intended by Papa. He was simply a man with a sense of humor. He loved to smile and for others to do the same. Soon after the wedding, Papa would be back plowing in the field, leaving his tracks in the fresh turned dirt, the left foot reaching out for more of the world.

He served as pastor for several different churches over a span of fifty-five years. At one church, Forrest Baptist, he preached twice each month for thirty-five years. For more than the first twenty-five years, he rode the fifteen miles from his house to Forrest Community in a horse-drawn buggy. Late each Saturday afternoon, he would drive his team of buggy horses to Forrest and spend the night in the home of a church member. The next day, he would preach in both the morning and evening service.

Following the evening service, Papa would get in his buggy, start the horses toward home and curl up in the buggy seat to sleep. The horses had learned the route and they consistently took the right roads back to the barn. When the buggy stopped, Papa knew his faithful team had arrived at his barn gate. He would feed his reliable horses and make his way into the house for a few hour's rest before starting another day of work on his "eight-hour system."

I never saw his buggy and team. By the time I came into life, he owned a 1927 Model T Ford. Papa was a large part of my life. I was age seven when I started to realize that Papa was the smartest man in the world.

The world was wonderful when I was seven. It was a world of discovery, excitement, and Papa. Some of the other grandkids called him "Grand Pa," but to me he was "Papa." I like to give different names to special people, because it makes it seem like they belong to me. Of course, my world at seven was a small one, but that did not matter. It was the only world that I knew, which made it a big, wide, new, and wonderful world!

Even then, Papa seemed an old man with his white hair that covered both his head and chest. To little boys, old men with white hair are supposed to be smart, and Papa never failed to know the things I needed to know. It seemed like no matter how difficult my question, Papa had the answer.

He knew all about mules, cows, and pigs. He knew how to treat the sore spot on a mule's shoulder with bacon grease. He knew how to drench a cow for worms with a longneck bottle and how to put rings in a hog's nose to keep it from rutting under the fence. He was a world authority on the benefit of snakes, carefully explaining that snakes could get into places for the mice and rats that were beyond the reach of the quickest cat in the world. Papa knew everything that was worth knowing, everything that grandfathers were supposed to know. It seemed his knowledge was without end.

But being old was just part of the way that he had acquired his knowledge. Papa loved to read and knew how to talk to God. His God-talking was none of that fancy stuff like I would sometimes hear at one of the churches in town. Papa would talk to God just as if God were seated right there beside him, sometimes it seemed He was. Every night Papa would read his Bible and talk to God about the events of the day. Sometimes he would tell God about his confusion, his doubts, and his lack of understanding of the mysteries of life. Mostly, he just asked God to guide his life, and mine too. It made me feel good when Papa would include me in his talk with God.

Even at age seven (and at age eighty, too) I sometimes wondered how God could think of everyone, especially of me. When Papa mentioned me in his talks with God, I knew I was being thought of and that would make me feel secure. On the nights that I knew that I had been called to God's attention, in bed I would hear the call of the Whippoorwill and think that God was talking to me. I have never known how to talk to God as Papa did.

But there was more to Papa's reading than just the Bible. He read those other books, too. Eleven of them. They were big and thick, and had dark blue, hardback covers. If they had been stacked on top of each other, they would have come up above my knees. But Papa did not stack them, he kept them on the shelf, next to his Bible.

On that shelf, above his table, the Bible was always on the left, and the big, blue books on the right. Papa called those big books his "Commentaries." No, that is not quite right; he called them his "Bible

Commentaries," as if the words belonged to each other and he could not use one word without the other. He said those big blue books had been written by men that had devoted their lives to the study of the Bible, and that they knew a lot more on the subject than he. I kind of doubted that, not that I had many occasions to doubt Papa about many things. But for anyone to know more than Papa just did not seem possible.

Not only would he read his Bible and those big, blue books, but he would also read his lessons and do his homework. He called them "correspondence lessons." Those lessons would come in the mail. Each Thursday he would say, "Son, go to the mailbox and see if I have another lesson assignment."

Down the dirt road I would go. I liked going to the mailbox. If it were summertime, I liked to feel the hot, dry dust on the road kind of gush up between my toes. That is, unless it was too hot and the dust would burn the bottom of my feet. When it got too hot, I would walk in the grass beside the road like Papa suggested. July and August usually put me in the grass. Papa knew about bare feet and hot sand and how it would gush up between one's toes. He was wise about all things like that.

I was always impressed when Papa's lesson plans would come in the mail. They came in a big, brown envelope. He did not get many big brown envelopes, just the ones that had "Howard College" stamped in the upper left-hand corner. (It is no longer called Howard College.

Today the school is called Samford University. I think I like the name "Howard College" better.)

It was mighty impressive to know that my Papa was a college student, there were not too many of those in my childhood world. It made me proud to carry that big, brown envelope back to Papa's house, so proud that I did not notice the hot, dry dust between my toes, even in July and August.

For every lesson received, in a day or two, I would take Papa's homework back to the mailbox. He did not have any big, brown envelopes in which to mail his assignments, he used large, white ones. He always wrote "J. Morgan Mills, Route 2, Reform, Alabama" in the upper, left-hand corner of the large, white envelopes that contained his homework.

The large, brown envelopes from Howard College and the large, white ones going back told me that this was Papa's most important mail. For less important matters, he sent his mail in smaller, white envelopes. His "J. Morgan Mills" in the left upper corner of the small envelope never seemed as important as when written on the larger ones. When one is seven, and has Papa as a teacher, one knows the important things.

It would make me mighty proud to see his middle name, (Morgan) on that envelope going back to Howard College. That is my middle name, too. I got it from Papa. I would sometimes look at the name "Morgan" being sent all the way from the Stansel Community of Pickens County to Birmingham, Alabama, and think that someday I might be a college student, just like Papa. I would think that if I ever became a student at Howard College they would already know my name.

After supper (that was what the evening meal was, this "dinner" business came much later in life) Papa would fire up the kerosene lamp that sat on his table, nearly under the shelf that held his Bible and those big, blue books. The he would get to his lessons and Bible reading.

Papa taught me that it was not wise to have the lamp directly under anything. The way he taught me was simple enough. Two or three years before I was seven he said, "Here Son, hold your hand over this lamp's chimney and feel the heat. Not too close, it may burn you, but close enough where you can feel the heat. We must never set the lamp directly under any thing because it might cause a fire." Does that not prove how smart Papa was? It seemed as if he knew everything that was worth knowing.

Papa would light that kerosene lamp and get busy with his reading and homework. It was that way every night, except the weekends when Papa preached at Forrest Church. I will tell you more about his preaching at other churches and baptizing folks in the creek some other time. For now, I'm just telling you about Papa's smartness, and some of the many things that Papa knew.

His knowledge seemed endless, like how to adjust the wick in the lamp. He not only explained about the wick, he showed me, too. He showed me that if the wick were too short, the lamp would not burn and if the wick were too long, it would smoke the chimney. "If you get it adjusted right, you get the best light and no smoke," he explained. Papa would check the kerosene level in the lamp, adjust the wick, and then to his Bible, big blue books, and homework he would go. It was the way that Papa did things.

A year later, when I was eight, Papa got an Aladdin Lamp. He would fill its reservoir with what he called "white gas." He showed me how to use the little pump on the side of the Aladdin Lamp to pump up the pressure of the gas in the reservoir, and how the fragile, white mantle of the new lamp was, and how much better light it made.

Even before Papa got the new Aladdin Lamp, he sometimes talked to me about light and how it could make everything better, saying, "Try to put everything in this world in its best light, it will make your world better. Put everything in its best light, and there will not be so much darkness." It seemed Papa was trying to tell me something special when he talked like that, like it was some lesson he had learned from his Bible, or those big, blue books, or from Howard College. At least it seemed that way.

It seemed he knew everything and tried to explain much of it to me. He knew about how Jonah had disobeyed God and got in trouble for not doing what God wanted him to. Papa knew all about how Jonah wound up in the belly of the whale and prayed for forgiveness and God saved him from death. He knew about Ezekiel and the sparkling wheels in the middle of the air. Why, he even knew about Nebuchadnezzar and his fight with the Egyptians.

I guess the best part was Papa's willingness to share what he knew with me, and his always finding the time to answer my questions. No matter what he was doing, he would stop and give me an answer. Take the quail with the broken wing as an example. Papa was working in the hay field that day, and I was playing close by in the corn. The corn had been "laid by." (All the corn plowing was finished, and the corn stalks were beginning to turn brown, awaiting the harvest.) When I first saw that crippled quail in the corn field, I knew I could catch her, what with her left wing dragging in the dirt and her being barely able to flutter and move on the ground. It sure seemed as if a seven-year-old boy could catch a crippled bird. She was in bad shape and just a few more flutters was all she had left in her. No bird in that shape would ever fly again.

I chased that bird a hundred yards, or so it seemed. (When you are seven and chasing a crippled bird, twenty yards seems like a hundred.) Several times, I got close. Real close. Just close enough to whet my appetite and get my bird-catching juices flowing. But never close enough to get my hands on that hen quail. I knew it was a hen, Papa had already taught me how to tell the difference between the hen quail and the rooster. In addition to the pigs, chickens, mules, cows, and snakes, Papa knew all about birds, too.

I got close enough to know that I could catch that quail in a few more steps. That hen was just about out of gas. She was on her last leg, or wing, I should say. I almost made it. There seemed like no way a crippled bird could get away from a seven-year-old. But it did. On my last try it seemed that hen, like Jonah, got some help from God. Up through the corn stalks she flew in a flutter and hurry, and was quickly out of sight. She kind of reinforced Papa's words that God works miracles. How in the world could a crippled bird get well so quickly, except with God's help? I knew that Papa would know.

He was riding high on the seat of the hay rake and saw me running across the field. He called the mules to "Whoa" long before I got to him. Stepping down off the rake, he took his large bandana out of his pocket and had the sweat wiped off his brow before I reached him. "Son," he said, "you look like you need to ask me something."

No sooner than I started telling what had happened then Papa got that crooked grin on his face, but he let me finish my story. Even before I told him about that crippled bird getting well so quickly, I knew I had come to the right source for an answer. I could tell by that look on his face that Papa, like always, understood.

He let me finish and said, "Let's let the mules blow for a few minutes and walk over here to the shade and talk for awhile. I put us a watermelon under that big oak this morning so it would not be too hot. I don't reckon you would mind if we cut that melon and ate while we talked."

Papa was in no hurry to satisfy my amazement of a quail with a broken wing being able to fly. We had pretty much finished off that Dixie Queen melon before he started to talk. "Son," he said. He most always started his talks to me with "Son". It was kind of like I belonged to him, which I did. He was mine, and I was his. That was the way it was with Papa.

"Son," he said, "there are many miracles in this world. Some say the miracles are the product of nature. I prefer to believe they come from God. That mother quail is just one of God's many miracles. You likely did not know she was a mother. You likely did not see her baby chicks on the ground, close to her when you first saw her, but they were there, you can be sure of that. I do not know how many there were, maybe a dozen or more, but you can take my word for it, they were there.

"When those chicks heard you coming through the corn, they squatted close to the ground and did not move. They just blended in with the dirt and weeds, but they were there. That is part of the miracle, they knew to just be very still and you likely would not see them.

"But, there is more to the miracle than that. The best part of the miracle was the mother quail acting as if she were hurt. Her dragging her wing on the ground and acting like she could not fly, and her fluttering around and keeping just out of your reach was part of her act. She knew that she could lure you away from her babies and she put on a good show for you. You took the bait and followed her. She led you away from her brood so they would not be in danger.

"That is the way that good parents do things, they always do what is necessary to protect their young. When that hen led you far enough away, she took to the wing. You can bet she circled around through the corn and that she is back with her chicks. Before we finish this watermelon, she will be back taking care of her young. When the sun goes down today, those baby chicks will be safely under the protective wings of their mother.

" Now, I have had all this melon I want. You sit here in the shade and polish it off. I need to finish raking this field before the end of the day. When I unhitch the team, I will let you ride one of the mules back to the barn."

Papa wiped his mouth, tucked his red handkerchief in his hip pocket, put some Beech Nut chewing tobacco in his mouth, and back to work he went. I ate my fill of the melon and marveled about how much Papa knew. In my eyes, he was the smartest man in the world. He tried to see things in their best light. To him, miracles came from God and nature was simply a part of God's work.

Now, in the twilight years of my life, approaching the age at which Papa died, I sometimes tell stories about Papa and the things he taught me. Recently, a friend called, saying, "Joe, I am doing a music program for a Fourth of July celebration at the Railroad Depot. I have invited my sister to sing God Bless America. I wish you would be part of the program and tell one of your stories about your grandfather. It is men like him that made America great."

I agreed to tell the story. In doing so, I realized that I had never thought of Papa as an American. To me, he was simply the man who paid his debts, sometimes called a stubborn mule a "Tom Fool" (the strongest language he ever used), read his Bible, talked to God as if he knew him, taught me so much of life, and plowed the earth, leaving a left footprint that reached out for more understanding of life.

American? Yes. The smartest one I ever knew.

A Talk with Billy

Sometimes I talk to old friends, even dead ones, and Billy had been dead for twenty years.

An old friendship sometimes fades out of sight until something comes along and stirs it into view, like seeing Billy's granddaughter yesterday. She was just a baby when Billy died, he hardly had the chance to see that granddaughter and hold her on his lap.

Maybe Billy can look backward from that mysterious place that now holds him and see that grandchild. Billy now knows a lot more about things like that than I. I hope I get to talk to him about that part of the mystery of life when we next speak. I should have asked him about that yesterday when I talked to him for the first time since he died. But, I was so busy doing all the talking, telling him about things in my life, that I forgot to ask about that. Billy always was a good listener.

That is the nature of folks like him; they have more of a gentle, listening streak than talkers like me.

I well remember that day twenty years ago when I last saw and talked to Billy in his hometown of Athens, Alabama. I do not know why I went by his law office that day long ago. I was in Athens and ready to leave and something told me to drop by and talk to Billy. I am glad it happened that way.

"Come on in, Joe. Gosh, it is good to see you"—that's what Billy said those many years ago. Talking that way was his manner. He could be busy as all get out, yet he would act like he was glad to see you and that he had the rest of his life to just spend with you.

We talked for a while that distant day of yesteryear. I do not remember much of what we talked about. I wish I could say he talked about his grandkids in Huntsville. If I could say that, I could tell those kids and it would make them feel good. But that would not be honest. Besides, they are not kids any longer. They are almost grown, or at least they think they are.

Even twenty years ago, Billy and I were old enough, and had seen enough, and smelled enough, and tasted enough of life to know this growing up business of life is always unfinished. Maybe Billy talked about his new grandchildren when I went by his office that day, maybe he didn't. The only part I clearly remember is what was said as I was leaving.

"Billy," I said as I was going out his office door, "I did not have any reason to come by and interrupt you. I just wanted to tell you that I love you." Billy was a very loveable guy, really easy to love. Of course, he followed me to his office door that day (folks like Billy always *see you out*). He thanked me for coming by. After saying that, he said, "Joe, I love you too, and I hope to see you again, soon."

But, I did not see him "soon." I guess that is part of the mystery of growing up, not knowing how long *soon* will be. In fact, I had not seen Billy since that day. Haven't talked to him either, until yesterday. Even yesterday, like that day so long ago, I did most of the talking and Billy, still having that gentle way about him, mostly did the listening.

It is sometimes strange how the spirits of old friends come rushing up to greet you. That is the way it was yesterday. Billy had kind of faded into the past. It had been years since I had even thought of him. Now some folks would take that to mean that he and I must not have been such good friends after all. But Billy and I are not distracted by that kind of thinking. We have done enough of the smelling, feeling, and tasting of life to understand that a lot of *ooing* and *aughing* over each other does not have a damn thing to do with friendship. Now Billy, not having the streak of meanness in him that I have, would not say it that way. But he would agree with my saying it. I did not say that when I talked to him yesterday, I was too busy talking about my grandkids, and he was mostly listening.

No, I had not thought of my deceased friend for several years; that is until I saw his granddaughter, Andrea Ashe. I saw how old she was and some of her artwork that she had on display. Right away, when I saw her, I wished that Billy could be there seeing her art work, too. That's what brought him to mind, I wanted him to see that girl who now thinks she is almost grown up. Anyway, that is what put me to thinking about my friend.

I still had that girl and Billy in mind when I went through the door of the Old Church at Burritt Museum, atop Monte Sano Mountain in Huntsville. This was less than a half hour after I had seen Andrea Ashe and remembered, for the first time in many years, my friend, Billy Malone.

It seemed as if Billy met me yesterday at the door of the Old Church. It seemed as if he had just walked with me to his office door in Athens and said *I hope to see you again soon* and was now opening the door of the Old Church for me almost twenty years later. Old spirits operate however they wish. Tradition and a lot of *ooing* and *aughing* do not bind them.

Old spirits, just like friendship, have nothing to do with how large a house one lives in, how fancy a car one drives, how fancy one's clothes are, diamonds, and things like that. When one has sampled as much of life and Billy and I, we know things like that are as worthless as a bucket of cold spit. That's why old spirits and good friends call it *ooing* and *aughing*.

When Billy met me at the church door yesterday, there was none of that worthless, gushy stuff. There was no embarrassment that I had not even thought of him for years. Time shared by spirits of old

friends is too precious for foolish things like that. I had some things
I wanted to share with him, and, like always before, he had the time to
listen.

So, yesterday, I talked to Billy at the Old Church. There was
some fellow playing a guitar and singing, and maybe fifty other folks
were there. I did not want to disrupt the little concert, so I silently
spoke to my friend. No sooner than I say that, I realize that I must
have disrupted Billy's listening to the music. Maybe that was the reason
he was there, he wanted to hear some traditional music. I did not think
of that.

Or, maybe he was there because he knew I needed to talk to
him, that I needed to walk some old roads and plow some old fields
with him. I hope that is the reason. Whatever the reason for his being
there, Billy, like always, was gentle and let me do most of the talking.
Not once did he act like he was irritated because I was keeping him
from listening to the guitar and singing. His spirit just stuck close to me
and listened.

I believe he still had that gentle smile on his face, but I did not
actually see him. I just felt him there. That is the way of old spirits, one
just feels them and knows they are real close. No, I did not actually see
Billy, yet, it seems I did. It seems I saw his face and the gentle smile
that he always wore on his lips. No one else saw him, but I think I did.
Mostly I just talked and he mostly listened.

While the fellow strummed his guitar and sang his songs, under
my breath, I told him about seeing his granddaughter. "Billy," I said, "I

saw Andrea Ashe today, not more than an hour ago. I am not sure how she spells her name, but for folks like you and I, we know correct spelling is just so much *ooing* and *aughing* and has little to do with real living and loving. Anyway, old friend, however she spells her name, I saw her and the art work she had on display, and wished you could be there with both of us."

I went on silently talking to Billy in that old church building for almost two hours. I told him about my grandkids and the things I had done with them. I told him about how lucky I have been, about what great teachers those grandkids have been, about how they call me "Hoss," and how that came to be. I told him about how my grandkids inspire me to write simple poems and stories, about my telling them hundreds and hundreds of stories over the years, and about my worrying about their future and wanting a good life for them. I just poured it out to Billy, and he listened. Now and then, as I talked, I could sort of see his face, I know he was smiling. He always smiled when he listened.

The fellow with the guitar said he would do two more numbers and then bid us farewell. I knew it was time for me to do the same with Billy, at least for then. I think we will pick it up again some day right where we left off, but for then I knew it was time to go. I knew it was time for old spirits to say *I've got to go now, but I will see you soon*. I realized, almost too late, I had talked too much and there were things I wanted to know about Billy's present life—how it is in that mysterious place that everyone seems to talk about, but no one seems to know about. I wanted to know if he could see and hear those grandchildren of his. I wanted to know what his thoughts were and if he ever got to go fishing or to football games. Looking back, I now realize there were a thousand things I should have asked him.

I wish I had asked him about this business of growing up and if the "up" ever stopped, or if the "up" turned into "down?" I wish I had gotten Billy to tell me just where "hereafter" is, and what it is like, and if there is any established *pecking order* there, and if the little babies that did not make it in this world ever *grew up* in the next? There are many things that I should have asked Billy while I had his attention at the Old Church yesterday. At least, it seems I could have asked him how long *soon* was. Yet, I had done most of the talking. I felt bad about that, and still do.

"Billy," I said, "I hope I have not made you feel bad by telling you about my grandkids and all the good times we have had. I hope my telling you about my grandkids did not make you sad about missing yours. That was not my intent. Maybe I should not have told you about those things. Billy, I have talked too much. It is your turn, what would you have me tell your grandkids the next time I see them?"

He, I am sure, smiled his gentle smile. Now I did not see the smile, but the way he spoke let me know he was still smiling. Billy said, "Joe, gosh it is good to visit with you again. I am glad to know that you have not gotten wrapped up in all the silly and frivolous things of life. I am even gladder that you told me about your grandchildren. Thanks for doing that, it meant a lot to me. When you see my grandchildren, just tell them about how it is been with you and yours. Just tell them that, had I been around, it would have been pretty much the same way with them and me. Tell them it would not have been exactly the same, because we are two different people, but it would have been pretty much the same. If you would let them know that, I will be most grateful."

That is the way it was yesterday when I again talked to Billy. The man with the guitar stopped his playing and singing and I knew the time had come. It was not *soon* yet, but it was time to go. Neither Billy nor I were ill at ease because I had not thought of him for years. That would be *ooing* and *aughing*, and life, both here and there, is too short for that. He and I met at the Old Country Church. I talked and he listened. When the music and clapping stopped, I could feel Billy's hand on my arm as he saw me to the door.

Country Store

The country stores of my youth were all very different, yet, in many ways the same. Like so much of yesterday, these stores are no longer with us. For those with an interest in what they were like, a word picture is attempted.

In appearance, most country stores had a "shotgun" nature about them, long and narrow. Most stood on rock pillars, some close to the ground. Some had a small, narrow front porch. Benches in front of the store were common, either on the porch or in the yard with their backs against the front wall. Weather permitting, two or more men might be seated in front of the store, But there seemed to be some unwritten rule against a woman sitting in front of the store. Cats, dogs, and men—yes; women—no.

Many of these stores had a single gasoline pump. If the store were built too close to the fronting gravel road, the gasoline pump, when added later, would be located alongside the store. Metal drums, accommodated with a drum pump, dispensed kerosene, a necessity for most customers. I remember kerosene selling for five cents a gallon, and gasoline for sixteen cents a gallon.

Many customers used snuff or chewed tobacco. Spitting on the floor inside the store was frowned on. A centrally located wood-burning heater provided warmth. If a fire was burning in the stove, opening the stove's door and spitting into the fire was acceptable. Poor aim and missing the mark brought a frown from the storeowner.

Typically, the store's double front door opened to a middle isle with long counters on each side. From front to back, shelves lined the walls behind the counters. A narrow path, just wide enough for the clerks to squeeze past each other when going to and fro while attending to the customers' needs, separated the counters and shelves.

A few of the stores had freestanding glass display cabinets with glass fronts that occupied a part of the row of counter space. Some had smaller glass-enclosed display cabinets that sat on top of the counter. Most candy was of a hard variety, something that weathered the heat well. It was displayed in bulk, in glass jars that sat on the counter. In large measure, cookies were displayed in glass jars in bulk form too.

A large, cast iron, wood or coal burning stove occupied a portion of the center isle space, its six inch stove pipe extended upward through the roof. Sometimes, the stovepipe would extend upward eight or ten feet and then make a ninety degree turn to exit through an exterior wall. Stovepipes taking this ninety degree turn frequently were supported by bailing wire wrapped around the pipe and attached to the store's ceiling above the pipe. On a cold winter day the store's hot stove drew a crowd.

During the winter months, it was common to find several straight-back, caned-bottom, mule-eared chairs close to the stove. (The mule-eared chair got its name from the two back legs that extended from the floor upward, and above the top "ladder" a few inches, thus giving the appearance of a mule's ears pointing to the sky.) Often the chairs would be centered on a wooden checkerboard. During the lean years, and most of them were lean during my youth, if a wood checkerboard could not be afforded, then one was drawn with a heavy logging pencil on a piece of cardboard. Plastic checker pieces came far in the future. Wooden checker pieces were rarely seen and frequently lost. This was not a problem. The caps from soft drinks were always available. One checker player would turn his bottle tops up, the other turned his tops downward. Checkers were played for pleasure, no betting on the game was allowed. Even if it had been allowed, few had the money to bet with.

Following the long center isle to the rear of the building usually led one to a double door that opened into an unheated storage room in the rear. The storage room was for bales of hay; sacks of cow, mule, and chicken feed; flour; unopened boxes of canned goods; excess gallons of syrup; five gallon cans of lard; and other staples that would replenish the goods sold on the grocery side of the store. Two or more cats were permanent residents of the storage room and store, effectively maintaining control of the mice and rats. Seldom was the storage room used to house any of the dry goods that were sold on the opposing side of the store.

Continuing one's walk from front to back through the storage room would lead to another double door and onto a small loading dock in the rear of the store. The height of the loading dock was a standard five feet to match the normal height of the sideboard of a wagon's bed. Seldom were horses used, except an occasional buggy horse for the more affluent.

In larger country stores, for reasons that I cannot explain, most grocery items were displayed and sold from the left side of the store as one went from the front to the back, and the dry goods vended from the right side. In the smaller stores, the grocery and dry goods were frequently mixed and found on both sides of the store. Many of the smaller, more remote stores had no back storage room, just the one large rectangular room.

Paper sacks were available in some stores, but sparingly used. It was cheaper to wrap the purchase in brown paper taken from a large spool. Most wrapping paper was about eighteen inches wide and torn to the desired length by the clerk from the spool with the aid of a spring-loaded, straight edge device that gripped the top of the roll of paper. Tearing the wrapping paper in the right length was looked on with pride. The storeowner frowned when the paper was torn too short, but most of these pieces were saved for use with another customer. The owner's frown was even greater when the paper was torn too long, these sheets were usually used and the customer walked out the door with two or three inches of unnecessary paper. (It was not uncommon for a student's homework to be handed back to the teacher on used brown wrapping paper.)

The paper sacks were used for eggs, dried beans or peas scooped from a box or barrel, and other merchandise that did not lend itself to wrapping. Finely spun cotton wrapping string made its way from an upright spool through an overhead ring and dangled near the spool of wrapping paper. The clerk held the loose end of the wrapping string in place with one hand over the paper that enclosed the wrapped goods while maneuvering the string around the package so as to form an "X" in the middle. Often the clerk would hold the string tightly between his teeth to break off the desired length. The use of too much string brought a frown from the storeowner, but not as great as the frown of too much wrapping paper.

Customers frequently bartered with the storeowner; fresh eggs for coffee, tomatoes for flour, potatoes for sugar, or fresh vegetables for a pair of socks. The coffee beans (sometimes referred to as "them coffees") were stored in a box, measured out by volume, or by weight in the more modern store, and ground by the clerk to the customer's satisfaction. Some liked their coffee fine-ground, others thought the flavor was better if the coffee beans were coarse-ground. The hand-cranked coffee mill generated a nice coffee aroma.

Many goods carried a plural designation. They were often called "them coffees", "them cheeses", or "them syrups." The cheese was cut from a large hoop with a downward motion of the hand-operated cheese cutter. Calculating a true pound of cheese before the cut was made was a work of both science and art. The uncut hoops of cheese were received in round, wooden crates with the enclosed round hoop wrapped in a gauzelike material. The total weight of the hoop was stamped in blue ink on top.

Most hoops weighed about fifteen pounds. After the hoop was removed from its wood crate, it was placed on a turntable, cheese-cutting device equipped with a large, ugly looking cutting blade, much like the blade of a guillotine. A downward pull of the cutting handle forced the blade through the hoop below, producing a wedge-shaped slice of cheese. A cut of approximately one-fifteenth of the total diameter of the hoop would result in one pound if the hoop weighed fifteen pounds.

Once cut, the remainder of the hoop was seldom covered. The customer had the right to sample the cheese before purchase. A request for a "tad of them cheeses" signaled that a sample was desired and the clerk, carefully positioning the cutting blade, would shave a small slice from the hoop and hand it to the customer. No attention was given when the clerk used his bare hands to cut the cheese and pass the sample over the counter. Nor were there any requests that the cheese-cutting blade be cleaned.

A wooden cutting board and butcher knife lay nearby for slicing the bologna. An occasional housefly was not considered a serious threat. Sometimes the clerk would wipe the knife blade on his not-too-clean apron. The local health department was occupied with more important things, like the control of head lice and internal parasites that seemed to make school children their targets of choice.

(The schoolteachers distributed small metal cups with removable lids for the students to take home and use for the collection of stool samples. One was instructed to print their name on the label, collect the specimen, and return the feces-filled metal cup to the teacher. The health department would collect the samples for analysis. Evidence of an internal parasite brought free medication and instruction for its use.)

Flies in the store were discouraged by double screen doors at the front of the building, but often greeted by the large open door at the rear. During fly season, a hand-pumped fly sprayer would give the store, for an hour or so, a strong smell of fly spray. Most of the time, the store clerk would place a wooden shipping crate over the cheese while the spraying was in process, and the already-cut-stick-of-bologna would be covered with wrapping paper. In addition to the fly spray, there were the ever present fly swatters, frequently called "fly-flaps."

Even before the Great Depression years, flour, horse and cow feed, and some fertilizers were sold in printed cotton sacks. When emptied, these sacks were thoroughly washed and converted into dresses, shirts, and underwear for the family. Sack patterns often changed, which was a mixed blessing. The change offered more variety and less opportunity for the embarrassment of being seen wearing the same color dress or shirt day after day. Frustration came when the homemaker had saved one particular flour sack, but needed two for enough material for a garment and the pattern changed before the second flour sack could be had. (My sisters frequently wore dresses made from these sacks. I do not recall wearing shirts made from flour sack material, but it is likely that I did.)

Rarely during my youth did these stores that were located away from the small towns have electrical wiring. Kerosene lamps provided the light after sundown. Beginning in mid 1930, the small stores in the little towns started being "wired for electricity," as it was called. With such wiring, wire cords would drop from the ceiling, attached to a pull-chain socket and a naked light bulb.

The insulation on the electrical wires was very poor. Frequently the positive and negative wires were installed parallel to each other, but ten inches apart. This was to avoid any arching of the electrical charge from one wire to the other. With electricity came refrigeration and the disappearance of the icebox in which the soft drinks were kept. The iceboxes, both in stores and homes, sat above a funnel that, in turn, sat in a hole that was drilled through the floor below. The water generated by the melting ice in the box, using this conduit, made its way to the ground below without wetting the floor. Typically the ice truck came by two times each week on Mondays and Thursdays.

Ice manufacturing plants were in the neighboring towns, making large rectangular blocks of ice. As recalled, each of these large blocks weighed 300 pounds. These large blocks were loaded on the ice truck and sold by the iceman in smaller blocks, depending on the customer's need, as the ice truck made its way though the countryside. The iceman would use a common ice pick to carve the larger block of ice into smaller "weights." Weight was a relative term, depending on the skill of the iceman's use of the ice pick and how much the large block had melted along the way. Twenty-five pounds was the smallest weight available. The twenty-five pound block of ice at the end of the route on a hot day was never as large as the twenty-five pound block at the beginning of the day. At the time, life was simpler. Getting a smaller weight of ice at the end of the route was not viewed as being unfair, it was accepted as a condition of living near the end of the route.

Toilet facilities inside such stores, whether in town or countryside, were virtually unheard of. In town, toilet facilities were available in the public buildings. But these, as did the water fountains in such buildings, carried the ever present signs that read *Whites Only.* On rare occasions, the small stores outside the towns would have an outdoor toilet standing a few yards from the rear of the store. These carried no signs, but it was understood that they too were for *Whites Only.*

Some of the white customers had sufficient financial strength to establish a line of credit. Typically these were called *Charge Accounts*. As the depression deepened during the 1930s, these credit arrangements lessened. The bookkeeping was very simple, but as varied as the imagination. Often the merchant kept all records of accounts receivable in a single, hardbound ledger book with the customer's name shown at the top of the page. Debits and credits would be noted on the ledger sheet as they occurred. Sometimes it might be months before a bottom line balance was established.

A sales ticket with a duplicate copy being retained by the merchant was even more rare. Often the entry on the ledger sheet left much to be desired as to what had been sold or what had been charged for each item. Sometimes the date of sale, along with the total, was noted. Other ledger entries might show only a dollar total, without a date of sale or description of merchandise. Other store types might have used equally primitive bookkeeping methods.

On occasion, there was a crude secondary record of the credit sales. This came as a result longhand figures reflected on a paper sack or a piece of the wrapping paper that the customer carried home. At the store, the merchandise selected had been placed on the counter and the store clerk would use the bag or paper to note the prices and make a tally of the total. Rarely were adding machines used, and rarely was interest added to the unpaid accounts. In a very real sense of the word, the customer was at the mercy of the storeowner in the determination of the balance due on the account.

The store served several functions—commercial, social, and sometimes, religious. The customers of my youth would mostly arrive at the store riding in a mule drawn wagon, the more fortunate in a Model-T Ford, or, even better, a Model-A Ford. (My grandfather, a small farmer and Baptist preacher, had a deluxe, four-door 1927 Model-T Ford.)

Saturday shopping at the store often saw the entire family arrive in the wagon. Early arrival assured a better parking place for the team and wagon. There were no traffic jams and seldom did the farmer hitch a kicking mule to a wagon. Mule runaways were rare, but always exciting. The horse was more excitable, which is one of the reasons it was seldom hitched to the wagon. It was a serious transgression to hitch both a mule and horse to the same wagon. Having a "matched pair" was a matter of pride.

On Saturdays, the customers would first attend to their shopping and then to the visiting with each other. During the winter months, the center isle would sometimes be highly congested with bodies. Conversations were interrupted with the necessity to look for someplace to spit the brown liquid product of snuff or chewing tobacco. In the warmer months, the socializing was more frequently conducted under the shade trees that always seemed to be a part of the setting. The summer months were the ones of choice for the itinerant preachers that gravitated to the captive audiences close to the store. It was not uncommon to have a Baptist preacher fully primed with the spirit on one side of the store and a Methodist preacher loaded to the lips with a sermon on the other side. Drawing a larger audience, like having a matched pair of mules, was a matter of great pride. Seldom was a collection plate passed among those in the standing audience. Spreading of the gospel was considered fair compensation for the preacher. The chill of winter would diminish the "call to preach."

Often the local politicians, while running for office, would visit the stores, shaking hands down the center isle as they made their way in and out of the store. The front steps of the store was a favorite platform from which the promises of public improvement were made. In 1946, James (Big Jim) Folsom stood on the front steps of such a store in the community of Pickensville, Pickens County, and made his campaign talk for the Governorship of Alabama.

Pickensville sat on the east side of the Tombigbee River. A hand-operated ferry was the only means of crossing the river to the Mississippi side. No sooner than Big Jim finished making his promises than someone in the small audience standing in front of the store asked, "Jim, if we elect you governor, will you build us a bridge over that river, so we can get to the Mississippi side?"

Immediately, Big Jim led the small group down to the bank of the river. There, he walked north a few yards and stopped to look across the river. He then turned and walked south a few yards and stopped to peer across the river from that spot. After several such trips and "surveys," he took the heel of his big size 14 shoe and knocked a small hole in the dirt. Pointing down to the small depression in the ground, he said, "Boys, when you elect me governor, I will build you a bridge and right here is where we will drive the first construction stake." Big Jim was elected, but he was long dead before a bridge was built.

The stores reflected the social customs. Profanity, or even off-color, suggestive language was simply not heard in the presence of women and children. Among the whites, the youth always said "Yes, Ma'am" or "No, Ma'am" to the ladies. The white youths were not expected to show the same deference to the black adults, it was neither forbidden nor practiced. It was a rare occasion during the 1930s and 40s for anyone in a public place to appear to be under the influence of alcohol. Hard drugs were something that one might read about, but were not available. The only exception to this rule was a rare addiction to morphine that sometimes followed its medical usage.

When I was a boy, country stores were a large part of one's social world, that and churches. The country store is now a thing of the past, replaced by the supermarket, department store, and (curses) the convenience store. I liked it better the old way, a sure sign that I have grown old.

Jimmy

Ageing is rewarding in many ways. One of which is recalling those who have touched my life in a positive manner, such as Jimmy.

I acted as his eyes for a year. Or, did I? At the end of the year, and even now, more than fifty years later, it seems he had better vision than any man I have known.

It is impossible to forget my first day on the job as Jimmy's employee. Understandably, I was trying to make a good impression. Jimmy and I sat in his office and chatted for a few minutes before I stepped into the reception room to retrieve a client's file. I returned to his office, leaving the reception room door standing half open. We talked for a while longer before Jimmy arose from his chair and stood behind his desk. We continued our talk, with Jimmy standing.

It happened rather quickly and certainly without my expectation. Jimmy walked around his desk and suddenly stepped in the direction of the reception room and the door that I had left standing half open. Before I could say anything, much less intervene, Jimmy walked nose first into the edge of the door. It sure seemed I was off to a poor start in my new job as Jimmy's law clerk. I immediately suffered what the old folks sometimes called a "serious sinking spell."

Jimmy, regaining his balance from his unexpected collision with the door's edge, turned in my direction and grinned through his lips that were a mass of scar tissue, saying, "Damn, I need to watch where I am going." Jimmy was blind, or at least society treated him as if he were blind. I, too, thought Jimmy was blind when I first started clerking for him. It was later that I came to realize the keenness of his vision. In working for Jimmy and getting to know him, I found a hero. Now, more that fifty years later, he is still my hero.

Jimmy, during World War II, had gone ashore on Iwo Jima with the 4th and 5th Marine Divisions in February 1945. More than 900 ships were used to transport Jimmy and his fellow United States Marines to that stinking, pork chop shaped speck of volcanic rock some 600 miles from Tokyo. As the troop ships had made their way toward battle and certain death for many, Tokyo Rose, in her rich, cultured English voice taunted the marines, claiming that when the fighting on Iwo Jima ended there would not be enough living U. S. Marines left on Iwo to fill a telephone booth. She was wrong. Many marines died, but many, like Jimmy, survived to become splendid examples and possibly America's greatest generation.

Of the eighty-odd Congressional Medals of Honor the U. S. Marines were awarded during some 1300 days of World War II fighting, almost one-third of them would be awarded to the marines for their fifty days of fighting and dying on Iwo Jima. (One Medal of Honor winner on Iwo was only sixteen years old, so determined to have a part in the fight that he stowed away on a troop ship to get there.) Jimmy did not get a Medal of Honor. Leaving various body parts and eyes scattered on the beaches of Iwo was commonplace. Medals of Honor were not awarded for commonplace events.

It was not easy for Jimmy to get to Iwo. He was too young for that war, or at least his mother thought so. Jimmy had pestered her almost from the beginning of the war to let him join the Navy, but she refused to sign the papers. Without her signature, he was too young to join. But persistence finally paid off, and his mother ultimately caved in and signed for him. Mid 1944 found Jimmy as a proud marine. He had not yet graduated from high school, but he was on his way to Iwo.

Twenty-two thousand well-trained and well-armed Japanese soldiers were defending Iwo; it was considered part of the Japanese mainland, and their homeland had not been invaded during the past 4,000 years. They were fanatical fighting men who would fight to the death. Only 216 of the Japanese soldiers were alive when the shooting stopped. The U. S. Marines suffered more than 30,000 casualties, 7,000 of whom died.

It was a brutal fight, of that there can be no doubt. Admiral Chester Nimitz would say of Jimmy and others like him who fought, bled, and died there, *"Among the Americans who served on Iwo Island, uncommon valor was a common virtue."*

Jimmy lasted longer than many of those who arrived early on that Iwo beach where there was no place to hide. The black, pebble-sized grains of volcanic sand defied the digging of a foxhole. One marine would describe it as being like trying to dig a hole in a mound of shelled corn—no sooner than a shovel full was removed, that it immediately refilled. Jimmy lasted, as I recall, four days before his lights were put out forever.

He never knew what hit him. Seldom in war does one know what takes them down. Whatever it was, it got him in the head and face and left him vulnerable to a door standing half open. But whatever hit him did not rob him of spirit and humor; he could still hit a door, nose first, and look around with a grin on his face in the general direction of where his new law clerk sat and say, "Damn, I need to watch where I am going."

This was my first, and lasting, impression of Jimmy; a blind man who was determined to watch where he was going. I say blind, but was he? If one has better vision than I, should I ever consider him blind?

With the body parts that still clung to his frame, Jimmy was shipped back home. Many, like Jimmy, were loaded into the large hospital ships, given the best care that circumstances of war could provide and told to "Hang on marine, we will get you home." Some did not complete the voyage. Those who died on the way back home, still dressed in hospital garb, were placed on a wooden board, covered with the flag of their country, and let slide into the great Pacific Ocean. The flag was saved to cover the next dead marine. Jimmy, one of the lucky ones, made it back.

I do not know the number of reconstructive surgeries he underwent and I am sure the doctors did their best for Jimmy and others like him. Even with the doctors' best, his face would remain a virtual roadmap of scar tissue left by the shrapnel and surgeon's knife. For the rest of his life, he wore a crooked smile and talked a little more out of one side of his mouth than the other. When one came to understand the reason for Jimmy's somewhat twisted and contorted face he became a handsome man. After the surgeons did their best, Jimmy was assigned to a rehabilitation facility in Philadelphia, living in a halfway house on the road back home to Alabama.

There, in the City of Brotherly Love, Jimmy was patched back together and made ready to go back home. In rehabilitation, he was paired with another marine that had the bad fortune of being fitted with one glass eye, but the good fortune of having one of his God-given eyes still in place and somewhat in use. The one natural eye that remained was impaired, but it was good enough to guide the two rehabilitation buddies onto the streets and into the everyday walks of life in Philadelphia.

It was common procedure to pair one with no sight perception with another that could see, at least a little, and to encourage the pair to put on their civilian clothes, get out on the streets, go to the restaurants, movies, bars, and work their way back into the mainstream of civilian life.

One evening, Jimmy and his glass-eyed buddy, dressed in their civilian clothes, made their way to the bar stools of a local tavern to enjoy the libations of the city. Soon Jimmy heard a third voice, coming from beyond his one-eyed friend. This third male voice was upset, even angry. This third voice protested the poor state in which the civilian population found itself. This unseen voice complained that new cars could not be purchased, gasoline was rationed, and various consumer goods were in short supply. The government, according to the protester, was showing favorites by giving everything to the military and saving nothing for the civilians, and that seemed unfair.

Suddenly, Jimmy heard this third voice begin to spit and sputter, and it seemed the owner of that negative voice half-fell from his bar stool and was heard no more.

"What did to you to that guy," Jimmy asked his buddy with the glass eye?

"I did not do anything," his friend responded.

"Come on, tell me what you did. I heard what he was saying about how tough it was on the civilians, and I know you did something. You know I cannot see a damn thing, tell me what you did," Jimmy urged.

"Well," his buddy replied, "I really did not do anything, but it seems that guy kind of choked up when he found my glass eye in his drink." Jimmy Turner really chuckled when he told me of that episode.

Jimmy made it back home with his Braille writer, a gift from Uncle Sam. Jimmy even made it back to his old high school and got his diploma. And then he decided to tackle college. As recalled, he was the first of his family to be so bold—there were no college men in his lineage. That Braille writer seemed to work magic in his life; that and the wonderful girl, Louise, who would become his wife and life-long companion. Louise offered Jimmy encouragement and hope. She urged, "Why not become a lawyer? Come on, Jimmy. You can do it!" And he did. For good measure, Louise became a lawyer too. Not to be outdone, their children became lawyers. Not a bad legacy for a man who society said could not see.

After getting to know him, it was hard to remember that he was blind. How could one be blind when Louise would take him out to the country roads, where there was no other traffic, and let Jimmy drive the new car they purchased? Jimmy wanted to "Try it out, to get the feel of it." And he did. If the lawn mower needed fixing, Jimmy could handle that, too. He still had good hands. Whatever hit him on Iwo did not injure his hands. Why else did God give him hands, but to use them?

Jimmy loved to "watch" movies with Louise, and he "saw" just about every football game the University of Alabama played, baseball and basketball games too. He just could not see half-open doors, with these he needed to "watch where he was going."

I had the good fortune to clerk for Jimmy for a year, my senior year of law school. I read law cases to him, sat in when he talked to witnesses and clients. Even went to the Alabama Supreme Court and sat by his side as he argued, and won, an appeal. On the way down to

Montgomery that day, as we headed to the Supreme Court, Jimmy said, "Joe, if we win this case, I am buying the beer. Hell, if we win, I may even drive us back to Tuscaloosa." It was a few weeks later before we got the good news from the appellate court. Jimmy had won, and he bought the beer.

My year with Jimmy gave me experience and insights beyond comparison. When I earned my law degree, Jimmy and Louise honored me by asking if I would like to be employed by their firm. (I wanted to practice law in Huntsville, Madison County. Elijah Berry, my forefather, had moved there in 1826.)

I will never again meet anyone whose so-called "serious handicap" meant so very little. Jimmy seemed oblivious to his loss of sight. I never heard the man say anything that suggested self-pity. To the contrary, he was high on life and all that was in it. This good friend and inspiration practiced the profession of law for fifty years. His vision was far better than mine; he saw things clearly.

Not long before I left Jimmy to come to Huntsville and begin my law practice, I asked him, "Jimmy, what do you think you would have done with your life had you not lost your eyesight?"

Jimmy thought for a while before responding, "Joe, we never know where a road not taken would have led us." Jimmy pondered the question awhile longer and continued, "My granddaddy worked all his life in the woods, cutting and hauling pulpwood to the paper mill. My daddy did the same thing. I guess if I had my eyes, I would be out cutting wood and hauling it to the paper mill."

Jimmy died in 2002. I am indebted to many for the good examples that have been set for me. The great example of Jimmy is far from the least. This story is told in tribute to a man I consider a Great American! One of the best I have ever known.

Good Friends

I never knew his name or shook his hand, but we became friends. He lived in a house about a mile from mine. Weather permitting he sat on the left side of the little front porch of his house. For several years, twice each day going to and from my office in town I drove past this man who became a true friend.

Linda, my wife, and I had built our home in his neighborhood. I judged him to be more than twenty years older than I. It seemed that he and his porch were one, that they belonged together. Living there before I moved his way gave him the better right to expect me to be the first to wave as I passed by. But the man did not stand on the tradition and ceremony of city folk.

In spite of his better right to wait for me, he usually waved first. Sometimes I would see if I could beat him with the wave, and a few times I did. But our waving was not a competitive game. It was friendly waving. One would have to live in the country to understand what I mean in saying it was honest country-style waving. There was no pretense, no shame, and no show and tell. It was just honest-to-God friendly waving, not meant to impress or curry favor. It was simply the right thing to do. It was the kind of greeting that I do not see from the front porches of the big houses in town. Only those who have lived in the country will understand.

My wife and I had moved into his domain. From his waves I understood he made us welcome to the community. Possibly unknown to me he had left his porch and passed by our place as Linda and I hammered and nailed our home together, board by board, making it grow from the ground up. If he passed and saw us cutting, sawing, hammering, nailing, and sweating, I am sure he approved. Regular waving teaches one many things about the other person.

My wife and I had built our country home with our own hands, working nights, weekends, and holidays for more than three years. I had drawn our construction plans on a brown grocery bag. We moved into our home during constructions while it was still no more than a shell. The house had no interior walls, and only the sub-flooring. Lumber, saws, nails, and tools occupied what is now our great room.

The fiberglass fibers covered our bodies as we gave our home a generous wrap of insulation. At the time, our bath facility was not adequate for the job of fiber removal, but the nearby Flint River was. We used the "Baptizing Hole" that had the reputation of washing one's sins away. It got most of the fiber and hopefully some of the sin. Some may have thought we were crazy. In some ways we were.

Ours is an all-wood home, inside and out, crowned with a tin roof. We proudly proclaim, "There is no sheetrock in it." Mindful of the great difference, we call it "our home," not "our house." It is a friendly, happy home; like the wave of the old man who sat on his porch, never failing with his happy wave.

For the first year we lived in the sawdust as we built our interior walls and doors. Linda cooked our meals from an electric skillet and washed our dishes out of what is now our utility sink. Several times, we took our dirty bodies to the Baptizing Hole.

I made all our kitchen cabinets, facing them with tin in which Linda, with hammer and awl, punched various patterns and designs using quilting patterns as a guide. It was a wonderful time of life, and the little man on his porch was, from its beginning, a part of it. His friendly wave, with that left hand, sent warm thoughts and happy feelings our way.

As I passed his house each day, weather allowing, he was seated in his rocking chair, always wearing overalls and a long-sleeved shirt which was sometimes red, other times blue. He never failed to wave. I never saw him getting up or down. Just sitting, his feet in brogan shoes, rocking his chair and waving.

On occasion, a lady sat in a straight-back, mule-ear chair on the right side of his porch. I assumed it was his wife. I never liked her as much as I did him. She never waved. She was not the rocking chair, waving sort. Maybe she did not see well. Maybe she just did not like to wave. Maybe she had grown up in a big house in town. She and I never became close friends.

I could tell by the way the man waved that he did not watch the violence of television, or read of the problems of the human race in the newspaper. I could also tell that if he had been unable to wave his left hand, he would have waved his right. Regular waving for about ten years let me know things like that.

Winter months would drive my friend from his porch, back into his little house. I knew he was at home by the smoke from his chimney. I never saw his woodpile, but I knew it was wood smoke rather than coal from its different color and better smell. Each day during the winter months I looked for the chimney smoke. I knew that was his way of winter-waving. I responded to the smoke by waving back. (My friends in their big houses in town do not know how to winter-wave. Their loss.)

Seems like it was the spring of '93 when I looked in vain for the return of the little man to his porch. Spring came early that year. He was always rocking and waving by the time the Purple Martins returned to the pasture gourds. For more than two weeks that year I looked for the wave of his hand. The smoke of winter was gone from his chimney. Where was my friend?

Sadly, I told my wife, "The old man is gone."

"He will be back," she answered, "he will be back."

Most of the time she was right about such things. This time, I hoped for her to be right, but I feared that she was wrong. I never saw his wave or the smoke from his chimney again, but I remember him still. Most friends come and go in life. A few remain. The little man and his honest-to-God wave remain with me.

Who was that man in overalls, long-sleeved shirt, and high-top shoes who waved to me? Was he all of us? Or none of us? Was he a stranger? Or my brother? Does he yet wave to me in the wings of the Bluebirds, Monarchs, and Swallowtails? My head tells me he has gone, yet my spirit says he remains. So much of life now seems that way, a struggle between head and heart.

Now retired from the things that once took me to the town with its big houses and the people who fear to wave, I do not pass the little house as often. But when I do, I always look for the chair that no longer rocks and the hand that no longer waves.

Mostly now I just sit on my home porch, marvel at all the boards that Linda and I sawed and nailed, listen to the squeaking hinges of the doors we made and hung, sometimes recall how crazy we were to wash our bodies in the Flint River, attempt to write, and look for someone to whom I may wave.

Reprehensible Lawyer

It was to be my first trial in Scottsboro, Alabama. I had been a practicing attorney hardly more than a year and I was led to believe that the Scottsboro attorney who would oppose me in the trial was the Devil incarnate. If not that, as least his identical twin. (I will call this attorney "Bill Morrow.")

It seemed as if each Huntsville lawyer who was aware of my upcoming trial with Bill Morrow as opposing attorney saw fit to offer warning of my imminent dangers. Some of the milder cautions included:

"Did you say that Bill Morrow is on the other side? You had better watch that son-of-a-bitch."

"He knows every trick in the book, and many that haven't been recorded. He'll use every one of them."

"Morrow! You can't trust that bastard. Don't believe a word he says, if his lips are moving, that's a sure sign he's lying."

"Bill Morrow! You had better keep your eye on him during each recess or he'll have one of the jurors out back of the courthouse talking to him."

I could go on indefinitely with the gratuitous admonitions this young lawyer received about the opposing attorney, but I have related enough for you to understand my concern. I was scared to death without all this input from my colleagues about the evils of Bill Morrow. I was young and this was only my second or third jury trial.

(Looking back more than fifty years, I now realize that some of the warnings I received were sincerely offered. Others were part of the hazing process by the older lawyers, my initiation into the fraternity of trial lawyers.)

What a way to start a trial career! I was led to believe the opposing lawyer belched fire; that when he spoke, the courthouse shook on its foundation. I drove the forty miles from Huntsville to Scottsboro believing that Morrow ate gunpowder for breakfast and horseshoe nails for lunch. I thought that each morning before leaving home he had his wife whip him with an ugly stick just to get him in the proper frame of mind. I had been told that Bill Morrow had been known to chew a young lawyer in one bite and then spit him all the way from the Scottsboro courthouse steps to the east side of Chattanooga, Tennessee. My drive to Scottsboro that Monday morning to meet Bill Morrow was one of the longest of my life.

I managed to get to Scottsboro, find a parking place, and make it on trembling knees into the courtroom. Judge Snodgrass, the trial judge, took the bench, called the court to order, and reviewed the fifty-nine cases that were on the week's trial calendar. My fright and intimidation was enhanced when I reviewed the list. Bill Morrow was listed as trial attorney in thirty-eight of the fifty-nine cases. The docket made it appear that Morrow could single-handedly whip the entire bar of Alabama. The Huntsville attorneys had warned of Morrow's experience. Even so, I was not prepared to fight Goliath! I looked around the courtroom for some place to hide, but had no such luck.

Most of the Jackson County Bar was present when Judge Snodgrass rapped his gavel for order. All attorneys, except one, appeared to be in a jocular mood. Among the happy lawyers, there was talk of the college football games played over the past weekend, and the upcoming Alabama/Auburn game. Except for the one man who sat against the back wall with a stern look on his face, there was much laughing, joking, and telling of funny stories. Not seeing any man with horns, and never having met Bill Morrow, I was not able to identify my opponent. I hoped that he was not the man sitting against the back wall with the large frown plastered over his face.

Judge Snodgrass appeared to be a kind man and tolerated the jest of the local lawyers very well. He allowed the local attorneys to exhaust the replays of recent football games before starting the docket call. Names of the trial attorneys in each case were shown, along with the parties, on the docket list.

Each time the first nine cases on the docket were called, the man with the frown on his face, the one who seemed to like isolation from the crowd, the one who did not seem to know how to smile, the one who sat by himself in the courtroom, arose from his chair and ambled to the bench to talk to the judge. By this time it was evident, even to a beginner like me, that this was Bill Morrow. He looked bad! He sort of mumbled, in a bad way, when he spoke to the judge. I know it was my imagination, but it appeared that even Judge Snodgrass was afraid of the man. Things were not looking good for the new kid on the block.

Finally, case number forty-two on the docket, my case, was called. Lucifer arose from his chair against the far wall, and with difficulty I was able to get to my feet and move toward the Judge's bench. I let Morrow lead the way, I dared not walk in front of him. My knees shook with each step and continued to knock against each other as I stood before the judge. I dared not stand as close to the judge's bench as Morrow. He placed both elbows on the judge's bench and acted as if the place belonged to him. I had a strong urge to urinate, but figured that was not the best time and place.

The judge greeted me with kindness, he knew I was scared to death. He welcomed me to his court and explained that my case was near the bottom of the docket and might not be reached that week. As the considerate judge explained things to me, Morrow appeared to glare in my direction. As Morrow glared, he seemed to bare his teeth and I was reminded of the warning that he could chew up a young lawyer and spit him all the way to Chattanooga. Not that I needed it, but I was reminded of the Bible story of Abraham leading his son, Isaac, to the mountain for sacrifice. Morrow played the role of Abraham, I was Isaac.

On the spot, I developed serious reservations about law practice. I felt I had made a grave mistake in my career choice. I felt a strong urge that I not only needed to urinate, but do number two as well. I wanted to run, to hide, and to vanish. All the while, Morrow seemed to glare in my direction and show his teeth. Soon his mouth seemed equipped in a manner that would have been the envy of the largest saber-toothed tiger that ever lived.

I tried to find solace in the words of the judge that my case might not be reached for trial that week. If this happened I would not be offered for sacrifice until a later time. I had slim hope that my case would never be reached for trial. Trial work had lost its potential glamour, let someone else do it!

After a few moments standing before the judge, which seemed like 900 years, I shook my way back to my chair and tried to more or less remain seated as the remainder of the docket was called. My shaking was so great that my fanny was bobbing up and down, around and around. I was sometimes in my chair, most times out. Not wanting to appear sacrilegious, I silently prayed that all the cases in front of mine would be tried instead of settled. I did not wish Judge Snodgrass any harm, but I hoped the cases in front of mine would keep him busy for the next forty years. Morrow, back in his chair against the far wall, glared at me, opened his mouth wide so I might see his long teeth, and remained master of all that he surveyed.

In addition to being scared and having the never ending urge to soil my pants, I was woefully ignorant of how things worked in the courtroom. Once the entire docket was called, which took about an hour, Judge Snodgrass started a recall of the same cases to determine which ones, during the interval, had been settled by agreement and which ones would actually go to trial.

In this second call of the docket, various excuses for delay were offered by the lawyers: one lawyer had a toothache, another a doctor's appointment, witnesses could not be found, lawyers had to be in other courts, parties were sick, some at the point of death, it seemed. A big dove shoot in Kennamer's Cove seemed to require attendance of more than half the local bar, and one lawyer was so bold to explain that his wife wanted to get pregnant and he wanted to be at home when it happened. A thousand reasons, all good and sufficient to the kind judge, were offered as to why the cases in front of mine could not be tried that week.

Worse yet, all of Morrow's other cases seemed to be settled to Morrow's satisfaction. As these cases were called the second time, Morrow seemed to walk to and from the judge's bench with a swagger. He walked with a smirk on his face, an appearance of dominance and satisfaction. His opposing attorneys walked to and from the judge's bench with appearances of just having their tails kicked, and what little tail that was left seemed tucked between their legs. All too quickly, my case, which was near the end of the docket, became the first for trial.

I felt the urge to reexamine my belief in prayer. I had earnestly sought God's help in seeing that all the cases in front of mine would be reached for trial and that mine would never be reached. Prayer had failed me. My next urge was to call my wife and tell her to sell the toilet seat because, henceforth, I would have no need for it, that forever after my ass would belong to Bill Morrow.

The rush of events precluded my following either of these urges. Judge Snodgrass called out, "Mr. Morrow and Mr. Berry, are you men ready to proceed with trial?" I was too ignorant to say I wanted to go on the dove shoot, or that my wife needed to get pregnant, and I was too scared to run.

Mr. Morrow looked at me, licked his lips, smiled, and shook the courthouse with his announcement. "Judge, I am always ready!" The lion had roared and I experienced what my grandmother called a "doomsday sinking spell." Too afraid to speak, I nodded "yes" to the judge's question.

All too quickly the trial began. From the outset, Mr. Morrow was an ideal example of courtesy. He was the epitome of kindness, yet, in no manner condescending. He appeared ready to extend every favor, dispensation, indulgence and service to the opposing young lawyer that circumstances would permit. But I was not to be taken in by such a clever fellow. Not only was I armed with the warnings of the Huntsville

Bar, I was also well versed in the good Southern Baptist doctrine that the Devil took many forms and wore many faces. There was no doubt in my mind that Morrow was, figuratively, patting me on the back, looking for a soft spot in which he would stick his knife.

There were few spectators in the courtroom during the trial. The local bar, except Mr. Morrow, had gone to the dentist, the dove shoot or possibly to impregnate their own wives or someone else's as soon as their cases had been continued. Some of the courthouse square checker players drifted in and out of the courtroom as the trial progressed, I assumed they wanted to see the next young lawyer that Morrow would crucify.

The only consistent courtroom observer was a little lady who sat in the middle of the front spectator row. The little lady was more than eighty years old, possibly ninety. She was frail, her back badly bowed and she walked with the aid of a heavy cane. She wore a rather stern appearance and seemed to spend most of her time staring at Judge Snodgrass. Several times, during recesses, she tried to get the judge's attention, but without success. She obviously did not like to be ignored and her astringent appearance hardened.

Just before an afternoon recess, I had occasion to cross-examine a young lady that, on direct examination, had styled herself "an eyeball" witness to the occurrence that had given rise to the litigation. My cross-examination of this young lady was the only part of the trial that went reasonably well for my client.

I got the young witness to admit that she had a somewhat limited opportunity to clearly see what had happened that evening. Among other things, the young lady admitted that the lighting was poor and she was some distance away. The event had occurred about midnight and the young woman admitted, with great hesitation, she was somewhat preoccupied at the critical moment. Her preoccupation involved the back seat of an automobile and a local businessman whose wife was out of town. I did not insist on the businessman's name or a graphic description of their encounter.

My cross-examination of this young lady was, without doubt, the high moment of my trial. In fact it was the only good moment, but it did not last. I felt a fleeting moment of satisfaction when the young lady was excused from the stand and Judge Snodgrass announced the afternoon recess. My brief moment of satisfaction of accomplishment was not to last.

Rather than leave the courtroom during the recess, I busied myself preparing for the next witness. I stayed at the counsel table and Judge Snodgrass, I thought, stayed on the bench. I paid no real attention to whom, if anyone remained in the courtroom with me. My thoughts were on Mr. Morrow. I desperately reviewed notes and shuffled papers, trying to prepare for the onslaught of future witnesses Morrow would present. It is hard for a freshman lawyer to keep his head above water; I needed more than a life raft or buoy. My mind left no room for doubt, Morrow was up to something. He had been too nice, he had been lulling me to sleep. Any moment now, Mr. Morrow would become half crocodile and half barracuda, lusting for a young lawyer to devour. Morrow would surely resume the trial riding a wildcat, spurring it with a bolt of lightening and beating its flanks with a rattlesnake. I could feel it coming. My reverie was suddenly broken with, "I'm gonna whup yore ass!"

The unexpected words came from the spectator section of the courtroom. I looked up, expecting to see Mr. Morrow. At last, I thought, his true colors are shining through, he is coming after me! I looked in the direction from which the words came.

To my great surprise, it was not Morrow, but it was the little old lady that had been sitting on the front row and carrying the big walking stick. Law professors had never told me trial work could be this exciting. The little lady with the big stick was going to give that Judge a good caning. She was headed toward the bench, moving as quickly as age and infirmity allowed.

My God, I thought! This is going to be something I can tell my grandchildren about. It is not every day a lawyer gets to see a judge get his "ass whupped."

I turned in my chair to look toward the judge. I wanted to see how he handled this delicate situation. (This was not the time and age when every courtroom had security personnel present. I doubt that Judge Snodgrass ever had a regular bailiff while he was on the bench.) My second "My God" of the day was when I realized that Judge Snodgrass was not on the bench. In fact, he was no place to be seen.

There was no one in the courtroom except the little old lady, the big stick, and I.

Understandably, my attention was immediately refocused on the lady with the stick. No sooner than she passed through the gate separating the bench and bar from the public than she made a right turn, in my direction.

Hellfire and damnation! This lady was not after the judge, she was after me! Although I didn't realize it until later, the young lady I had just cross-examined was the great-granddaughter of the little lady who carried the big stick.

Realizing that some have led a protected and sheltered life compels a digression on my part. In Alabama, and most of the South, there is a world of difference in the statements of "I am going to whip your ass" and "I'm gonna whup yore ass." The former suggests that serious thought is being given to the subject; the latter, particularly in 1960 Scottsboro, Alabama, meant that absent Divine intervention your ass is going to get "whupped."

As the little lady and the stick came my way, discretion being the greater part of valor, I started backing up. With strong dedication of purpose, the little lady came forward, stick and all. With even more dedication of purpose, I backed some more. The more I backed, the quicker she stepped. I was rapidly running out of room and she was between the gate and me. I have no recollection of what, if anything, I said. I had one recurring thought: being in my position was no way to win a fight with a great-grandmother, particularly because she had the stick. In such a situation, one is licked before the fight even starts.

I literally backed as far as I could go, into the corner of the courtroom, ducking and dodging every step of the way. My advantage of youth and agility was counterbalanced by her dogged determination, cunning and guile. To this point, I had not been hit. There had been several near misses and I was out of retreat room.

I do not know where he came from, my mind was on more serious things, but there he was. I witnessed a transfiguration, a miracle before my very eyes. Lucifer was transformed into an angel. Not just an ordinary angel, a guardian angel. Mr. Morrow had stepped between the near victor and the already vanquished. He had the little lady in one hand and the big stick in the other. He led her out of the courtroom and shortly came back to check on my well-being. The trial continued, neither lawyer said anything to the judge, and Morrow won the case, fairly so.

In later years I had occasion to oppose Mr. Morrow in several other trials. He never lived up to his advanced billing of being a lawyer I "needed to watch." I always found him to be a worthy advocate and a man of his word. I developed a friendship with this attorney, one that I value. He died several years ago and I miss him.

Thanks Mr. Morrow, but for you in my first Scottsboro trial, my "ass would have been whupped" in more ways than one.

(Writer's note: *The above story is based on an actual occurrence in Judge Snodgrass's courtroom. All essential details are accurate; the only exception being the reasons the lawyer's gave to get their cases continued. In that particular I took a storyteller's liberty of embellishment to add flavor. The Judge Snodgrass depicted was the father of Judge John David Snodgrass, who sat on our circuit bench in Huntsville and, like his father, rendered good service for his community.)*

Putting Things in Perspective

Somewhere along the road of life I have heard of finishing schools for girls, private schools that emphasize cultural studies and prepare students for social activities. If I have ever met a graduate from such a school, none of the social graces have rubbed off on me. I am pleased not to be burdened with too many social niceties.

Although not one for girls, I attended a different sort of finishing school. My school was not for refinement of intellectual and artistic tastes, unless one considers learning about crap games, poker games, whiskey drinking and other things as being of the self-improving nature. My school was not listed in any Ivy League catalog. It was located in North Africa. I not only attended this poor-boy finishing school, I completed my studies with honors and without being placed in a single jail. Looking back sixty years, I realize this "school" in a distant land probably provided the best part of my education.

Before enrolling in this school, for about a year and one-half, I attended what is now Auburn University. (Back then it had the mouthful name of "Alabama Polytechnic Institute.") Note that I say I "attended" that school, meaning I was, most of the time, present there. My attendance at Auburn is not to be confused with my being a student there. Being faithful to a well-defined high school habit, I have no recollection of ever opening a book outside the classroom while enrolled there. I had no idea of what I wanted to do with my life. That was just as well, because I had no money for either college or anything else. I did have, for my first year at Auburn, a $250.00 Sears, Roebuck & Company scholarship. This scholarship was unrelated to academic achievement. The only way to obtain this money was to be very poor. In that regard, I was well qualified.

The kind man who would later become my father-in-law arranged an entrance exam for my finishing school by making an appointment for me to be interviewed by Mr. Clyde Shepherd, Jr. of Atlanta, Georgia. This was in 1951. I was age twenty.

Mr. Shepherd's construction company had a contract with the United States Government to build an airbase in Libya, Africa. At the time, our government was building several airbases that encircled Russia, providing the means for our heavy bombers with their payloads of destruction to reach the interior of that country in the event that the ongoing cold war became hot. I hitchhiked from Auburn to Atlanta for my interview. There, before seeing Mr. Shepherd, I boldly completed the employment application form for employment as a heavy equipment operator. (I had never been on a piece of equipment that was powered with a diesel engine.)

Called into his office, I took the chair in front of Mr. Shepherd's desk while he reviewed my application. On the application form, in its "work experiences" section, I had honestly listed a variety of prior jobs describing many things except the operation of heavy equipment.

Mr. Shepherd reviewed my application, gently smiled, and asked, "Joe, what is your experience in operating heavy equipment?"

"None" was the only answer that I could give.

"What makes you think you can operate heavy equipment?"

"Mr. Shepherd," I said, "if others can do it, I can do it." This, too, was an honest answer. For most of my life, I have felt that if others can do something, so can I. I still feel that way.

The kind man smiled and said, "I believe you can," and gave me a job in Africa. I had passed my finishing school entrance examination. (I have maintained contact with Mr. Shepherd for almost sixty years. The last time I spoke to him, he was ninety-eight years old.)

I spent the night in Atlanta after seeing Mr. Shepherd, going the next morning to a doctor for a physical examination and receiving various inoculations required for an International Health Card. I recall receiving eight shots, including Tetanus, Typhus, Typhoid, Smallpox, and Yellow Fever.

The doctor giving the examination and shots first said that I would receive one-half of the shots that day and was to return two days later for the remainder. I explained that I was taking final examinations at Auburn and needed to immediately return to school, and further added that I did not have enough money to spend another night in Atlanta. Hearing my plea, the doctor gave me all required shots at the same time, with the caution, "These will likely cause you to develop a fever and you should not drive a car."

There was no danger of my driving something I did not have. Leaving the doctor's office, I made my way to the street that carried traffic in the direction of Columbus, Georgia, and on to Auburn, Alabama.

My reliable hitchhiking thumb got me to the southwestern outskirts of Atlanta before the ill effects of the eight shots began to take control. Realizing that I was suddenly very sleepy, I made my way back into the city to the Greyhound bus station. There, I was informed that all the money that I had would get me a ticket to Columbus, Georgia, with about fifty cents remaining in my pocket.

On the bus to Columbus, I passed out and went into a deep sleep. At Columbus, the bus driver had to shake me awake. Once awake, I was greatly embarrassed. The fly of my pants was standing open. I have always wondered if some damn pervert on that bus had attempted to take liberties with a young man that was on his way to a finishing school. I closed the fly of my pants, disembarked the bus, stuck out my thumb, and made my way back to Auburn where I got passing grades in all subjects for the quarter. Prep school was behind me. I was now headed for a different world.

My employment contract included a prepaid airline ticket from Atlanta to Tripoli, Libya, plus arranged and prepaid travel accommodations. With a seasoned and very nice construction worker, Marion Blackmon, I flew from Atlanta to New York City. (My reliable thumb and considerate motorists who gave me a ride had let me travel in several states of the South and

Midwest, but I had never traveled to the northeastern part of our country.) In New York City, we met eleven others, all seasoned construction workers, going to the same job. The thirteen of us took a flight to Amsterdam, Holland, with intermediate stops at Gander, Newfoundland and Shannon, Ireland.

I will never be able to explain the reason for a most unusual occurrence in Amsterdam. We had been provided first class tickets and travel accommodations, but the mysterious event in Amsterdam was far beyond "first class."

All passengers, except the thirteen of us going to Tripoli, were offloaded from the plane in the usual manner, going though the terminal and customs. The remainder of us were held on the plane while the others disembarked. The plane was then taxied to another part of the airport, where our luggage was loaded into a waiting van to be transported to our hotel. A well-dressed gentleman came onto the plane and asked the thirteen of us to go with him. He led us to two stretch limousines that were waiting at the foot of the plane's ramp. I do not remember ever seeing a limousine before; I was more of a mule-and-wagon type. The first limousine I ever saw, I rode in it!

Completely bypassing the terminal and customs routine, these two limousines transported us off the airport some distance to a complex of large, impressive buildings. It appeared to be a complex of government buildings, but I cannot be sure—it was during early evening hours, with little available light. There, we were escorted into one of the buildings and down its long hallway into a very large dining room. I had never seen a "supper room" like it. My finishing school had taken a quantum leap!

The large dining table and its decorations are impossible for me to describe. I do recall that the table was covered with a beautiful linen cloth and the eating ware were arranged several places deep on either side of the china dishes. The room seemed filled with the flags of the United States and tulips. Every turn of the eye brought more American flags and another crop of tulips into view.

About six or eight men, all in white dinner jackets and white gloves were there to serve us a meal, the likes of which I had never seen before, nor have I since, nor will I ever again. The entire event defies description.

We were served a meal that was fit for royalty, at least eight courses. When one has just enrolled in a finishing school, one does not count. My most vivid recollections of the occasion are the manners and conduct of those dignified men who served our meal and the silver-serving cart.

The place and its splendor simply did not match those seated at the table. It was a gross mismatch! It was not unlike thirteen hogs dining at a king's table. Possibly I had the best knowledge of which fork to use, and I had none. It was a comic affair! Yet, the men who served us so well kept their dignity and reserve. They stifled their shock and dismay, and acted as if they were accustomed to slopping the pigs.

To the great credit of these men, the only signs of disbelief that I saw were, on occasion, when the shock was too great, their eyebrows would twitch, like a rabbit's nose sniffing a carrot. Other than this, they were gentlemen to the bone. (Think of the typical English butler that we sometimes see in a movie.)

After dessert, a large silver-serving cart was rolled into the room and around the table. This cart was filled to the brim with miniature liquors of various kinds and description. Until then, I thought that all liquor came in either a half-pint bottle or a fruit jar.

As the silver cart was pushed around the table, the man who appeared to be in charge announced, "You will have a long flight to Tripoli, we serve you with some bottled cheer to help you along the way."

When the cart was pushed to me, the man to my left looked at me and said, "Boy, you are not old enough to drink very much, so fill your pockets for me." I obeyed his demand.

The splendid meal that defies fair description was concluded and we were transported, again in the two limousines, to our hotel for the night. The next morning we were placed on a charter flight via KLM Airline and flown to Tripoli, with an intervening stop on the Mediterranean Island of Malta. Malta still bore the signs of the devastation that it had suffered during World War II, which had ended only six years earlier.

I will never know who hosted this fantastic meal, or who was expected as guests. I have always felt that American diplomats were expected. Needless to say, diplomats are not what the host received. It is and always will remain a delightful and fond memory of mine. One may safely assume that on seeing the splendor of this beautiful dining room and experiencing such a magnificent meal, that my eyes stood open as wide as moon pies.

The thirteen of us were the only passengers on the Tripoli flight, plus enough of the liquor miniatures to provide "cheer" for the trip. The two female flight attendants (they were called "hostesses" then) managed to control the masculine urges some of the men demonstrated by breaking out enough playing cards to start two poker games. The remainder of the trip was uneventful.

My years in Libya were, to say the least, filled with things good and bad. I was able to visit Italy, Switzerland, and the south of France while living in North Africa. In North Africa, I visited the beautiful ruins of ancient cities founded by the Phoenicians more than 1,000 years before Christ. Leptis Magna, located on the coast of the Mediterranean Sea about 100 miles east of Tripoli, was once an important port city of Carthage, and then of Rome. The ruins of this city are counted as some of the most spectacular in the world. The places and things I saw made me realize the smallness of the world in which I had live thus far. And during my lifetime along came the invention of the Hubbell Telescope, and the smallness of my world became even smaller.

I worked daily, and often ate, with the Muslim Arabs. Not once did I see nor sense any hostility on their part toward the Christian visitors in their country. To the contrary, they made me feel like a welcomed member of their family. I have nothing except fond memories of my Arab friends.

I experienced many of the things I never wanted my children and grandchildren to do. Poker and crap games were my teachers. My two times of drinking an excess of whisky were enough to let me know that it was neither a fun nor safe thing to do.

Now, during these winter years of life, I realize that my best education came from events and people outside the classroom. Had there been such a thing as a finishing school for boys, I would not have had the money to pay the tuition. Even with the entrance fee, I likely would not have joined the class. I would have found such a school too snobbish for my simple taste.

Many of my friends with deep religious convictions believe, or so they say, that God plays an active role in directing our lives. (I sometimes think of them as the "gospel mill" crowd.) My life does not seem to have happened that way. I am never certain how much of life has occurred according to my own plan, much less God's. More and more, where I have been, what I have done, and where and who I am seems the product of chance. It was not planned that way, but that is the way it turned out.

Possibly I learned more useful things between ages twenty and twenty-five, when I was not in school, than any other period of my life. Those were the years that took me far beyond the small world that I had lived in before. Those were the years of sowing wild oats to the wind and often reaping the whirlwind.

Some of those years brought a bumper crop. Those years and all that was in them was my finishing school.

Those years were a great teacher. The hard-earned lessons are best remembered. How well I recall one event that left its mark. I had been in Africa about a year when one night found me in a bar in Tripoli with Pete Quattlebaum, a heavy equipment mechanic who worked on the same construction job as I. Pete was about thirty-five years old, stood at least six feet and three inches, and weighed about two hundred forty pounds. He had an abundance of body hair and looked more like a gorilla than a man. Pete was a hard-fisted, whiskey-drinking, woman-chasing, poker-playing, red-necked, giant of a man who loved a fight and was good at the game.

We had not been in that bar long before a seaman off a British merchant ship came through the door. The man was a stranger to us, obviously merely passing through the city. This man appeared to be about the same age as Pete and equally matched his size. These two big bulls, Pete and the seaman, looked each other over for about thirty minutes. Pete and I sat at one end of the bar and the British seaman at the other. Slowly the alcohol consumed by each, and that mysterious chemistry that sometimes goads grown men to act like juveniles took control, and these two giants started a fight with each other. They fought inside the bar. They fought outside, onto the sidewalk. They fought out into the street in front of the bar. The crowd wisely made no effort to intervene. None of the spectators dared step in. These two men engaged in the bloodiest, goriest fight that I have ever witnessed. Certainly, I have no desire to see its likes again.

It was a very equal contest. Finally, Pete put the seaman down for the last time. (Pete, too, had been down several times.) The merchant seaman was prostrate in the middle of the street. He raised himself to his knees and elbows to catch his breath, spitting out a mouthful of blood, and possibly a tooth or two. The man finally regained his feet and turned to look for Pete. Pete, though on his feet at the time, was in essentially the same condition as the seaman. Turning, the seaman spotted Pete in the crowd and took a step in his direction. Pete drew back his right fist, making ready to hit the seaman with another blow. At this time, the seaman raised both arms into the air, signaling surrender that the fight was over. Pete lowered his fists.

What happened next left an indelible and positive memory. Once Pete dropped his fists, the seaman stepped over to Pete with his right hand extended and said, in a strong Cockney accent that cannot be duplicated, *"Matey, I just want*

to shake your hand and tell you that you jolly well
whipped my tail."

The seaman advanced to Pete, shook his hand, and
turned and walked away. As he departed, he squared his
shoulders and walked away with dignity.

I never lost that image, what a wonderful lesson I was
taught. I admired the loser of the battle more than the victor.
That stranger showed me how defeat should be handled. He had
given the battle his best effort and had lost. It seemed as if he had
given himself credit for having done his best and accepted the
fact that on that day, and at that time, his best simply had not
been good enough. He congratulated the victor and walked away
with an attitude that seemed to say, *"Maybe we will meet again.*
Maybe next time will be my time".

Since that day, I have come to realize that there are many
battles in this life. Most of them are emotional. Some we will win,
others we will lose. Since that day, many years ago, I have lost my
share of the battles of life. In losing, I have always tried to
remember the example of that stranger that fought so well, and
lost.

Now, almost sixty years later, I still see that man who lost
that fight and extended his hand to the victor, and I yet hear his

words, *"Matey, I just want to shake your hand and tell you that you jolly well whipped my tail."*

Such were some of the days and nights of my finishing school, all of which have been a great teacher.

Tucking Cousin Johnny Away

Cousin John was one of my few wealthy relatives and he never changed the style of his neckties. He always wore those big wide ones, about five inches wide across the bottom. I would sometimes look at those neckties, think about the money he had, and wonder why he did not get something more stylish.

When I first met him my necktie was about one inch wide. His had me beat by four inches. He was habitual with his wide ties, he never missed a step. When he found a good thing, he stuck with it. But, it turned out that he knew what he was doing. He taught me that one should be patient in life, that if one just waits, the same thing will, like a merry-go-round, come around again.

He had good timing, too. By the time he died, those big wide ties were back in style. Cousin John had timed it just right. But I must admit, his timing darn near ruined me. It is fifty years later and I still get flashbacks of what I experienced the day I helped tuck him away. The old folks would call it a "sinking feeling," a feeling like you are going down to your knees and won't ever be able to get up. I remember it well.

Six of us were asked if we would transport Cousin John on his last earthly trip. One cannot refuse that kind of request. When the bugle blows, one must step forward, no matter what the cost. This is particularly true if the deceased had money. Rich folk, even dead ones, are entitled to special attention, just in case…well, just in case.

I knew Cousin John had been partial to hot buttered cornbread with lots of sugarcane syrup poured over it. And I knew he could eat more fried chicken than a boatload of Baptist preachers. I agreed to help plant my cousin with full knowledge that he would be a heavy load—I was a lot younger and stronger then. Besides, he had lots of money and there was an outside chance I might be mentioned in his will. It was a long shot, but I wanted to be in good standing with his nine children, just in case.

So I agreed to meet the other five pallbearers at the church the day they planned to tuck Cousin John away. We were to meet the hearse when it backed up to the front steps of the church, unload Cousin John, and carry him up the steep steps and into the church. Three of the five were standing at the foot of the steps when I arrived. I was relieved; it appeared they could handle their share of the anticipated load.

The hearse arrived and backed up to the church before the other two pallbearers arrived. It was a hot August day and the four of us stood under a nearby shade tree, waiting for our other two helpers. The family and friends of the deceased were already in the church and its organ was groaning as only a Baptist church organ can groan when a prominent member dies.

After waiting twenty minutes for the other two pallbearers, a long, black Buick Roadmaster pulled into the parking lot. The young driver got out, opened both back car doors, and assisted two elderly men from the Buick. The two appeared to have a combined age of at least 175 years. Both were short in stature, one appeared to weigh about ninety pounds, and the other one was on the lean side.

The two old men toddled toward the front of the church. As they approached, one pallbearer spoke to me, saying, "Let's assist these gentlemen up the steps. Our help has not yet arrived." I agreed to this. It appeared that we had plenty of time and the old men appeared to have plenty of need. The church organ continued its moan and groan.

Soon there would be moaning and groaning of a different nature. The two old men hobbled over to the four of us and said, "We are here to help bury Cousin John." The able-bodied four of us let out a collective groan. Getting Cousin John into the church and then into the ground had taken on a new dimension. My first impulse was to run like hell as fast as I could. Then I thought, you know, that long shot thought about the money and the will—stranger things have happened. So I decided to stay the course.

The service was already more than a half hour late in beginning, so quick planning was called for. I suggested that we put the ninety-pounder in the middle on the left side of the box, and put the less-than-ninety-pounder in the middle on the right side. This arrangement would leave one able body on each corner of the coffin. Without a second to my motion, parliamentary procedure was ignored and the execution of the plan began.

I purposely placed myself on the left corner, in front of the ninety-pounder, so I would be in front as we carried John up the steps. If the load shifted toward the rear as we went up, I did not want it landing on me.

Cousin John was a big man, probably weighing close to 325 pounds. He required an extra large box. I had seen him at the funeral home the night before. He was dressed in his best suit and wore one of his big wide ties. I calculated that his wide tie weighed at least five pounds. (When we planted Cousin John, it seemed that tie weighed at least ten times as much as my first calculation.) John was eighty-three years old. The two middle pallbearers carrying his box up the steps were each older than John and only slightly livelier.

Miracle of miracles, we made it to the top of the steps without a mishap, thanks to the two strong pallbearers bringing up the rear. At the top of the steps, two funeral home men unfolded an accordion-like dolly. The coffin was placed on it and Cousin John was rolled in fine style to the front of the church for the service.

While the preacher was saying nice things about John and likely hoping that the church would receive honorable mention in John's will, I learned that the two more-dead-than-alive pallbearers were named Bob and Charlie. Both took a nap while the preacher said grace over John. While those two slept, I whispered to the others, "I will take the left rear going out, be sure Bob is in the left middle and Charlie is in the right middle." (If the load shifted going down the front steps, I wanted to be bringing up the rear so I could land on top.) My co-conspirators nodded their heads in agreement. After the preacher did the best he could for Cousin John, the two funeral parlor men rolled him to the rear. We had to shake both Bob and Charlie awake before we could follow.

Alas, the best laid plans often go amiss. Following the dolly out the exit aisle and taking positions to lift the coffin from the dolly for the hazardous trip down the steep front steps, Charlie wound up on the front left corner, Bob on the left rear, and me in the left middle.

As I almost single-handedly lifted the coffin off the dolly, all three of my good buddies on the opposite side looked at me and grinned. One of them winked. I knew that I was in trouble, very likely serious trouble.

Our exit plan was to go down the steps, then manually carry Cousin John about seventy-five yards across the church parking lot to the adjacent cemetery and the open grave that had been prepared, extra wide, just for him. Even before we started down the steps, that seventy-five yards across the parking lot looked like seventy-five miles.

I got lucky going down. The two men from the funeral home were carrying the folded dolly down the steps, taking it to the hearse that had been parked in the shade. As we started down, both Charlie and Bob stumbled at the same time, almost falling. Both funeral home men dropped the dolly and let it make its way down the steps on its own. At the same time, both men grabbed a corner of the box and we all made it alive, except John, of course, to the bottom of the steps.

The funeral home men had had enough. One propped Charlie under the left front corner of the box and the other propped Bob under the left rear. I was still in the middle. This accomplished, the funeral home men grabbed their dolly, put it in the hearse, and burned rubber as they left the parking lot. The three pallbearers across the box grinned again, and this time all three winked at me. I was beginning to feel very alone.

The near fall coming down the steps seemed to jar both Bob and Charlie awake for about ten steps. Very quickly thereafter my situation became critical. With every step, my load got heavier. And heavier. And heavier.

I leaned forward, busting a gut and gasping for breath, and said, "Pick up, Charlie." Charlie could neither hear nor pick up.

I leaned backward, busting another gut, and said, "Bob, we are about to lose Cousin John! In the name of God, pick up." Bob seemed as if he heard, but he manifested no "pick up" ability.

All the while, I did a side step carrying one hundred percent of the left half of the box and all that was in it. My faithful friends on the other side of the box continued to grin and wink. One even snickered!

Twice Charlie stumbled and fell. Going over him was impossible; I had to hold Cousin John with one hand and pick Charlie up with the other.

About thirty yards from the open grave, my load got about ninety pounds heavier. I looked back to try to determine what had added the additional weight. Bob had crawled on top of the box and gone to sleep.

What I did was not a nice thing, but I had only two choices. Either I could swat Bob off the box and let him fall to the pavement, or drop my side of the box and let both Bob and Cousin John roll to the pavement. I chose the course that was calculated to cause the least disturbance and preserve my small chance in John's will. I gave Bob a roll. Some kind soul picked him up, brushed the dirt off, and led him away. I never knew what happened later to Bob, and I do not care to know.

With just one additional stumble and fall by Charlie, he and I made it to the left side of the open grave. As we sidestepped our way alongside the opening and I looked at the three grinning hyenas on the opposite side of John, Charlie disappeared. He was there one moment and gone the next.

The parade had to be halted while I held the coffin with one hand and pulled Charlie out of the grave with the other.

That is the way it was when we tucked Cousin John and his wide tie away. I got no mention in his will, but I did get a triple hernia out of the deal. Although not getting any of Cousin John's estate, my concluding words of that day have become world famous. As we lowered Cousin John into the ground I shouted, "FREE AT LAST! FREE AT LAST! THANK GOD ALMIGHTY, I AM FREE AT LAST!"

At a later time, another man used my words and became famous for them. Possibly you have heard the other person's words. If you were within a ten-mile radius of the cemetery the day I helped tuck Cousin John away, you certainly heard mine.

(Writer's note: Any resemblance of any person, living or dead, is purely coincidental. I exaggerated about the three hernias. It was only two, or possibly the whole affair never happened. You be the judge.)

Delta Queen

The Delta Queen, the last of the smoke-and-soot-belching paddleboats to part the waters of our rivers, slipped by me this morning. I had read in *The Huntsville Times* that the old riverboat was making her way up the Tennessee River and would pass Huntsville in route.

I had intended to be at Ditto's Landing, south of Huntsville, Alabama, as she passed by on her way to Chattanooga, Tennessee to become a thing of the past. According to the newspaper, she was destined to drop permanent anchor in the big bend of the Tennessee River at Chattanooga, there to be converted into a hotel. It grieved me to know that an old friend was to be permanently chained in place. She had been made to travel, to ride the currents, and dodge the snags and sand bars. Like a racehorse, she had been bred to run. Now she was to be shackled, hobbled, and put out to pasture. Old folk, like me, are sensitive to the injustice of being used, discarded, and locked away in some closet, or worse.

The Delta Queen and I are about the same age. I wanted to wave goodbye to her as she made her way up the river, never to churn the water and belch the soot again. Waving farewell seemed like the least I could do. But in the early morning hours, under the cover of darkness, she caught me napping and passed me by.

Yet, I know it was not she that planned to slip by in the night. Even in my slumber, I know the ways of those so cruel as to permanently chain the Fair Lady to anchor, never to see Paducah, Memphis, Natchez and New Orleans again. I know there are those who crucify beauty, charm, and heritage in the name of profit. They often work their dirty deeds in the darkness of night. Old men who love old boats understand such things.

The truth be known, I really wanted to do more than just wave to her as she made her last journey. Old friends are owed more than a mere wave of my hand. The Fair Lady was due to have a part of my spirit keep her company as she, like a terrible thief, was to be bound in stocks and pillory, never more to sound her whistle and ring her bell for the next river's bend or landing.

No, a wave of hand would not have been sufficient. I wanted to be a boy again, standing in the night on the dark shore at Ditto's Landing, barefoot, in my overalls, with a lantern in hand to signal the captain. I wanted, in the darkness of night, to see the sparks from the stack jump toward the heavens as fresh hickory logs were fed into the Fair Lady's furnace. I wanted to hear her as she rounded the bend west of Ditto's Landing, churning, belching, hissing, moaning, and groaning her way upstream to where I stood. I wanted to hear the pilot's voice above the hissing steam call out, "Pipe the port watch. Ditto's Landing, ho! All hands on deck to lower the plank for passenger. Mind the Cypress stumps. Careful, now."

I wanted to hear the answer come, "Aye, aye, Sir."

In my dream of things no-more-to-be, I wanted to be short the passenger fare and see if a quart of home brew would induce the first mate to turn his back while I slipped aboard and hid in the boiler room as the Fair Lady made her last run past Gunter's Landing.

Once past Guntersville, Bridgeport, and South Pittsburg, I wanted to hear the pilot's call, "Pipe the starboard watch. Make ready with the plank and chain. Ross Landing, ho! Steady now, mind the helm. Careful crew, 'tis port of last call!"

I wished to hear that last reply, "Aye, aye, Sir."

I wanted to hear the Delta Queen vent her steam for the last time, to huff and puff no more. I wanted to hear the splash of anchor at Ross's Landing, the place we now call "Chattanooga, Tennessee." I wanted to see and feel the ghosts of ages past walk her plank for the last time and hear her bell toll its last farewell. I wished to leave a part of me to the Delta Queen. The Fair Lady needs company. Forbidden fruit appeals to boys and old men who love old boats, un-hobbled horses, and children who can romp and play.

But the Delta Queen passed by Ditto's Landing in the darkness of early morning as I slept, leaving me with only my dreams of barefoot boys, riverboat gamblers, wood-fired boilers, hickory sparks that jump and grab for the stars, paddlewheels, hoopskirts, fiddles, banjos, and lady friends who pass me by in the night.

Letter to a Little Girl

January 20, 2004

My Dear Little Girl,

I write to you now and hope that someway, somehow, this letter reaches you twenty years from now. In a manner of speaking, this is a letter to you, Anna Kate, and Ethan—the three greatest grandchildren the world has ever known. But I address the letter to you, Little Girl, because you are so much younger than the other two and some of the things I will say are a bit too serious for a seven year-old girl.

I do not want to sound either melodramatic or morbid, but my almost seventy-four years of living, watching, and trying to understand life suggests that I might not personally be around at age ninety-four to hand you this note. After I finish writing, I will try to figure a way for a "special delivery" of this letter to you.

My little blue eyed girl, this letter comes from my heart; I say this letter comes from my "heart." Of course, that is a figure of speech. You and I have talked about figures of speech. We already know the human heart is just a big muscle that plays a very important role in our living. Let's just say that my words come from my soul, my spirit, or from that magic place where grandfathers keep and hold special memories of special people.

In writing these words, I reach way down inside myself and try to pull up some of those wonderful joys that you and I have shared. Although I cannot recall all things, I also cannot reach any deeper trying. Little girl, I scrape the bottom of my barrel trying to express the joy you have brought into my life. I reach way down into my heart, or guts, or whatever one wants to call it, recalling our lives together.

Of course, you are not the first grandchild in my life. You know about the other two and how much they mean to me, so nothing I say about you is to distract or take away from the equally good memories of the others. I guess one way to look at the other two is to realize how the things I learned from them helped prepare me for my love of you. They extended my reach and enlarged my capacity. They gave me a larger "love bucket." The three of you have been equally great teachers.

Life, it seems, is a building process. Each day and each person seems to prepare us for the next day and next person. Let's just put it that way. Let's just say that my loving the other two has helped me to love you and let's agree that my writing to you in this way is my way of writing to all three of you.

I will leave it to you to get a copy of this letter to Anna Kate and Ethan; that will take care of my "special delivery" to them. (Now, if I can just figure a way to get this to your hands in about twenty years.) When you give this to the others, do me a favor. Tell them my love for them is no less than my love for you. Tell them it is just different. Tell them it is different because all of you are different people and I found it impossible to love everyone in the same way.

Maybe other folks can love every grandchild in the same way, but I never mastered that art (or is it deceit). I have found that all of us have different needs, abilities, capacities, wishes and desires, and all these differences just made my relationship with every person a little different. So it was with the other two. Tell them that I am grateful for all the things they gave to me and all the things they taught me. One thing is certain about the three of you: you are all loveable people. There is a good lesson there. If you want to be loved, be loveable. The three of you have been great teachers about love, honesty, and openness. Three great teachers! I have been the lucky one.

But, back to you, my little girl. Back to you and why I write this letter, telling you things that you are now too young to understand, things that I likely will not be around to personally tell when you are older.

You came along at such a great time of life for me and you filled up such a big place in my heart. (There I go again, another figure of speech.) Maybe it would be better if I said you filled up my days and night, that you got inside me and caused our hearts to get twisted together in a tight knot. Do you remember that day when you were four and you twisted those little fingers together and held your hands out to me as I drove our truck? Do you remember that you held those twisted hands and fingers close to my face and said, "Hoss, mine and your hearts are twisted together just like this"? I almost died on the spot, my emotions almost choked me to death. Of course, you came to my rescue with a follow-up. You must have known that I needed some relief when you added, "They are twisted together so tight, it just makes my head itch." Remember? I will never forget, at least in this life and hopefully not in the next.

You were right, our hearts were, and still are, twisted together just the way you described. And the older two grandkids may take credit for that. They are the ones who started me on the road to letting my heart get twisted all together with the hearts of grandkids. I knew little about twisted hearts with kids before the other two came along. But they gave me a graduate study, they set the stage by expanding my ability to understand and love. See how this thing works for me? I can never love any two people the same way. Each one helps me in loving the next one. I do hope all three of you will see, feel, and understand what I am trying to say.

Yes, you came along when my need for love of a child was great. (I have a strong need for a child in my life.) I had retired from my work and renewed my interest in so many other things. Things like my reading, writing, gardening, story telling, teaching, and loving Nana. But, even with all those things, there was still a need for a child in my life. My kids were grown, and Ethan and Anna Kate were almost grown. Well, that is not quite accurate. That kind of a statement sort of flies in the teeth of what I have already said about the building process of life, about each day bringing something to stack on top of yesterday and the day before.

Let's just say the other two were old enough, when you came along, to begin to think that they were grown. In a few years the three of you will begin to think as I do. All of you will begin to see things differently, and begin to better understand that loving one person increases one's capacity to love the next person. It took me a long time to really figure that out, but you three are smarter than I and will understand quicker. By the time you read this letter, I think you will understand my meaning.

But, Little Girl, there I was, kind of standing pretty far along the road of life with my special needs, when you came my way. You had special needs, too. You seemed to need someone to hold and love you. Of course, you had your daddy; but he, like me in years past, was busy trying to make a living, trying to pay the bills, and do all the other things that daddies have to do. You seemed to need someone to give you a bath and then wrap you in a towel, sling you over his shoulder with your naked butt showing, and parade you around the house. We called this after-the-bath-ride a "Pig-tail Twist." If the weather permitted, we took that pigtail twist parade out into the yard, around the house and back again, your naked bottom mooning the world, all accompanied by your squeals of joy. What wonderful memories you gave to me!

You had need for such a ride, and I was so happy that I was there to twist that towel, and that I had the strength to do that parade with you. I hope you see this in your mind, even now, many years later, and I hope you see that grin on my face when you would say, "Don't stop Hoss. Let's do it some more."

I hope you and the other two see how my love for you was different. It had to do with circumstances. Your circumstance was different and so was mine.

Enough of being a teacher, you have heard enough of that from me. I just want you to understand, when you are older, how special you are and, as with Ethan and Anna Kate, how grateful I am for all that each of you have given to me.

Little Girl, for whatever my reason may be, I want you to remember the special times we had together. I do not fully understand my reason for wanting this, but I want it nonetheless. I suspect the emotions I feel are common to most, if not all, grandparents who have a younger grandchild who is too young for a *serious talk*. There are at least two reasons for my wanting to "reach back" from tomorrow and again touch you. The first is that you are now too young for serious talk. A child does not need such things. The second reason is that within a few years you will begin that awkward time of life that tends to temporarily separate the child from the adult, particularly an adult who wants to do some serious talking. I calculate this period of separation will last at least ten years and the time will have passed without my being able to tell you, as an adult, some of the things that I want to say. I fear it will be too late. (I do not fear death, but I would not want to walk that road without trying to let you, Anna Kate, and Ethan know the things that come from deep within me.) Thus, my special delivery letter to you, just in case I am not around.

So, in this manner, I try to stir old memories and joys. I want you to recall my joy and happiness in you. The things we did, the places we went, the new things we saw, and the games we played.

To name just a few: there were our rides in our truck, the first vehicle that you learned to "drive" while seated on my knees; the Eastern Box turtles, one of which you named "Alice Smith," and her trips to your kindergarten and first grade classes; the "poopy-tail" bull down in Mr. Red Patterson's pasture; the baby goats and kittens and the names you gave, "Danielle," "Courtney," "Fluff-ball," "Two Big-eyes," and the one that did not make it, the one you said you loved the best, "Goldie"; the chicken snakes we found in the tractor shed and driveway; the beautiful Copperhead snake we saw in Miss Alice's driveway; our trip down by the Flint River, both dressed in our Osh-Kosh overalls, to have the surprise pictures made for your Daddy and Nana; Bozo Black Butch, the invisible black crow that lived in our house, the only such bird in the world that cast a shadow; Betsy Farmer, the little chick-a-dee that we found; the Red Tail hawk with the injured wing that we took to the vet; the Ruby-throat hummingbirds that we caught and held for a few moments; the baby rabbit that Macon, our wonderful Labrador, brought to us as we hiked in the pasture; the first day I permitted you to walk alone down the driveway to the mailbox; the time I permitted you to climb the tall extension ladder that leaned against the house so you could closely see the baby Cardinals with their open mouths in their nest; our naps together and always holding hands; the many, many stories I told you as we rocked in *our favorite chair*; the stories I read and told to you at Randolph School; your seeing me on the roof of the house at age seventy-three and saying, "Look Nana, Hoss is on top of the house, now that is remarkable for an old man"; and the joy of hearing you and Nana talk and sing in the car as I drove.

My dear little girl, I could write for days of the wonderful things you have done for me, the things you have taught me, the joy you have brought to my life, and the wonders of being able to love someone so completely. I could write an equal time about the other two and the many joys we shared. But to write of them would be duplication, in large part, of what I write of you. The only difference being that with you I was building on what I gained from them. For this foundation, my heart is equally filled with joy, happiness, and good memories. So, in this way, permit me to use you as a conduit. Send copies of this long letter to them. Tell them I reach out to them, just as I reach for you.

The only real difference was that our circumstances were different. I had more time. I had a different need, which you filled in such a beautiful way. You had special needs, needs the other two did not have. So, you see, it was a different time and place. And I had the things the others had already given and taught me. That is the way of love. It is a matter of time, place, need, and opportunity to respond. So it was, and is, with you and the other two.

So it is with my need today; my need, in some manner, to reach from tomorrow back to today and touch Ethan, Anna Kate, and you again. Be safe, and well, and happy, and warm, and dry my little girl. Ethan and Anna Kate, you do the same. All be happy.

I will close by saying I remember telling all of you many different versions of my story of *how I got that hole in my lip*. As if you do not already know, all those stories were make-believe. When we meet again, I may tell you the truth of how I

came to have that little hole in my lip, or I may just tell you
another story. Only time will tell.

Thank you my child and children for being so good to
and for me. Much love from "Hoss."

(Writer's note: *With reservation, I include this letter among my
stories. It is a personal letter. I share it in the belief that the emotions
expressed are common to many grandparents and, for that reason, may be of
interest to others.)*

I'll Fly Away

In the manner of old men, he often reflects on things past and speculates on things future. Pushing the recall button of memory, he plays old scenes of life and wonders where most of his friends have gone. He knows his world is shrinking. No longer does he get to the yard by jumping off the edge of the porch, age had taught him how to use the steps. His closet, once filled with business suits, now contains only two, one for funerals and the other for weddings. He tries to avoid both events. Almost daily the span of his reach grows shorter, his grasp now exceeding his reach.

His once splendid vegetable garden was no longer planted. The weeds he had fought each spring and summer for many years have won the battle, now growing more than head-high. Cows and goats are no longer seen in his pasture. His two empty barns, with their open center hallways filled only with mazes of cobwebs, seem to stare toward his house, resembling question marks asking *where did everyone go?*

He has more time now to speculate about things of the future. What is there beyond this day? Where are the friends and family of yesterday? Is there really some life beyond this one? Some of his remaining friends seem so sure there will be another day, in another and better place. Try as he may, he can never develop the sense of confidence about the future. He has hope, but not the confidence of deep conviction. Often he thinks, *I think too much.* Not wanting to disturb the belief of others with his uncertainty, unless asked, he keeps his silence on this subject.

Sometimes he ponders the claims of different churches and denominations. Most all, it seems, try to sell a ticket to heaven. Churches had always wanted him to give his money to God, but they all gave local addresses for the mailing of his contribution check. Maybe, he thinks with a smile, the government needs to expand its consumer protection program and regulate the sale of tickets to heaven. Continuing his smile, he thinks the new program could be called *Truth in Heaven Ticket Sales* and government regulations could be written requiring proper disclosures. Life still had some of its lighter moments.

He finds many positive things about the smaller world in which he lives. Life is simpler. The shopping malls no longer offer any thing for sale that he needs or wants. His truck is almost old enough to vote, but paid for. Even better, other motorists give him plenty of room to park when he makes an occasional trip to the supermarket. If he has to "squeeze" into the parking slot on arrival at the store, when he returns with shopping bags in hand there will be no other vehicle parked within ten feet of his old, battered truck. Yes, his span of life is smaller, but it still has happy moments. The respect of an old truck by others is just one.

Loss of hearing is another. Hearing aids help, when he wants to hear. Most of the time he does not. He has found a beauty in silence. He has discovered that ninety-five percent of spoken words are not worth hearing. He loves books. Good books. Books that teach, not entertain. When cornered by a long-winded politician or theologian, his hearing aids' sudden *loss of battery powder* provide a perfect, inoffensive *escape route.* Sometimes he tells close friends that a hearing aid is one's best protection from a windstorm.

He is not unmindful of the many hands that have helped him along life's road. Living in a quieter, smaller, simpler world gives him time to think on such things. Most of those helping hands are now gone to that mysterious place from which no one he knew has ever returned. He tries to "repay" the dead by helping the living. He could think of no other method of repayment.

On occasion he searches his emotions seeking some attachment, some remote connection, to his great-grandparents. There have been eight of them, or so he had been told, none of whom he ever knew. His search is in vain. There simply are no emotional attachments to these strangers that he never knew; he is looking into the totally dark vacuum of ages past. He wonders, beyond two or three present and future generations, will it not be the same way with him? The old man wonders, *will anyone know I have walked this earth? What*

footprint will I leave? How will others know I came this way?
His logic tells him that someday he, too, will be a vague image of a great-grandfather that no one knew, merely one of an unknown eight. No sooner than he has this thought, a second thought occurs: *If one is to become an unknown, what does it matter if it is one of eight, or one of a million? An unknown is an unknown!*

Sitting by his window, watching the gold and purple Finch on their thistle feeder, he remembers the Eastern Bluebirds of his youth. Cavities in old rotted fence posts had been their favorite nesting place. Now the use of treated and metal fence posts has greatly decreased these nesting places and the number of Eastern Bluebirds has greatly reduced. Now he seldom sees a Bluebird and is saddened by the loss of this feathered friend.

He is led to ponder: *What if, when I die, I could leave the Earth with a few thousand more Eastern Bluebirds than there would have been had I not come this way? Would that not be a legacy of worth and value? The Bluebirds will remember, even if the great-grandchildren do not. Why not let the wings of the Bluebirds be my footprints?*

The old man resolves to do all that he can to reverse the trend of the diminishing Bluebirds. He decides to build and place at least 1,000 Bluebird boxes in the countryside, out in the open pastures and fields, away from people. He is diligent in his effort, building and placing at least two hundred birdhouses each year. It is good therapy, leaving little time to think of the scenes and loves of life that are now past, or what address to use when mailing God his money.

****

He did not keep count, but death found him far beyond his goal of building and locating 1,000 Bluebird houses.

Only a few friends and neighbors noted his dying. Deaths of old men are commonplace things. In keeping with his request, his graveside service consisted of his grandson reading the Twenty Third Psalm, his granddaughter reading a simple poem he had written, and a few friends singing the gospel song "I'll Fly Away." As wished, he was buried in an old pair of overalls. He had said, "Be sure they are old and comfortable, I will be wearing them for a long time. No starch, please."

Some said that a dark, overhead cloud blocked out the sun as his body was lowered into the grave. Others said the near-darkness was caused by an overhead flight of 20,000 Bluebirds that came to take his spirit to the heavens.

What do you say?

(Writer's note: The writer has made and placed more than 1,000 Bluebird boxes in the open fields and pastures, and continues with the project. In the rural community where he lives, the Eastern Bluebird is now abundant. The final scene in the story is how he would like for things to be, the remainder of the story describes how things are.)